IN THE HEAT

IAN VASQUEZ

IN THE HEAT

 ST. MARTIN'S MINOTAUR ≫ NEW YORK

This is a work of fiction. All of the characters, organizations, and events portrayed in this novel are either products of the author's imagination or are used fictitiously.

IN THE HEAT. Copyright © 2008 by Ian Vasquez. All rights reserved. Printed in the United States of America. For information, address St. Martin's Press, 175 Fifth Avenue, New York, N.Y., 10010.

www.minotaurbooks.com

Library of Congress Cataloging-in-Publication Data

Vasquez, Ian, 1966–
   In the heat / Ian Vasquez.
      p.   cm.
   ISBN-13: 978-0-312-37809-7
   ISBN-10: 0-312-37809-2
1. Belize–Fiction. 2. Boxing stories. I. Title.
   PS3622.A82815 2008
   813'.6–dc22

                     2008011732

First Edition: June 2008

10 9 8 7 6 5 4 3 2 1

For Pamela

ACKNOWLEDGMENTS

Special thanks to my mother and father, good parents who laid the foundation; to Markus Hoffmann, for his keen eye and splendid suggestions; to Lynne Barrett, a teacher whose voice I still hear just over my shoulder; to journalism colleagues past and present, whose daily work exemplifies respect for the reader; and for all Belizeans—*dis da fi you,* especially the park boys of my youth, with whom I swapped lies and lived stories that one day soon must be told.

IN THE HEAT

1.

MILES YOUNG WAS ready for the suffering. He began his ritual at midday, three hours before it went down: a cup of rich, bitter coffee; a bologna and lettuce sandwich, light on the mayo; a bathroom visit.

He left his house carrying nothing in his hands or pockets. Sammy liked to say to him, "You're acting like you're walking to your death, son," and though Miles would say if anybody was going to die, it would be the other guy, he knew this was the appropriate state of mind.

It was a clear afternoon, a good wind blowing off the Caribbean Sea, a faint, muddy smell of mangroves in the air. He headed south along the sea wall on Southern Foreshore, past the wooden colonial houses that had hardly changed since he was a youth running these Belize City streets. Even the potholes looked the same, the wooden rainwater cisterns in the backyards, the dark wooden lampposts.

When he turned the corner at Government House, that stately white mansion behind the wrought-iron fence where the British governors used to live, he was filled with pride, though he couldn't have cared less about the history. This was about hometown pride today, saying to the Mexican coming into his backyard, You're crazy if you think Miles Young will lie down for you in front of his people, and if you assume an older man is a cakewalk, you will leave here dented.

Somebody in a car waved and hollered his name. Miles smiled politely, trying to keep his head down, focus on this Ricardo Garcia he'd seen fight only in jerky amateur videos. A man on a bicycle rolled past, glancing over his shoulder with a grin. "Knock that mawfucka out, Miles." Miles raised a fist in acknowledgment, his smile feeling forced now.

Instead of the direct route via Regent Street, he opted for the quiet lane that led to Albert Street, if only to relax, clear his mind. The smell of wood smoke from a yard of rickety tin-roofed houses soothed him some. Clothes flapped on a line propped high with sticks. A little black girl peered at him through the slats of a fence. He didn't know her but he said, "Good morning, my dear Lisa."

"My name's not Lisa."

"Oh really. So what's your name then?"

"My name is Roylene."

"Of course, that's right. You're the pretty Roylene everybody's talking about."

A stout black lady came out of one of the houses with a basket of laundry. "Is you dat, white boy Miles?"

"Hey, Miss Mazy. Talking to Roylene here. She's so big for a two-year-old," glancing at the little girl.

Roylene looked all confused, turning to the woman, then back to Miles. "I'm five!"

Miles threw up his hands. "Well, imagine that. I'm so sorry," and Miss Mazy laughed, telling the girl, "He's only teasing you, pet." Miss Mazy walked over to the fence, holding the basket against a hip. "You ready, Miles?"

Miles struck a boxing pose. "How do I look?"

"Like a winner. But you'll take care of yourself today?"

Miles nodded, touched by the concern. He turned to Roylene. "I have a daughter a little younger than you, and when she gets to be your age? I hope she's pretty just like you. See you, Miss Mazy," waving as he walked on.

He reached Albert Street with thoughts of his daughter heavy on his mind. If he won today, bigger fights would come his way, he was sure of it. And bigger paydays, which meant security for Lani . . . Lani, Lani, your daddy's gonna be okay . . .

Then he was in the middle of the crowd at the gate to Bird's Isle, shaking hands, bumping fists, saying thanks and you better believe it when they told him to get the job done, Miles pushing through, people touching him—always happened, some fans just needed to touch you, be a part of the event or send you good luck through their fingertips. He went through the gate and crossed the long wooden footbridge to the isle, people dropping back, giving him his space.

Ahead, palm trees swished in the breeze. His pulse quickened as he neared the rust-spotted zinc roof that covered most of the plank bleachers and the basketball court where the ring would be. Miles took a deep breath and stepped off the bridge, back into the brutal game he thought he'd left forever three years ago.

At 2:48, the preliminaries were over. Sammy said, "Ready, Miles? Ready to do this thing?"

"Yeah, yeah, I'm ready."

"And what's this thing you gonna do?"

"Whip ass. I'm gonna whip this boy's ass."

Toby said, "Whose house is this?"

"My goddamn house."

"I said whose house?"

"My house, man, my house!"

"You better know!"

Sammy turned to the man at the locker room door. "Open up, the better man is coming through."

Dressed in a hooded white robe with black piping, Miles began hopping in place, the murmur of the crowd filtering into the room, bringing that tingle in the veins, the jitters that came every time. Toby stepped in front of him and Sammy took up the rear, and Miles pounded his gloves together and began jogging out the door.

The fans in the plank bleachers on either side of the door were the first to see him, and the cheers went up, the loud clapping. Booming dance-hall reggae started up from speakers on the stage, skinny black teens moving to it, a few waving bottles of Guinness. People crowded around Miles, Toby, and Sammy, but fans from the distant bleachers could've picked the trio out easily–two black men in ball caps and the hooded boxer. Toby, his cut-man, still on his side after all these years, leading the way across the sandy stage floor to the stairs; Sammy, his trainer and manager, with a hand on his shoulder now. The fans in the folding wooden chairs on the basketball court below rose from their chairs clapping, turning for a better look, talking excitedly.

He came down the stairs and lifted his eyes, smiled, gave them a nod. The place was packed, bleachers on four sides filled, the scuffed-up court jammed with people and chairs, leaving only a narrow aisle that led to the ring. Ricardo Garcia was already up in there, pacing around his handlers. Miles's mouth went dry, he could hear his heart beating while they took the long walk, his boxing shoes crunching peanut shells and *pepitas,* spilled popcorn, stepping over a beer puddle right before the ring stairs. Miles trotted up, ducked through the ropes and waltzed into the ring, and the cheers grew louder. People shouting his name. Raising and spilling cups of beer. Wide grins on a few faces he recognized.

When the announcer started the introductions, Miles started the slow belly breathing, slipping into that zone of focus, seeing but not really seeing the rusty iron pillars that led to the girders under the roof; glancing at the Mexican, who was also glancing at Miles. Miles raised his hands when they introduced him. He smiled.

In his corner now. Sammy kneading the back of his neck. Miles shook out one leg, then the other. He saw the Mexican smile and a fear rose up in Miles, a strange sense that he'd get hurt today. Something he hadn't felt before. His neck was tight. All the handlers began leaving the ring. Miles sucked in a deep breath, let it out slow, but a bubble of anxiety had lodged in his chest. He did some neck rolls to loosen up, watching Garcia, who was standing calm, with that smile. Feeling everything Miles was not feeling. Then the ring was empty except for the referee, a short man with slicked-back hair and a bow tie, and Garcia in his corner, gloves up, glaring now. Miles's last thought before he lifted his gloves was something he always told Lani: Be good, you hear?

The bell rang, and Miles lumbered across the ring under a hundred pounds of doubt.

2.

HE GLIMPSED HIS reflection in the car window and felt like a stranger to himself: cut bottom lip, swollen nose bridge, hot welt on his left cheekbone. He flopped into the backseat and held the icepack to his face, deciding to get the hell out of the game, but for good this time. One benefit of failure is to reveal the truth, and he was deluding himself no more.

The car nosed its way through the crowd of fans on Regent Street. People kept turning to look at the car, recognizing Sammy and Toby, then searching for Miles.

"Thing to do now is pick up your money from Manny Marchand," Sammy said, eyeing Miles in the rearview.

"Sweetest noise I've heard all day," Miles said.

He leaned his head back and gazed out the window, narrow streets littered with plastic cups, paper bags, the air smelling like dust and the sea. Dark wood-frame houses slid by in the late afternoon sun. Buildings with corrugated zinc roofs and leaning antennas. Skinny dogs poking through an upended garbage bin. Bicyclists darting around the slow Sunday traffic. The car crossed the old swing bridge, the river flowing murky and slow, crowded with ancient sailboats. A minute later they pulled into the gravel parking lot of the Radisson Fort George Hotel.

"Time to get paid," Sammy said. "How you feeling, Miles?"

"Aching all over. Pretty sure I'm still beautiful though."

Sammy turned around, looked his fighter in the eye. "Just wasn't our day. Happens to the best of us, but you did well in there most of the time, and I'm proud a you, boy. You got up off that canvas, you carried on. How we have to look at this, it's nothing but a setback. Toby and me still believe in you."

Jesus. Clichés to comfort him.

"That's right," Toby said. "Don't get down on yourself, hear?"

Miles nodded, released a breath he'd been holding for years. "This is it for me," he said. "I'm through."

Sammy studied him. "Give yourself some time, don't decide that yet."

"No, this is it, Sammy. I'm getting too old and too slow for this shit. In that ring today, all I did was think. Think and think and guess 'bout what I was going to do, how I'd set this guy up. Meantime, he's bringing it to me, beating my ass good. I'm only thirty-five, man, but today I felt like I was fifty, no exaggerating." He exhaled heavily, looked out the window.

"We had rewarding times. We traveled," Sammy said to Toby, "We been places, me and this boy."

"I hear that," Toby said.

"Mexico, Puerto Rico, Jamaica, Brazil . . ."

"Yeah," Miles said still looking out the window, "it was a great experience." He turned to Sammy. "Now it's time for something new, you know?"

Sammy nodded. The mild sea air wafted through the open windows. Then Sammy reached back and put a firm hand on Miles's knee. "Like I said, give yourself some time. You never know what tomorrow'll whisper in your ear. Life, son, life got this funny way of messing up your life."

* * *

They walked through the Radisson Fort George lobby, past the rattan chairs and paddle fans, the terra-cotta tiles and faux animal skin rugs of one of the priciest hotels in Belize. Sammy asked the front desk to please call a guest, the boxing promoter Manny Marchand. The woman said Mr. Marchand wanted visitors to meet him upstairs in the lounge.

Miles shook his head, remembering Manny had agreed to compensate him for training expenses in cash, but counting something like a thousand dollars in a bar was unwise. Unless, of course, you didn't have the cash.

Sammy said, "Let's see what story the fat man comes up with."

They climbed the stairs and strolled down a polished hardwood floor and through glass double doors into the lounge. They sat at the bar and Miles ordered a Heineken, Sammy asked for a glass of water, and Toby hesitated. Miles remembered Toby's weakness and told the lady he'd take a Sprite instead, easy on the ice.

Toby said, "Drink your beer, man. I got two months' momentum under my belt, don't worry about me." So Miles said, okay, the Heineken, while Toby settled for a Coke.

They sipped their drinks, Miles scanning the room. Then he saw Manny push through the double doors and come sauntering toward them, his three-hundred-pound girth wrapped tight in a powder blue guayabera. "Howdy, howdy, sorry for the wait," patting Miles on the back, nodding at Sammy. He pulled up a stool. "Didn't go quite our way, eh?" He pointed at Miles. "But you almost did it, almost had him in that seventh round. That son of a bitch got iron for a chin, though, right? Scotch rocks, hon," he said to the barmaid. He swung his attention back, nodding and smiling as if they were the best of friends. "So what can I do for you today?"

Hunched over his Coke, Toby mumbled, "You know what. Came to get paid."

"So then, let's talk," Manny said.

Miles said let's.

"I wish the outcome had been different, you know? You looked strong in there at times, but you had better days. Probably ring rust. What advice do we have for him, Sammy?"

"Far as advice goes," Sammy said, "I'd tell him what I always say. Make sure you get your money after the fight, win or lose."

Manny reached for his drink and took a sip. "Good advice."

"Sensible advice, seeing what a crooked business boxing can be, corrupt sanctioning bodies, shady promoters, all that."

Manny put his drink down. "Not sure where you're going with that. I'd like to think we can conduct ourselves like professionals here."

"With integrity, you mean? Pay fighters on time, the full contract amount, that sort of thing?"

"You have something you want to say to me, say it."

"Paulie Canto."

"Hell, I'm not even going to discuss Paulie Canto. That was two years ago. He sued, we're going to court, the law'll decide. End of story. What's that got to do with today?"

"Just the four thousand dollars I'm short, having been Paulie's trainer. But we're not going to have a repeat of that today, right? That's all I'm saying."

Manny took a long drink, licked his lips.

Miles said, "I feel it, you got some bad news. Just break it to me gently, I've had my ass kicked today."

Manny raised a palm. "A delay, that's all it is."

"You're a piece of work," Sammy said, shaking his head and looking away.

"You know how the banks are in Belize," Manny said. "I couldn't get hold of that amount of money in time and gate receipts won't be squared away till tomorrow. Had the money wired from my bank in Miami, but you know how it is. Should be cleared by Tuesday, no later."

"Meanwhile, we're waiting," Sammy said, "*been* waiting to get paid for training expenses, like it says in the contract."

"Well, seems to me you're not appreciating the fact that I didn't have to agree to that. We all know that kind of incentive is for top-rank fighters, champions. Very least I'd like you to acknowledge that."

Miles said, "So now you're stiffing me *and* insulting me?"

"Come on. What I'm saying here, I'm saying, I'd like you to realize that you're in a great position, that, hey, we put on a fantastic boxing card for the fans with a local hero"—he nodded—"a star treating fans to an action-packed main event, fans that have been starving for good pro bouts. Instead what I'm hearing are accusations and suspicion. Today shouldn't be a day for fears, gentlemen, but a joyous occasion. Miles Young, former world-ranked contender in two divisions, former North American Boxing Federation middleweight champion, the best prize-fighter Belize has ever produced is *back*. The man is *back!*"

Miles, Sammy, and Toby looked at each other, all smiles. Miles gave him a round of applause, the barmaid turning to look. Then Miles went serious and said, "Manny, please, inquiring minds want to goddamn know, when are you going to pay me? Let's deal with training expenses first."

Manny's shoulders slumped, he feigned a sigh. He said, "Okay, very well. How much I owe you?"

"To start with, and I think we all agreed, isn't that so, Sammy? You said you'd pay us the balance of training expenses in cash."

Sammy wagged a finger. "Cash, that's what you said."

Manny tossed back the last of his drink. He took out his wallet and peeled it open. "How much?"

"One thousand forty-five," Miles said.

Manny flipped through the bills in his wallet, tugged them out, and counted them out on the bar, hundreds and twenties. "Eight hundred twenty. That's all the cash I got on me." He pushed the stack over to Miles, who slid it over to Sammy.

The trainer folded and slipped them into his front pants pocket. "Which leaves a balance of two hundred twenty-five, in addition to the fight purse, which means the check will be for ten thousand two hundred twenty-five."

Manny stood up. "I could write you gentlemen a personal check now, or you rather wait until Tuesday for a cashier's?"

Sammy said, "Miles?"

Miles said, "I'd prefer the check now, actually." No second thought required.

Manny produced a checkbook and pen from his guayabera pockets and wrote out a check with a flourish. "All I ask," handing the check to Miles, "is you wait till Tuesday to cash it. Fair enough? Now, sir, some people outside who'd like to meet you, fans, want to shake your hand. Do them that favor?"

This surprised Miles. "After today?"

"Come on, Miles. These are diehards."

Miles exhaled. "If I must." He took a big swallow of his beer, rose slowly, saying to Sammy, "Won't be long. Once they see this face they'll want to get it over with quick."

The people sitting at the umbrella tables on the deck didn't resemble your average fight fans. They were overdressed couples with Caesar salads and margaritas, and white-haired American women who were probably hotel guests, not a diehard within miles.

Manny looked over his shoulder and said, "Let me talk to you a minute?"

Miles followed him downstairs to a wooden landing overlooking the garden and the swimming pool. Manny said, "Listen, Miles, I got a friend who wants to meet you, discuss something. Do me the favor and give her a few minutes tomorrow. I'll pick you up, take you to her place, maybe get some lunch after."

"What does she want to talk to me about?"

"Far as I understand, it could be of benefit to you."

Miles gazed beyond the white picket fence to the sea, waves splashing against the seawall, spraying high. "Manny, I just got beat by some mediocre dude I'd have wasted inside of three rounds not too long ago and I'm tired and hurting and just a little pissed at the world, so I really don't have time for games. So you tell me what your friend wants right now or let's forget it."

Manny put up a hand, saying, "Okay, look, it's a job offer. She wants you to find somebody for her. She'll give you the details."

"Somebody in the business?"

"No."

"Then . . ."

"Because you're the perfect man for the job. That's how she

put it. Listen, Miles, talk to the lady. It's an opportunity to make some money. While you ponder your next move. Let's be frank, boxing won't be there forever. Today was a tough day, tomorrow will be tougher. Incidentally, I mention to you Hakeem Wahed is making a comeback?"

"He used to be a world champ. Anybody can bounce back, he can."

"You might be right. But I'm thinking, from what I know about his, uh, pharmaceutical habits, it's not that he *wants* to come back, but he *has* to. He's got debts to service."

"Who doesn't? Why you think I took this fight?"

Manny pointed at him. "Exactly. He didn't have anything else outside the ring. But you, you could have other options if you start giving yourself the opportunity, see what I'm saying here?"

Miles said, "I'll listen to your friend, Manny. That's all I can promise."

"Good decision. Pick you up say around ten?"

Miles said sure, around ten, now if there was nothing else, he'd better be going, and as he turned Manny put a hand on his shoulder.

"Do something for me? For the time being, keep this between me and you?"

"I have no idea what you're talking about."

Manny clapped his shoulder. "Good man, good man."

They went back upstairs in the gathering twilight, Miles hoping he hadn't just agreed to something he'd regret.

3.

WHEN HIS FATHER died, Miles had returned to Belize after twelve years of boxing in the States and moved back into the house he grew up in, by the water on Southern Foreshore. It was a three-story colonial wood-frame built in 1938, with a garage and storerooms on the ground level and three huge bedrooms on the third floor; but what Miles really liked was the second-floor verandah with a swing that overlooked the sea and the sailboats and sand lighters and sugar barges in the harbor, the old Baron Bliss lighthouse on the other side. In the evenings Miles liked to sit down with a cool drink and feel the darkness fall and watch people passing by along the seawall, a quiet time.

He had been daydreaming about this pleasure all afternoon, but after the hotel he had to pick up his little girl from the babysitter's house. He drove to her home on Barrack Road in his father's old Taurus, wearing oversize sunglasses to hide the marks on his face. Alicia Gomez lived with her father above his barbershop called Gomez and Sons, though Mr. Gomez had no sons, only Alicia, who worked part-time in the shop.

As soon as he walked in he could see she was upset with him. She said, "You didn't call me. You said you were going to call me."

"I'm sorry. We went to see my promoter right afterwards."

"You know, I promised that I wouldn't bug you about the

fight, but you knew how I was worrying about you all week, all day today, and you couldn't keep a simple promise to let me know you're okay?"

"Listen, I said I'm sorry. It wasn't a good day. I lost, if you haven't heard."

"Oh, Miles. I know, I know, and look at your face," reaching out to him. "Take off those glasses, let me see your face."

Instinctively, he drew back. She reached out and clutched his hand and he gave it a squeeze and let go. "I'm just not in the mood to talk," he said. "Okay? Please? Where's Lani?"

Alicia frowned and stepped back. Miles looked at her and didn't know what to feel. He liked Alicia but sometimes he wondered if he'd made a mistake rushing into it with her, kissing her that one night she came to babysit Lani, starting something he wasn't sure he was ready for.

Alicia gathered his daughter's toys and sippy cups into a bag and didn't say another word. At the door he turned and said he'd call her. She rolled her eyes and gave him a dismissive wave.

Miles and Lani ate a supper of hot dogs and tortilla chips with salsa on the verandah, then he rocked her in the swing, Lani shrieking, demanding he push faster, faster. He gave her a bath, enjoying the ritual of filling the tub with tepid water and a capful of bubblegum bubble bath and swishing it, thinking this is what really matters in life, not boxing. Then he toweled her down, trying in vain to dry her properly while she danced and sang and struck poses in the tall door mirror. After that came a little warm milk and a minor struggle to brush her teeth, then a wet kiss and bedtime.

He popped two Advils and took a cold Belikin out to the swing. He sipped the beer, going over the day, trying to persuade himself that the fight didn't mean anything. Having no success, he got a *Newsweek* from inside and did his best to read a story about the latest round of Israeli-Palestinian peace talks. He went inside again, returned with the phone and speed-dialed a number.

When she picked up, he said, "What if a guy told you he's grateful for how good you've been to him and sorry for acting all awkward earlier and would be happy if you came over and let's chat, maybe have a drink with him?"

For a second, silence. Then Alicia's voice said, "I'd tell the guy it sounds like he's feeling sorry for himself and thinks this girl will feel sorry for him, too, maybe want to get into his bed to comfort him. I'd tell the guy no thanks and don't call me if that's the way it's going to be, I don't know who he thinks he's trying to use."

Click, she hung up.

Shit. Miles drained the beer. Alicia had him pegged. He sat there with a headache and the empty bottle. After a while he went upstairs to his bathroom to search for something stronger than Advil. When he opened the medicine cabinet a prescription bottle of pills toppled into the sink. The cabinet was jammed with more pill bottles his wife had left behind. Reaching for the Excedrin, he knocked down two more brown bottles and said, "Fuck, fuck, fuck."

He kind of lost it then, batting the bottles into the sink or onto the linoleum, making a racket. He remembered his daughter and stopped, surveying the mess. He picked up the bottles one by one, opened them and dumped the pills into the toilet, tossing the empties into the wastebasket. Ativan, Zoloft, Prozac, all the meds that never seemed to reach her, an assortment of shapes in white and blue and peach collecting at the bottom of the bowl. He flushed and watched them swirl out of sight. "So long, Abby," he said, feeling a touch melodramatic. He sat on the rim of the tub, thinking about her, his daughter sleeping down the hall, the house oppressively quiet. Truthfully, he told himself, he'd done his best. He'd been a good husband for those four years, attentive, faithful, more affectionate than he'd ever believed he could be. She was never coming back and he knew it and was trying to see how it could be his fault, something he was missing.

He went to his room, really exhausted now and hurting all over, and lay down fully dressed. He lay in the dark, eyes wide open, listened to the sea washing up against the seawall, the room, the walls seeming to breathe deep and slowly with him.

4.

NEXT MORNING, MANNY piloted the rented Cadillac down Princess Margaret Drive, the sea sparkling to the north. He'd talked nonstop since their drive began. First it was about the house he bought recently in Miami Beach, the thousands of dollars he was spending for renovations; then he asked if Miles had heard about how they shot Ray Escalante, the former government minister's son, in Corozal yesterday, how they clipped the old man, too, and he was in critical condition. Man, Belize was going to hell in a handbasket. Then it turned to boxing and money, Manny saying, "Of course, you don't have to answer this, but how much is Sammy getting from your purse?"

Miles, his shades on, looked at him and let the question hang for a none-of-your-damn-business moment.

Manny lowered the reggae on the radio. "What's the usual nowadays? Thirty-three percent?"

As if he didn't know.

"I'm hearing," Manny said, "some managers raking in thirty-five. That's crazy, man."

"Twenty-five percent," Miles finally said, "and that's for being trainer and manager. Sammy's a reasonable man."

"Good for you. I always say take care of number one first. Like this morning for instance, if the offer is attractive and you take it, the money will be yours a hundred percent. When was the last time you enjoyed that, huh?"

Miles looked out at the sea, thinking, Just shut up, Manny. Let's get there, get this over with.

They veered right on St. Charles Street in Caribbean Shores, fine concrete homes with terraces, lush gardens. Then they headed down St. Luke Street toward the seaside again. They came to a huge green house on the left with white trim, a verandah, and a rooftop terrace, a house he recognized.

Miles said, "The Gilmores, Nate Gilmore and his wife, what's her name again?" Miles snapped his fingers. "Isabelle . . . that's it. Am I right?"

Manny nodded. "So you remember them?"

"Sort of. They had a son used to go St. John's, a few years younger than me, Daniel I think his name is."

The gate was open and they drove up a brick-paved driveway, easing beside a silver Lexus. They walked along a brick path to the front steps, the yard sprawling and leafy with coconut palms and hibiscus and bougainvillea.

Miles said, "The sand and gravel business doing great, it appears."

"That and their others. They branched out."

A young Hispanic maid answered the door and told them in halting Spanglish to have a seat *por favor*, Senora Isabelle was coming in *un momento*. Miles saw Manny checking out her skirt as she stepped away.

They sat in a plush white leather sofa in a high-ceilinged room, sliding glass doors opening onto a terrace that overlooked the sea. An elaborate chandelier hung in the center of the room, reflected in the polished wood floor. The house was cool but there was Manny wiping perspiration off his jowls with a handkerchief.

He saw Miles watching him. "Boy, still trying to get used to this jungle heat. Living in the States has me soft." He gestured toward the other room. "Wouldn't mind getting myself a little maid from El Salvador, what you say, eh?"

Isabelle Gilmore flowed into the room wearing a billowing muumuu. "So glad you boys could make it, so glad." She and Manny shared pecks on the cheek, then she turned to Miles, who stood up. "Miles," she said, shaking his hand. "How are you? I haven't spoken to you in so long."

Miles couldn't recall ever having a conversation with her. He'd said hello to her a few times when he was a teenager maybe, but that was it. The maid had come into the room and Isabelle was saying something to her in Spanish, so Miles took the opportunity to gaze at Isabelle, the outline of her body shapely under the thin Hawaiian print, her sharp features and long black hair giving her classic good looks. No doubt the woman still had it, and she was about what, late fifties by now?

They sat down, chitchatted about the hot weather while the maid served them glasses of iced tea. Isabelle crossed her legs and said to Miles, "So when was the last time I saw you, and I don't mean on TV." Miles thought, now how am I supposed to know that? He was going to answer, maybe twelve years ago, when she said, "In Mexico City, the Valdez fight, I remember now. My husband and I were in Mexico on vacation and Nate, big fight fan that he is, we caught your fight at this old bullfighting arena. Yes, yes, we cheered you on so loudly, everyone started staring at us. And you won."

Miles smiled. "Ignacio Valdez. That's going back about ten years."

"Time flies. I remember seeing you packing groceries at Brodies during the summer, you were a teenager, and now look at you . . ." Her smiling eyes took him in. "All grown up, like they say. I heard you got married, had a baby girl. How's your wife?"

"Uh, fine . . . the last time we talked. We're separated."

"So sorry. She go back to Florida?"

Miles hesitated. "Yeah." How did she know that?

"My son, he used to get a vicarious thrill from the trouble you used to get into, the reputation you had. He'd always talk about you."

Miles said, "Well, I'm not sure I'm proud of all that. I was young, stupid. Thank God I grew up, right? So how's . . . it's Daniel, right?"

"Daniel is fine. He's a pediatrician, in Texas. You were expelled from St. John's, weren't you, Miles? I'm remembering something like that now."

All right, he was officially uncomfortable. She recrossed her legs, attractive legs for her age. Miles forced his eyes back up to her face. She said, "What was the reason again?"

He didn't like rehashing his youthful stupidity but was about to give a condensed version anyway when she said, "You punched a teacher, knocked him down. How could I forget that?" Right there, he heard a definite false note in her voice. "It was a big to-do, Joseph Young's son knocking out a teacher's front teeth in the chemistry lab."

Miles found himself smiling politely. He did not like this woman's style so far, the one-way conversation, her pretense.

"Brian Simmons was the teacher's name." She sipped her

iced tea. "But you went on to better things. You became a superb prizefighter. You had a gift, my husband used to say."

Miles said, "I did pretty good. Never won a world championship but I had my moments."

"You won that Castillo fight. I don't care what the judges say. Most people thought you won. Your first fight on HBO and the judges robbed you. But that's boxing, I suppose."

"I suppose," he said.

"You had quite a few fights after that. You beat Curry, whom no one gave you a chance against. You knocked out Azumah, the Nigerian, at the Mandalay Bay in Las Vegas. And that Johnson fight, a draw? Come on. People in Belize were angry for weeks." She tilted her head. "So not counting yesterday, you only lost two fights. That's a very impressive record."

Miles turned to Manny. "This lady knows her stuff." But he dropped the smile. He was uneasy, felt her heading somewhere he wouldn't like.

She said, "After Johnson, you had a couple more fights and then . . . nothing more. You just walked away. But I suppose if you hadn't retired then, you wouldn't have gone to work at the Pine Glade psychiatric hospital in Boca Raton, and you wouldn't have met a young patient there, and you wouldn't have been fired for what happened, shall we say, one passionate night?"

Miles sat up straight, trying hard to seem unfazed, like staring at an opponent across the ring. "What are you talking about?"

Isabelle smiled smugly.

Miles glanced at Manny, who shifted in his seat, wiped his face with the handkerchief. Miles said, "Lady, I don't know what your game is, but I suggest you tell me right now what you want."

"I would like to offer you a job," she said.

"Then offer me a job. Because I'm not sure if you expect me to be impressed or scared by what you think you know, but honestly I'm just a little impatient, so . . ."

Manny cleared his throat. "I've got a call to make." He pushed himself up to his feet and went to the sliding doors with his cell phone. He turned around and said, "Isabelle, maybe we should cut to the chase?" then walked outside.

Isabelle was still smiling, and Miles didn't like it. He said, "You might want to tell me what this job is 'cause in ten seconds I'm walking through that front door and it's see you later."

Isabelle pursed her lips and examined her fingernails. "I apologize if I offended you. That wasn't my intention." She gazed at him with a soft expression, all her arrogance gone. She said, "You know, your hospital liaison might seem troubling to some, but for me it's just information. My point of view as an employer is I need to be comfortable, know as much as I can about someone I want to hire, and whom I intend to compensate very well."

Miles leaned back, interested but keeping his face stone bored. "This the part I say, 'Really? Oh, please tell me more?' You want me to say that?"

"It would move things along if you did."

Miles just looked at her.

Isabelle said, "If this makes things any better, it's not like your life is a secret. You're well known; Belize is a small place and word gets around, rumors, half truths. A person can siphon out the facts. Information can be obtained if you really want it, so not that it matters, but my husband is from South Florida, as you may know, we go to Miami occasionally, ever since my husband's diagnosis. His doctor helped confirm for me what happened at the hospital."

Miles said, "Diagnosis?"

"My husband has Alzheimer's."

"I see." Then, quickly so as to be cold, "So what's the job?"

"Ironically, it's about getting some information for me."

"And that is . . . ?"

"I want you to help me find my daughter." Isabelle paused, drew a deep breath. "Rian is seventeen years old. She left home a couple nights ago. She was last seen with a young man she calls her boyfriend. I haven't seen her since, I don't know who has, and I've talked to her friends, her teachers, her . . . boyfriend's father. I don't think she's left the country. I have people, friends at the airport, at the Guatemala and Mexico borders, customs people, who've been on the lookout for them, but so far? Nothing. This guy she's with, he's twenty-five. You know who Marlon Tablada is?"

"The police inspector?" Miles remembering a wiry, handsome cop from his youth, a spit-and-polish dude who enjoyed roughing up street punks and whom a younger Miles had had a couple confrontations with.

"*Former* police inspector. He retired a few years ago and started a security firm. Anyway, Marlon Tablada is the father of Rian's boyfriend."

"Hold up." Miles sat forward. "That's why you haven't gone to the police or something? I mean, why're you coming to me?"

Isabelle sipped her drink, set it down carefully on the end table. "I've already filed a report with the police. I'm still waiting to hear back from them. Let me explain something to you. You haven't been living here so maybe you don't know. Marlon Tablada, let's just say he's not the kind of person you want to associate yourself with. A few years back, when he was still on the force, they brought him up on racketeering charges, said he was accepting bribes. He got off. Of course. Belize is small and as they say, if enough people say it's so, if it's not so, it's nearly so. Anyway, I did speak to Mr. Tablada on the phone yesterday, apprised him of the situation. Asked him if he knew where his son might be. He said he didn't know. Said he and Joel, that's his son, Joel and he aren't close, that Joel has lived with his mother since he was about sixteen and they hardly see each other. Basically, Marlon Tablada is not interested. Which is fine with me. You see, Miles, aside from my daughter running off with this, this *blockhead,* the other upsetting thing is she's stolen a substantial amount of cash from me."

Another pause. Maybe Miles was expected to fill it with the obvious question, so he obliged. "What do you call substantial?"

"About ten thousand dollars. My own daughter."

Miles said, "Huh," thinking, damn, lady, what the hell are you doing with ten grand cash lying around the house?

Isabelle must have read his mind because she said, "My husband had this longstanding practice of paying some of our workers in cash. The truck drivers, the gardener, the maid, they prefer it actually. Saves them a bank trip, saves us, you know, paperwork. At any rate, lots of people do it and we got burned. By our own daughter."

"So you want me to help you get your money back."

"I want you to help get my daughter back."

Miles nodded. "And explain to me now why I'm the man for the job?"

Isabelle said, "Three reasons. First, because you're Miles Young, national sports star. Like I said, Belize is a small place. Word gets round that you're looking for Joel Tablada, he might just show his face. Like, why is the boxer Miles Young looking for me? Second, because you're Miles Young, a boxer, and Joel is a personal trainer at the new gym out on the Northern Highway. A boxer seeking the services of a personal trainer? That's reasonable to assume, nothing strange about that. Third, because you're Miles Young, and let's be honest, your name commands a certain respect on the streets."

It all sounded logical enough, but Miles wasn't sold. He said, "Okay," nodding to show he was considering when what he was really thinking had to do with personal trainer Joel Tablada, who was probably all fit and brawny and who would understandably be quite pissed when the privacy he and his girl wanted was intruded upon. That was a possibility, and Miles had only vague memories of street fights, having dropped that tendency around the time he picked up boxing, learned some discipline. Because that's what boxing had done for him, disciplined him, so he didn't like being viewed as some goon or gun for hire, and in fact he was mildly insulted when she said his name commanded respect, because she wasn't talking about boxing, she was implying he'd know how to handle himself on the street, as in two grown-ass men brawling bare-fisted, anything goes. Like he was stupid enough to throw down over some issue that had nothing to do with him.

He drank half of his tea in one gulp. Chewed on some ice while she watched him. "I don't think I'm the right man for this job. I'm a boxer, ex-boxer to be honest. Not a bodyguard, not a private detective, and if you really knew anything about me? You'd know I'm just another version of Joel Tablada."

She said, "What do you mean?"

"That patient you mentioned became my wife, but I guess

you already knew that. Not that it's anyone's business, but after she was discharged from the hospital, she moved in with me. Despite what her father wanted. He was a lawyer in Boca Raton, prominent guy, didn't want his Abby going too far down the social ladder. Abby went back to college, though, graduated, got a job. We were doing fine until the old man threatened to disown her financially if she didn't move back home. So what happened? Abby and I grew closer, then we got married, and to get away from her family's harassment, we moved to Belize. I wasn't good enough for her father but I was good enough for the only person that counted and that's Abby. The same with Joel, he's maybe not good enough for you, but he is for your daughter. Point being, two people really want to be together, all of God's money can't stop them from being together. So I find your daughter, bring her back home, what then? You have a cage big enough to lock her up in?"

Isabelle Gilmore was bobbing one of her crossed legs. "You're completely forgetting the fact that my daughter is seventeen fucking years old. Okay?" And with a quick smile she returned to her ladylike self. "My daughter's still too young to know what you love isn't always what's best. Joel Tablada is a bad influence. I want Rian back home, and I want this man out of her life. Wouldn't you want the same thing? Wouldn't you be outraged if your teenage daughter stole your money and ran off with a man? I'd like to think so."

Miles finished his drink. She had him there. "Sure, but maybe I'd focus on my money first, because human beings, they're just harder to control. Most of the time, young people will do as they please, screw the consequences. Especially if they're in love."

"If Rian runs back to him then . . . her loss, I tried. But I have to try. It's my responsibility." She raised her voice toward the other room. "Rosa, *trageme el sobre arriba del pupitre en mi carto.*" Then she turned back to Miles. "Three thousand dollars. You take the job, that's yours up front."

Said it without blinking.

The maid came into the room, gave her a manila envelope. Isabelle brought it over and sat beside him, close enough so that he smelled her hair, strawberry shampoo. She slid the contents of the envelope onto her lap. A slip of paper with names and numbers, two photographs, and a check. She handed him the photos, one a close-up of a smiling girl with shoulder-length black hair, thick eyebrows, pretty in any man's book.

"That's Rian, about six months ago," Isabelle said, then pointed at the other photo, "and this is Rian and Joel about a month ago, the most recent picture of them together I can find." The photo was unfocused, grainy, the pair posing on the side of a dirt road, a small house on a green hill in the distance behind them, somewhere in rural Belize. Joel was a light-skinned black guy, sturdy, a fraction taller than Rian.

Isabelle said, "I think they're planning to elope. Rian will turn eighteen on Friday, that's four days. My daughter has a U.S. passport, so going to the States won't be a problem for her. I know Joel has ambitions to go back to school, study exercise physiology or some such thing, and he wants to live in the States, like which Belizean doesn't? If I had to guess, they're lying low till she turns eighteen, they make it all legal, and leave. I just don't know where they are and I need to know. By Friday."

She picked up the check. "This is yours, if you take the job, do my legwork, ask questions for the next four days. You'll give me the names and phone numbers of everyone you speak to, or where I can find them." She held up the slip of paper. "I've got names and numbers here of a few people who might help. I've spoken to some of them already, but you never know. And let me tell you something else. You find Rian, you bring her here or tell me where to get her? I'll write you another check to make it an even six thousand. How does that sound."

"Three thousand more."

"That's correct."

That was almost what he'd make for the fight after giving Sammy and Toby their percentages. The offer was seductive, but if Marlon Tablada was a person you wanted to avoid, why would he, an ex-boxer looking for a new trouble-free career, risk dealing with this character? Miles didn't feel entirely comfortable, considering how she came on at the start, trying to imply she knew what kind of man he was. He looked at the photos, thinking here was a woman who saw a faded boxer, had a way she could use him because he was just rough enough, wave money in front his face and voilà. She probably thought she smelled desperation. Nope, he was better than this. He put down the photos.

"Thanks, but no thanks," he said with a smile. "Maybe you're better off getting a private detective, somebody like that."

Her face hardened. She began shoving everything back into the envelope, saying, "You know very well Belize doesn't have private detectives." She walked over to the terrace door and called, "Manny, I need you in here."

Manny came in, glancing at one, then the other, holding the cell phone like a prop. Isabelle left the room. Miles watched Manny sit down heavily, the closer come to close the deal. "Miles," he said, elbows on knees, fingers laced.

"Manny," Miles said, brow knotted, acting all serious.

"So you won't take the job. Is it the money?"

"Oh no, the money's very nice. It's just that, let's just say there's more to me than money."

"You know, I wouldn't have asked you to come here if I didn't think this was something you could handle, something that would be financially rewarding to you at this point in your career."

"What point would that be?"

"You know, you've seen better days, you're–"

"–all washed up?"

"That's not what I'm saying. Miles, listen to me, I've known this family for years, I've known Rian since she was a little girl and it hurts me to see this beautiful young lady ruining her life like this, it really does, but imagine how Isabelle feels. Ten thousand times worse. It's her *daughter*. You could relate. And you could help, you really could. What's happening to Isabelle, when people hear it's Marlon Tablada's son"–Manny dusted off his hands, zipped his lip–"conversation's over. You might be the one person some people will speak to. Okay, we agree the money's good. Remember I told you about Hakeem Wahed making a comeback? What if I said I spoke to his promoter on the phone last night and that Wahed wants to make his comeback against you?"

Miles couldn't help but smile, heartbeat quickening, liking what he was hearing, realizing at the same time that Manny had set him up yesterday. *Incidentally, I mention . . .*

"Tell me what you got on your mind, Manny."

"What I have here is a fantastic opportunity for you, Miles, a comeback after your comeback. Wahed was originally matched up with a journeyman out of New York, but the guy broke his hand in training, so that leaves the date open for an opponent and that's where you come in. The fight is in three weeks, the Miccosukee Indian casino outside Miami. The deal is, you pick up what the other guy's purse would've been, something like twenty thousand U.S., and that's far more than what you made yesterday. Tell me, how many fighters get a *second* second chance?"

Miles's head was buzzing, and he stopped himself from chewing the inside of his cheek, a nervous habit. "I accept this job to look for this girl, this fight is mine, in addition to the three thousand plus three more if I find her, that's what you're saying."

Manny said, "That's about the size of it," and grinned like a man thinking, I got you now.

And maybe he did. Because how could Miles refuse this offer? If the rewards didn't match the risks was how. Miles took a long breath and sat up, Manny looking at him, waiting for the yes. Miles said, "Give me a minute," and got up, went out to the terrace, Manny saying, "Take your time."

Miles stared out over the silty waves, the mangrove islands in the near distance, a balmy breeze on his face. A Cessna was coming in for landing. He slipped on his shades and watched it roar toward the municipal airport a few hundred yards north, the sound fading, leaving Miles wondering: How did he look to the passengers staring out–like the owner of this huge house? Like he belonged here? Or did he look like what he really was, a man who was nearly broke, whose wife had halved their small joint account before she took off. And now an offer comes along and what do you do? Put pride ahead of it. And that's why only talk of boxing could put him in a mood to reconsider. Boxing had a serious hold on him. That's where his pride lay, in the craft that took him years to learn, and Manny knew it. In this sport filled with dark deals and shifty characters, Miles had found respect, an identity. People of all stripes had propositioned him at the peak of his career with "business investments" and usually he could sniff out their intentions within a heartbeat and tell them to be gone and sweat no doubts because he had money in the bank and a career to lean on. But with those days well behind him, he didn't have that luxury anymore, and stepping in the ring to prove himself again, make some money? Why not? He'd been doing it all his adult life.

He kept thinking about the money he could make. Man, pay off the house in Miami he'd bought when his career was hot, start saving for Lani's college education . . . So much he could do.

However. Come back down to earth. First rule, the number one principle in negotiations, an article of faith after a few dozen pro bouts: Never accept the first offer, negotiate up, and bluff like you're prepared to walk out.

Manny was still sitting there looking confident, ankle on knee, straightening his pants crease. So Miles hit him with, "Whose idea was this?"

Manny looked up. "What's what?"

"The fight. Whose idea."

Manny hesitated. "I heard about it, the other guy hurting his hand, and I thought, well, you know, I thought about you."

"So it was your idea."

"I wouldn't say completely."

"Bullshit. Tell me."

Manny nodded. "Okay, I admit. I approached them, Wahed's people."

"When?"

When Manny hesitated again, Miles said, "So you talked to them after the fight yesterday, after I got beat, and they said sure, we'll fight that loser."

"Look, Miles, you've been in this game for years, you know exactly how it is. Everyone's looking to make money with the least risk possible. This is business, no hard feelings."

"Oh, I understand fine. Wahed doesn't want to tie into somebody that might whip him. I don't blame his management, but it's interesting how you waited till I lost, contacted them knowing how ripe I look for the plucking now. You made your deal easy, you got your percentage for bringing me in, the man you promote, your side of the deal all sealed, now you're telling me to accept this job, go looking for a young lady I've never met when I should focus on training, and on top of that accept just twenty thousand to face somebody skilled like Wahed, get my ass beat, and be grateful? How much *you* making?"

"One second there, Miles." Manny put both feet on the floor, sitting tall. "You're talking like you're the boxer that won the fight yesterday. No disrespect but come on, you're not in the position to be making demands for a bigger purse, you know that. You're being unreasonable."

Miles gazed at him, then casually glanced at his watch. "Got to pick my daughter up from the babysitter. Guess we better get going. You want to take me home now, please?"

That stopped Manny. He said, "Have a seat, Miles. Let's not be so hasty."

"We're gonna talk dollars, or you gonna sit there and blow smoke up my ass? I don't have the time, I'm growing old as we speak."

Manny wiped his neck with his handkerchief, examined it, and folded it into a shirt pocket. "Twenty-two thousand, I'll see what I can swing to get you twenty-two. How's that sound?"

"You have all morning for this?" Miles shaking his head. " 'Cause I don't."

"You can't be serious."

Miles plopped himself on the sofa, shaking his head, really pouring on the flabbergasted act. "Apparently, you need me to remind you that you're the one coming to me saying it means a lot to you to find this girl. You need me to remind you that you're looking at a boxer who was ranked one of the top five middleweights by every sanctioning body for five years running. How I wasn't even a champ but HBO signed a two-fight deal with me seeing as how I was a crowd-pleaser and one of the smoothest tacticians to come around in years, and stop me while I'm tooting my own horn since I *shall* continue as long as you keep conveniently forgetting. Tell Wahed's people shame on them if they forget that the two years when he was champ, he refused to fight me, making excuses all day long because he knows how good I was. Put my name on a poster and hard-core fans will show up, name recognition alone. You know it, I know it, Wahed and his promoter know it, so don't shortchange me and ask me if I'm serious when you're the one playing games."

Manny took a moment. "How much?"

"Thirty thousand." When Manny threw him that stunned look, Miles added, "Take it or leave it," and stood up, wishing himself good luck.

One Mississippi, two Mississippi . . .

"Let me think about it," Manny said, pushing himself to his feet. He shrugged. "That's the best I can do at the moment. Got to talk to Wahed's promoter." He walked away toward the other room, not looking too happy, paused at the hallway door and called out for Isabelle. Then he walked right in.

By that move alone, the easy familiarity with the house, Miles suspected that Manny and Isabelle were more than mere friends.

She came out, her expression saying she knew where things stood. She said to Miles, "Thanks for coming," then looked to Manny. "I suppose it's up to you to do your best," and it sounded like an order. She turned on her heels and walked off. Not even a goodbye.

Miles said, "Isabelle."

She stopped, turned to look at him haughtily.

"Little something stuck in my craw," he said. "That part about me being fired from the hospital after one 'passionate night'? Good detail, but totally false. You shouldn't believe everything you hear. Truth is usually in the middle somewhere, that's what I think. Maybe even with this story you're telling me about your daughter. You know?" Miles smiled. "Have a good day now."

At the corner of St. Thomas and Princess Margaret, Miles told Manny to drop him off here, a friend lived down the street he wanted to say hi to, pop in. Manny said, "You sure? It's a good walk back, you know, and it's hot as hell." Miles said he'd be all right, shook Manny's hand and got out of the car. "Call me with some good news," Miles said. Manny tooted the horn twice as he drove away. Miles waited until the car was out of sight down St. Thomas, then he turned and walked in the direction they'd come from.

He took the street that led to the municipal airport, passing the sagging chain-link fence of the National Stadium. He veered right on St. Charles Street, going back into the heart of Caribbean Shores. He turned left on St. Mark, passed the tall homes with burglar bars and high ironwork gates on both sides of the potholey asphalt that dead-ended at the sea. He picked his way over bottles and cups and paper trash scattered in the wild grass and stepped onto the seawall. Turned to the right and gazed at the back of Isabelle Gilmore's house. The breeze felt cool on his neck and scalp, but he wasn't really enjoying it. Doubt was scratching at the back of his brain. Something just didn't feel right about this woman, this job. But, man, the money was so damn good. What was he expecting to see staring at her house like this? Maybe he just needed to walk, work things out in his head.

He headed up the seawall, passing the private piers on the left and the expansive backyards on the right. He was approaching the Gilmores' pier and through the tall trees in their yard, he thought he saw someone coming down the stairs. He walked a bit farther and saw it was a woman, dressed in a dark jacket, a skirt, and high heels. Isabelle. Miles turned back, not wanting to be seen. He thought he'd better quit this stalkerlike crap and get his ass home to Lani and a nice, hot lunch. He strolled up St. Mark and turned right on the corner, thinking about grilled cheese sandwiches and tomato bisque maybe, and how bright the day was, and he put a hand over his eyes like a visor.

That was the move that probably saved him from being recognized. He heard cars coming up behind him, stepped to the gravelly verge, and watched a Land Rover roll past, followed by a Lexus and another Land Rover. It took him a couple of seconds to realize that it was Isabelle Gilmore's Lexus, and then like someone catching a joke late, a bad joke, it hit him what the signs on the sides of the Land Rovers said: TABLADA SECURITY.

Miles covered his mouth against the dust, watching each vehicle stop at the corner and turn left, an even distance between them. He stopped walking. What the hell was that? If he wanted to give her the benefit of the doubt, he'd say that wasn't a security procession he just saw, that was mere coincidence. Didn't she just finish badmouthing Tablada, saying he was a problem? That scratching in the back of his head was starting up again. Hell, he wasn't even hungry anymore.

About eight o' clock that night Miles was reading *Goodnight Moon* for the third time to Lani before putting her to bed, Lani snuggling beside him with her stuffed panda bear. She pointed to the bruise on his nose. "Ohh, Daddy, you have an owie."

"Yes, it's just a little owie, it doesn't hurt. Let's read, baby."

"You were boxing?"

"Yes, sweets, I was boxing." Miles concentrated on the page.

"You, you fighted with a man?"

Miles exhaled. "Come, Lani, let's read."

She said, "Did Mommy reach yet?"

The question threw him for a second. Then he understood. "Yes, she reached, but now she has to rest."

"Then she won't be sad anymore?"

"Yes. But she may have to rest a long time."

"Then she will come back and be with me?"

This question struck him in the center of the chest and he had to turn his face away. The phone rang downstairs in the hallway, saving him. He kissed Lani, told her to keep reading, he'd be right back. "But I don't understand the writing," she called out after him.

It was Manny on the line. "You got what you wanted. It's a deal. Thirty thousand. Just got through to Wahed's promoter. He agreed, reluctantly. You're lucky."

"Naw, I wouldn't say that. I'd say I'm deserving. I'll need to see a contract now."

"I'll bring it by in the morning. Along with the envelope from Isabelle. Who's pleased about this, by the way. She wants you to start tomorrow."

Miles said soon as he had the contract in hand, her check deposited, he would, and he bid Manny a good night.

Back in the bedroom, Lani was asleep, as quick as that. Miles moved her to the center of the bed, drew the covers up to her neck the way she liked, and flicked off the light. Standing there in the dark, staring at her, he thought about the deal he'd just made, a sweet deal because a boxer negotiating his own fight was a rare thing. But this came at a sacrifice. He wanted to spend more time with Lani, build a connection so strong she'd never find reason to fear he'd leave her as her mother did. But now he'd accepted a job that would put him on the streets several hours a day, looking for someone else's daughter and taking attention away from his own at a critical time in her life. And even if he found Rian Gilmore in the next few days, he'd still have to devote long hours to training. To counter the rising guilt, he turned his thoughts to the money. The money. He left the room, feeling better, just a touch, that he was out of retirement yet again.

5.

THEY WERE IN Sammy's old car, creeping with the morning traffic over the Pound Yard canal bridge, heading downtown on Orange Street. The day was a scorcher, but Sammy had the windows open, arguing that running the air burnt more gas. The street was noisy, horns tooting, bicycle bells, pedestrians, hip-hop pounding from big speakers outside a music store. The contract lay on the seat between them, four paper-clipped pages.

Sammy was saying again why he wasn't comfortable with the arrangement, not that he thought Miles shouldn't take the fight, just that he worried about the distraction, especially with a short-notice fight like this when you needed intense focus. "We need four hours a day minimum," Sammy said, talking with his hands, "including roadwork, heavy bag, speed bag, ropes and mitt, some strength training for your legs, and sparring, definitely lots of sparring to get your timing right. Thing is I want to know, where you gonna find the time to look for this girl. Worries me, Miles."

A stray dog trotted across the street in front of the car. Traffic was bumper-to-bumper, the street narrowing to no more than fifteen feet. Chockablock houses, wood, concrete, concrete and wood, all with corrugated metal roofs, loomed on both sides. "I'll play detective in the afternoon," Miles said. "Morning for training, afternoon for the job, what's so hard about that?"

"Ahh, but your mind, I want your mind on one thing. And what about Lani?"

"I'll take care of that," Miles said, thinking of Alicia and knowing they'd have to clear the air soon.

"This contract," Sammy said, "let's get this squared away first. Pete will scrutinize this thing properly, make sure all the t's are dotted and the i's crossed, you know?"

Miles looked at him. "No, not really."

"How you mean?"

"Because I'm pretty positive, last time I checked, that you *cross* t's and *dot* i's."

Sammy grinned. "Just wanted to see if you're listening."

"Uh-huh, sure," Miles said. "Listen, about this purse. Twenty-five percent is yours, nothing changes, okay, Sammy? Don't want you thinking it's different now, me getting this fight on my own, all that."

Sammy turned his head and regarded him. "You're a good man, Miles. I don't care what they say about you."

"Yeah, yeah . . ."

"Thank you," Sammy said.

"No problem," Miles said. It was the least he could do. He'd left Sammy twelve years ago for better opponents, bigger purses in the States, and when he returned they had renewed their relationship with ease, no bitter feelings, sealed their agreement with a hug and a handshake, no paperwork necessary. Sammy was his friend; it was that simple.

They parked in front of the wooden bungalow on the riverside on North Front Street where Pete Leslie, Sammy's lawyer, had his office. The secretary, a striking brown-skinned woman with long hair pulled back and pinned in a bun, told them to go ahead into the office, Mr. Leslie was expecting them.

Pete was sitting behind a desk covered with neat stacks of papers, dressed in a tie and crisp, long sleeves. He looked like a studious schoolboy, and Miles would've trusted him even if he wasn't Sammy's nephew. He was a quiet, sober man, grounded in a way Miles had never been. They shook hands all around, Pete gesturing for them to sit down. The rattling a/c wall unit provided some relief.

"Miles, I'm sorry I couldn't make the fight Sunday," Pete said. "Took my kids to the cayes, but I heard you almost finished it in the seventh round. I'm glad you're fine, though, you look good. So, where's the contract?"

Sammy gave it to him and explained quickly how Miles had come by the fight, Pete nodding, and when Isabelle Gilmore's name came up, he made a slight face. Sammy said, "Something wrong?"

Pete said, "No, no," waving the contract. "Let me peruse a minute." He sat down, hunched over the pages, reading, flipping through, Miles growing anxious. Pete looked up after a while. "Well, nothing strange here, as far as I can see at the moment. Your standard contract. I'll need more time to examine it more thoroughly, though." He raised his voice toward the closed door. "Rita, if you could come here, please?"

The secretary came in and Pete asked her if she could run off a copy for him and also one of the ones from the warehouse the other day, please? She said sure, did he know where he wanted to order lunch from today, the lady from Maria's called a minute ago asking did they want Jamaican meat pies or the stewed chicken special. Pete stroked his chin, mulling it over. She said, "More time?" and he answered, "Yeah, I'll tell you later," and his eyes followed her out the door.

"So, nothing untoward in there," Sammy said, tilting his chin at the contract.

"I'll give it a thorough read, Uncle Sammy, but what I see so far looks on the level."

"What I mean also is everything, including Miles having to find this Gilmore girl. I'm asking because when I mentioned Isabelle Gilmore just now, you looked for a second like you swallowed something bitter."

Pete said, "Really?" He adjusted his tie. "No, I just . . . I don't want to say . . . I guess I'm thinking that I would, and this is just me, I'd be very careful entering into any business with the Gilmores. I mean I don't want to alarm you, it's just that this family has a . . . what could I call it? A secret history that's not so secret, let's put it that way." Pete clicked a ballpoint pen in and out, glancing at Miles.

"Thank you, Pete," Sammy said.

"Sure . . . for what?"

Sammy shifted in his chair so that he was facing Miles. "A warning coming from me maybe wouldn't have meant anything, me and Miles being too close."

Miles said, "I understand." He said to Pete, "Funny you tell me that about the Gilmores. Isabelle told me more or less the same thing about somebody else, this guy Marlon Tablada. It's his son the daughter ran off with."

"Marlon Tablada," Pete said and passed a hand over his low-cropped hair. "We're entering deeper waters now." He pushed his chair away from his desk and leaned far back, the leather creaking.

"Now you really have to tell me something," Miles said.

Pete expelled a lungful. "Okay. This is the deal. Isabelle Gilmore is married to Nate Gilmore, as you may know. What you mightn't know, and I'm telling you not because you're my client but because you're Uncle Sammy's friend, is that Nate Gilmore is one of the biggest, if not *the* biggest money launderer in Belize. Now, me being a lawyer let me back up here and ask that all this stays in this room since no charges that I know of have ever been filed against this man. But, hey, it's common knowledge. Look, the Gilmores own a few businesses. You've got the sand and gravel delivery business, not that I've seen many of their trucks around town. Then you've got a jewelry store.... What else, you've got..." Pete drumming the desk.

"A restaurant," Sammy said.

"Yes, on Barrack Road, Sir Nuncio's. Nobody's ever in there, I hear. Opens only Thursday to Saturday, something like that. But still in business, mysteriously.... What else... I think that's it. Okay, so what you have here is a man—or woman now, since I'm hearing that Nate is getting senile—a woman who owns these businesses through which money flows, and lots of it, considering how well the Gilmores live. But none of the businesses seem to be thriving. Yet here are the Gilmores living in affluence. The thing that's no mystery, that everyone knows, is that Nate, from way back, in the eighties when Mexico devalued the peso drastically and Belizeans started pouring into Chetumal by the truckloads to shop, remember that? Anyway, back then, Nate started converting your Belize dollar—not into pesos but U.S. currency. Everybody honors U.S. dollars. Banks have strict limits on the amount of U.S. they'll give you, but Nate would give you as much as you wanted–if you didn't mind paying a little higher exchange rate. That's how Nate got started. Pretty soon after that, Mr. Belizean drug dealer flush with U.S. dollars after shipping weed to Miami or wherever, he hears that Nate Gilmore buys U.S. dollars, so needing to deposit his profits in the bank without raising red flags, he goes to Nate, makes the conversion to Belize dollars. Doesn't care about Nate's high exchange rate because, hell, he's raking in so much money it's just a drop in the bucket. 'Course, Nate begins working it both ways, U.S. currency to Belize dollars, Belize to U.S. When drugs come into this country, like cocaine, foreign traffickers need to be paid, in U.S., and Nate becomes the man to go to. He supplies large sums of U.S. to whoever wants to do business. Pretty soon Nate's side business is Nate's biggest business, but he needs a front. Or in this case, a sand and gravel business, a jewelry store, and a restaurant."

Miles said, "That way the money they make looks legit, is what you're saying."

Pete nodded. "You got it. The businesses conceal the source of the money, wash it. Could I ask you something? How much is Isabelle Gilmore paying you for this job?" He held up a hand. "You rather not say I understand completely."

"Naah. Three thousand for a week, three more if I find the girl."

Pete passed his hand over his head. "Don't know what the going rate is for private investigation in the States, Miles, but that's an awfully big wad to be spending in Belize. Again, I only want to put a bug in your ear about what I know. Be careful.

What I'd suggest is get as much of your money up front as you can."

So Miles told him about the check, already deposited, which seemed to ease Pete's mind; Pete nodded, and that eased Miles's mind. But he had to ask one more question. "Marlon Tablada. Know anything about him I should be aware of?"

Pete rolled the chair forward and dropped his elbows on the desk. He said, "All right...again...this stays here." He paused. "Isabelle Gilmore told you something to the effect that Tablada is what? Somebody you would want to avoid?"

Miles said, "A man you don't want to be associated with. But listen," and Miles told him about what he saw the previous morning, Tablada Security Land Rovers sandwiching Isabelle Gilmore's silver Lexus.

Pete snorted. "Who do you think is responsible for the Gilmores' security? Way back when he was an inspector and now with his own security firm, it's always been Marlon Tablada. He's on Isabelle Gilmore's payroll."

"He works for her?"

"Does jobs for her. Might not be reflected in her books, but he does jobs for her, no doubt about it." Pete leaned back. "Listen to this. I have a colleague, an attorney I won't call by name, did some contract work for Isabelle Gilmore a year or so ago and he told me something that I'm telling you knowing full well you're not relaying this to anyone, understand? Okay, what happened, a couple days after he billed Isabelle Gilmore for services, she came to his office and paid him personally, in cash. Over two thousand dollars. Took the money out of this black Samsonite briefcase, he says, counted out the money, all crisp hundreds and twenties. Handed them over to him like here, no big deal, got lots more where that came from. And you know what? She does. Because my friend said right before she closed the briefcase he saw more cash in there, several stacks all neatly arranged. So anyway, my friend, he gets curious, asking himself how could this lady have no fear walking around with all this money? So after she leaves he goes to his window, watches her walk out into the street, you know, see if anyone's with her, and guess who he sees in a Land Rover waiting for her?"

Miles said, "Marlon Tablada."

"That's right," Pete said. "Tablada Security Land Rovers escorting her to wherever she was going with all that cash. She's talking to you with a forked tongue. Tablada and her husband go way back, according to what I hear. When you're in big-time currency conversion, you deal with certain types of people in certain private, out-of-the-way places, like spots out on the Northern Highway, hotel rooms, you can imagine it, and everybody's suspicious or nervous, and I'm pretty sure they come armed. Tablada used to accompany Nate Gilmore on some of his transactions, so people have said. What better protection than a police inspector? He's off the force now but still doing the same thing for the Gilmores, apparently. Look, I'm hitting you with a lot of information, but these are things I think you ought to know."

"Definitely," Miles said. "I appreciate it."

"Keep your eyes open and just be careful. I guess that's what I'm saying."

Miles nodded, smiling politely. For a second he had a notion to forget the deal, take the money back to Isabelle and say, due to information just received I must respectfully decline your deceptive offer. Then the notion was gone. He had too much attached to the job now, such as his fight, which meant money in the bank at a time when he had no solid plans for another career. Then there was this lunatic pride, a boxer's curse, which prevented a guy from admitting he didn't have the skills anymore, his reflexes were gone and that another victory was out of reach, would be always out of reach, like a title, like a ghost.

He thanked Pete for everything, Pete saying no problem. Sammy and Miles got up.

Rita waltzed in without knocking and put some papers on Pete's desk. "I made two copies, and here, take these back. These are the warehouse contracts from *last* year."

Pete said, "Oh, geez," and looked up at her like a chastened kid. "Sorry."

"Silly," she muttered, smiling.

Sammy glanced at Miles. Proper papers in hand, Rita traipsed back out. Sammy said to Pete, "You'll call me then?"

"Certainly. Give me a couple hours. You'll be home, Uncle Sammy?"

"Sure. Where else a retired man's got to go."

Miles turned and opened the door to leave, but paused, hand on the doorknob. Sammy hadn't moved, rooted to the floor staring at his nephew.

"How's Debbie and the kids, Pete?"

"Fine, they're fine."

"Tell them I say hello."

"I will."

Sammy cocked his head toward the door. "Pretty good secretary you have there. You should keep her as that, as your secretary. Know what I mean?"

Pete nodded quickly, adjusted his tie, began rearranging papers on his desk.

"Don't make the same mistake I made, you hear? Listen to a man who's going home to an empty house he lives in all by his lonely self."

Pete said, "Okay, Uncle Sammy." He looked at his watch, then picked up a manila folder, and found a paper inside that was suddenly interesting. He read it, avoiding eye contact.

Sammy watched him a few seconds until Pete raised his head. "Take good care," Sammy said. "Call me." He walked past Miles and out the door.

Pete lifted a hand in goodbye and buried his nose again in the folder.

Sammy proposed they go somewhere, grab a bite and discuss the upcoming fight. Miles wanted to eat, just not at a restaurant, and nothing too elaborate. He was craving *panades* or *salbutes,* something crunchy and greasy and down-home. Sit with it at the seawall in the shade of the lighthouse with a frosty bottle of Coke. "Any nice and nastys nearby?" he asked Sammy.

Sammy said he knew just the place and they drove down Queen Street to Daily, left on Eve Street by the seaside and made a U-turn to pull up in front of a vegetable market slash shop slash open-air restaurant on Barrack Road.

There were tables and chairs bolted down to a sagging wooden porch at the right of the shop. They ordered a dozen *panades* from a lady behind a grill-window, pepper and onion sauce on the side, a dozen *garnaches,* too. Then they sat under a fan, sipping bottles of Coke from straws, and waited out the slow service, cars and bikes passing by on the narrow street, the smell of cooking sharpening their appetite.

A good decade later, the lady slid their food wrapped in two packages of butcher paper out of the hole in the grill. "Mista, your orda."

The food tasted finger-licking worth the wait. Miles ate into Sammy's share, Sammy didn't mind. Miles made a mess, used a bunch of napkins. Sammy said, "Enjoy the grease now, you have to lay off this stuff for the next three weeks."

Miles said he knew, stuffing his mouth with fat pieces of *panades,* the fish hot and tasty inside the crunchy fried corn.

Sammy wagged a finger. "That beer you had at the Radisson Sunday. Hope you enjoyed it 'cause you know that's out during training."

Miles swallowed, going after the last *garnaches.*

"How much you weigh right now?"

Miles took a bite, said through his food, "About one seventy-five?" But it didn't quite work so he swallowed and said it again. Damn, the food was dee-licious, tasted like it did when he was a boy.

"That's where I want you to be," Sammy said. "The fight's at super middleweight. You lose seven, eight pounds during training usually anyway so you'll have no problem making the one-sixty-eight limit. Won't even have to fast a day or nothing like that. We start roadwork tomorrow morning, four miles as usual since you already have a good base. The gym after that, we work the bags, do some strengthening exercises. Easy for the first few days, give your body time to recover from Sunday. Sparring, now, that we don't begin till next week. I'm thinking of using different guys for this one," and he began listing a name of potential sparring partners from Belize's slim pickings.

Miles half listened, savoring the last of the lunch. The food had awakened a nostalgia in him that he was having a hard time containing, and his gaze wandered over Sammy's shoulder, down the street toward the silty waters. Remembering when he was a little boy walking home from school along the seawall, bookbag slung across his shoulders. Skipping flat stones on the waves. He must have been six, seven, just a few years older than Lani was now...Where had all the years gone? A little boy with large dreams of being a doctor-lawyer-actor-basketball-player-hero. The boy becomes a teenager with an attitude, smoking weed, fighting easily and often. The teen becomes a faded boxer wanting to revive a career that had fallen one step short. And this may be why life is sad.

Sammy was talking about Hakeem Wahed's southpaw style and Miles nodded, hearing "straight right hands will do it," while he thought about Lani, the jewel in his life, his one defense against the past.

"You listening? The right hand, we'll have to keep snapping that right. Tell me one southpaw not vulnerable to that? Wahed has this crouch, I remember it. Goes down, fires right, left, right body shots, *pow, pow, pow,* leans into you and comes up top with a vicious, vicious uppercut, beautiful thing. We'll work on how to stop that. We'll get you so that you have him thinking twice about...Well, I be sugared, I'm wasting my time here. You're off in the clouds, son."

Miles didn't bother defending himself. "Sorry. I'm thinking I better get going. Got to pick up Lani from the babysitter. It's a new babysitter. We'll continue this talk tomorrow, okay?"

"Miles, a fighter without enthusiasm is no better than a masochist. You sure you want this fight? I'm not talking about the money, I'm saying the *fight.*"

Miles mused on the question. Yesterday the answer would have been, "Of course, I do." And today? He truly didn't know.

He said, "Yeah. I want the fight," trying to convince himself. Boxing demanded so much of you, and he didn't know if he had anything left to give. As of this minute his mind was not in the game.

Sammy looked down at the table. "This is the reason why this job hunting for this girl is troubling me. After a long career like yours it's hard to get yourself up for a fight, you need to bear down, no distractions."

"I know, Sammy, I know. Things will turn out all right." Miles needed to believe this. He exhaled loudly, not wanting to talk anymore, just missing his daughter like crazy. He hoped for her sake, for his health's sake, that he would catch Sammy's fever before he walked into that ring again.

6.

RIAN GILMORE LAY on the bed, hands laced behind her head, staring at the thatch ceiling. On the other single bed, on the other side of the travel bags, backpack, muddy shoes, and dirty clothes strewn on the plank floor, Joel Tablada lay dreaming, curled in the fetal, twitching. He mumbled something she couldn't decipher. Until a few nights ago she didn't know he talked in his sleep. How could she—she'd never spent a full night with him. Their longest time sleeping together was the night in her bedroom while her mother had a cocktail party downstairs. Already that seemed ancient history.

She swung her legs over and put her bare feet on the floor and stared at Joel, feeling that something was wrong. Woman's intuition. Her mother liked to say, "Oh, just woman's intuition" when she believed Rian was doing something behind her back that she couldn't prove. Rian raked her hair back and tightened the band around her ponytail, wondering why she was wasting mental energy on that woman.

They were in the most isolated hut at the Makal River Ecolodge, behind tall banyan trees at the far edge of the clearing. The nearest hut was about fifty yards away, giving them the privacy she wanted, had insisted upon. Still, she looked through the window screens in a complete 360 before she reached behind her bed, felt the briefcase handle, and pulled out the Samsonite. She rolled to the combination, snapped the latch and opened the briefcase gently, like handling glass. Eased the top half back to the bed and gazed at what was inside. A shudder passed through her. It always did that to her—the money, all stacked and rubberbanded into tight, neat blocks, always triggered a delicious fright in her. It was, she realized it just this second, like a sexual thrill. Maybe because it was dangerous, having stolen money in your possession, and so freaking much of it.

Rian grabbed two blocks—how much was that?—set them aside. Locked the briefcase, jammed it back behind the bed, and one minute later was walking across the grassy clearing in flip-flops with the money in her backpack. Passing the other huts, she couldn't shake the feeling eyes were watching her through the screens. Probably no one was, all the guests were out canoeing on the river or hiking the trails, mountain biking, anything but minding her business. She knew this logically, but logic had nothing to do with fear and paranoia like a bad marijuana high.

About a half mile up a rocky side trail, she found the white Camry Joel had gotten last night, hidden behind tangled bush and trees. The backs of her knees were sweaty, her T-shirt pasted to her skin by the time she finished huffing and puffing up the incline. She noticed Cayo plates on the car. She fished the keys out of the backpack, unlocked the doors, and sat in the front passenger seat.

She removed the money from the backpack and looked around for a hiding spot, reasoning that this was a good move, stashing some of the money away just in case they got caught or the briefcase was stolen. The glove compartment was too obvious, and the stacks too bulky to shove under the seats. So she split the blocks and pushed some bills under the passenger seat, lodging the wad between the springs and the seat frame. She did the same on the driver's side, then popped her head up, looking around, just in case. Jungle everywhere. The tweet, tweet of birds, cicadas humming. And a disgusting humidity. She was covered in sweat. She started the car and turned the air full on, sat there awhile cooling off.

She got curious and started poking around in the glove box, maybe see where Joel rented the car, and that's how she found out that it was Harry Rolle who owned it. Said it right there on the registration. She read and reread it, fuming as she connected the dots.

So that's why Joel said he'd handle exchanging the car. Come to the gym like you're there to work out, but have your bags packed in the trunk, he said. I'll be waiting, he said. So she pulled up behind the gym around five o'clock Friday and he was there waiting with a stuffed duffel bag, looking handsome and buffed as usual, but fidgeting like a little boy. On the drive up the Western Highway he kept repeating himself, saying they'd spend a couple nights at a hotel in Belmopan to, like, celebrate, then head out to the Macal River Ecolodge, hidden and isolated, stay there until her birthday, get married, and say hello U.S. of A. Pity they didn't have time to get her a fake birth certificate. Anyhow, first they had to ditch her car to avoid being tracked so easily, exchange it for another, and he had a friend in Cayo who could arrange that. Then he asked, where's the briefcase, and she said, exactly where it was five minutes ago when you last asked, Joel, under the spare in the trunk. Yes, okay, that's right, he said, knees pumping.

She walked back quickly to the hut. Joel was awake, gathering clothes and shaving kit to take a shower in the middle of the day like the hopeless neatnik he was. On his haunches, bent over his duffel bag, he looked up as she walked over and sat on the bed. "Where'd you go?"

She watched him. "For a walk."

"With the backpack? Hey, you see my red shirt, the Gap one?" Rifling through his clothes.

"That one, on the chair over there?"

"Yeah, there it is. Forgot I took it out. You went far?"

"No. Where did you get the car from again, Joel?"

"San Ignacio, I told you." He stood up holding up a pair of khaki pants to inspect. "This supposed to be wrinkle free? Look at this, I can't wear this."

"You're in the middle of the rain forest, Joel, who's gonna care. It looks fine."

"Hey, you never know. Jane might come swinging out the trees searching for a mate. Tarzan's got to look snazzy."

"Uh-huh. So, Lord of the Jungle, whose car is it?"

Joel shook the pants out, slung it across a forearm. "I got it in San Ignacio, I told you. Nice, right?"

She said, "And you told me you can't stand Harry Rolle, yet you borrowed his car?"

Joel sat on the bed. "How do you know . . . You looked at the registration."

"Yup."

Joel shrugged. "Hey, he did me a favor. Yes, so I don't really like the guy, but if somebody could help you . . ."

"Harry Rolle is the only person who could help you?"

"Why you getting so upset?"

"I'm not upset, I'm just, I'm just *flummoxed*," thinking, Jesus, I sound like my mother. "You're forgetting who the Rolles are, Joel? Oh, nobody special, just the most notorious drug family in Belize, that's all, what's the big deal."

Joel sucked his teeth, tossed his clothes and shaving kit on the duffel bag. "I don't understand you. Harry is the one guy who couldn't care less about me and you, what we're doing. He's probably got so much to hide himself, he knows exactly where we're coming from. All I told him was me and you wanted some privacy. I told him your mother objected to us being together and would maybe track the car. So he lent me his. That's the reason I gave him, that this was just a little trip together."

"My question is," Rian said, "why go to the Rolles? You don't like them, you don't trust them. They're your father's friends, not yours. I never hear you talk about Harry Rolle except when you say you can't suffer the guy. What's going on, Joel?"

He leaned over, put his elbows on his knees, and picked at his cuticles, not saying anything.

She said, "You told your father about the money." Said it cool and confidently because she knew it was true.

He raised his eyes, went back to his fingernails.

She said, "That's why your father got involved, suggested we switch cars, suggested we go to the Rolles for another. I can't believe you did that. In fact, wait, I can, except I don't know why you'd want to do it. Babe, I know you'd want a better relationship with your dad but why did you feel like you had to tell him about the money? Was it, like, to impress him? Because that's what I think." She sat forward, took one of his hands. He held on limply. "Babe," she said, "how much did you tell him we took?"

Joel kept his eyes down. After a moment, he said quietly, "Twenty thousand. What we took."

"Only," Rian said, "only I took more than twenty thousand."

Joel sat up straight, pulling his hand away. "What are you talking about?"

"Let me show you something," Rian said. She walked to the other bed, tugged out the briefcase, opened it wide and turned to show him.

His mouth dropped open, his eyes went round, he looked almost comical. His eyes darted from the money to her and back. "Shit...oh, my Christ...that's more than..." Searching her face in puzzlement, he said, "Girl, what did you do?"

It was probably the first time she heard him curse. "Now you see why I'm worried."

He came at her, grabbed her shoulders and shook her, saying, "You lied to me," the briefcase tumbling out of her hand, money spilling out.

"Stop," she said, "stop it," and tried to slap him, make him let go of her.

But he seized her wrists and they struggled, tottering around before he pushed her backward onto a bed and sat astride her, the two of them breathing hard.

"Let...me...go," she said, bucking and windmilling her legs to try and throw him off. But he was too heavy. His face came close, and swear to God, she had to control herself she wanted to bite down on his nose so hard.

"Why," he said.

"Why what?!"

"Why'd you lie to me?!"

"What's gotten into you, why're you freaking out like this?"

"Because . . . you, because . . . I feel betrayed."

"*What?*"

He shook his head, eased his grip, and sat straighter. "You could've been honest with me. You know me, Rian, you know I like it when people keep to their words and be honest. What kind of person you think I am?"

"Get fucking off me, Joel."

He glanced at the floor. "All that money. How much is . . . Where did you . . ." He threw up his hands and swung a leg off her. "I don't even want to know." He jumped up, pushed open the screen door and went out onto the porch.

Rian lay there a minute, rubbing her wrists, thinking, Jesus Christ, this she did not expect. She gathered the money off the floor and returned it to the Samsonite, locked it and tucked it back behind the bed.

Joel was lying in the hammock, one foot on the floor. His head was turned to the view of the jungle sloping away to the north, the river gurgling faintly beyond that.

Rian stood watching him. "I'm gonna tell you something. Don't ever touch me like that again. Don't ever."

Joel pushed off with one foot, rocking the hammock. When it slowed down he looked up at her. "Okay."

She walked over the railing and stared out at the jungle, her back to him.

"Rian? Why?"

"Because she spent all the money from the trust, Joel. The trust that supposedly was for me when I turned twenty-one that I told you about? One of my aunts is the executor of the trust. My family kind of helps out my aunt financially, basically supports her, so she's scared of my mom. Well, my mom told my aunt that she needed her to sign off on a withdrawal. And guess what?"

Joel didn't answer.

Rian turned around. "There's no more money left in the trust. She spent it all, just about. My aunt called my brother Daniel crying and Daniel called me. My aunt's been signing off on withdrawals for months and now she's all guilty that my mother's gone and drained the trust."

"But that money, it isn't the same amount, it's not like it came from the trust. Right?"

"I know that."

"You're crazy, Rian. We're about to get ourselves in big trouble. I just hope you know that. The kind of business your mother's in, some of that money . . ." he shook his head.

"Some of the money might belong to the Rolles? Yes, I realize that."

"Then you're really crazy."

"That I might be. Everybody always said I was. That's why you like me. I'm the crazy girl that would sleep with you in her bedroom, don't forget that night, how my mother was right downstairs having her cocktail party and we're upstairs fooling around. That's me, so why're you so surprised now?"

"Why did you do it, Rian?"

"Because you dared me, and you took off your shirt and looked so–"

"No, no, God, the *money,* why did you take that much money?" He pushed himself up and stood beside her. "You said it would be a small amount, something that would take her a long time to miss." He pointed to the door. "That seem like a small amount to you? Why did you have to take so *much?*"

"I don't know. Because it felt right at the time? I don't *know*, Joel, I just fucking took it. Maybe 'cause I hate my mom, maybe 'cause it's not only the trust but that she's cheating on my dad and she deserves it, how's that sound? Or maybe because it was there, like the man said who climbed Mount Everest?"

Joel looked at her. "Would you stop?"

Rian brushed strands of hair away from her eyes and turned away. She stood staring at the jungle until Joel put a hand on her shoulder. "Rian?"

"You're asking me why I did it. It's like you don't believe anything I've told you about my mom. She doesn't give a shit about me, Joel, not about me or my father, my brother, no one but herself. My mother's all about appearances. Has always been. God, if people would only know, Isabelle Gilmore, the head of the Hospital Auxillary, head of this committee and that board, if they only knew what she was like. Can't even admit to herself her son is gay."

"Your brother's gay?"

"Yes. And I'm the ungrateful, rebellious daughter my dad spoiled. Know what my brother says? He says he thinks my mother has always been jealous of me, all the attention my dad used to give me. I didn't want to admit that for so long but it's true, it's so true. Know what else, what else is really silly? Anytime my mom and I have a quarrel? She makes this big show of changing something in her will. Won't say what she changed but she does it like to threaten me or something. It's so absolutely fucking stupid. How pathetic a mom is that, right?"

For a long time, neither of them said anything. They stood side by side staring into the trees. Rian wiped her eyes, went to lie in the hammock. After a while, Joel burrowed in beside her.

He said, "I know your mother isn't the nicest person on earth, but I didn't mean to upset you. I know she can be a . . . be like, difficult."

"You could say the word you wanted to say, I don't mind."

"No, she's still your mother."

"You're such a good boy," nudging him in the ribs, Joel flinching with a grin.

"You understand what I'm saying? I'm very worried, I won't lie to you."

"I know you are. But I refuse to feel sorry about what I did."

Joel exhaled loudly, dropped his head back, and stared at the ceiling. The wall hooks squeaked as the hammock rocked. "So, your brother's gay?"

"Sounds like you find that fascinating."

Joel rolled onto his side and pretended to choke her.

"I'm teasing, I'm teasing." She pried his hands off her neck, laced his fingers with hers. "Danny came out of the closet a couple years ago. Not that I didn't know already. My mother thinks his roommate is 'such a wonderful friend for him.' Fooling herself. As if anybody couldn't tell about Danny. We are what we are, and she's a manipulative bitch. There, I said it." Rian shut her eyes and nuzzled into Joel's neck. After some time, she looked up. "What's wrong?"

He shook his head. "Nothing."

"What's wrong, Joel?"

He shook his head again. "I told you about my father, right? Marlon Tablada, macho police inspector, how he used to enjoy batting me around when I was younger, told my ma it was to toughen me up? Yeah, well, my old man used to think I was gay. I'm serious. Called me a homo, all the time. Like when I couldn't open a ketchup bottle or lift something heavy? I'd get peppered with the names. Faggot, queer, batty boy, queen, fairy, nine-dollar bill, you name it he called me it. Young boy getting called these names, know how that makes you feel?" Joel looked as if he tasted something sour. "He used to tell my ma he was worried about me. One time I remember, I was playing basketball at Bird's Isle, I was supposed to paint the fence that day but I thought maybe I could get in a game or two, then run back home and finish up, you know?"

"How old were you?"

"Fifteen, sixteen maybe. So anyway, I'm playing basketball out there, constantly checking my watch. Even then I liked wearing a watch, never took it off, which my dad found strange. So I'm playing, having fun even though I couldn't play too good, just kind of learning the game back then. Running up and down burning some fat. I wanted to be lean, lean because I thought it would make my dad happy, see me looking all athletic. You know I was kinda chubby?"

"So you told me. Hard to believe."

"I was. So I'm trying my best out there, having a blast with my friends, and I happen to look up. And who's there, the only person sitting in the bleachers watching? My pa. Just watching, no expression. How long he'd been there I don't know. Didn't even acknowledge me when I looked at him. Right away, I remembered, *the fence*. So I stopped. Told my friends I had to go. I get off the court, my pa comes down, not saying a word, walks out with me. He's all quiet, doesn't look angry, happy, anything. Me, I'm all tense, trying to play cool, you know, just waiting for him to cuff me behind the ears any second. When we crossed the long bridge he asked me if sometimes I'm afraid I might fall into the water, the bridge being so narrow and me being so clumsy, or something dumb like that. I was like, what? to myself. Then he started up about how painful it was to look at me trying to play a sport that didn't suit me, was I trying to embarrass him or something. I wanted to say, but you're the one always tells me I should play basketball, get exercise, but I couldn't bring out the words correctly. I was confused, and scared, because you don't talk back to my father. Never. Then he starts mimicking me, stammering the way I was stammering, right there in the street. Some boys walking ahead of us looked back and broke out laughing at me, and my father, man, he just loved having an audience, and so he kept it up. Man, that was hard to take. I almost wished he would hit me instead. We get home, he made me finish the fence and start on the house that same day. Then he told me I was going to paint the entire house by myself that summer, he wasn't hiring anybody to help me. Middle of the summer, sweating like a dog. It took me two weeks. And I missed the summer hoops league that started up at Bird's Isle. Know what he said to me? Why didn't I try out for a team, if I was going to be a fat-assed mommy's boy all my life or was I going to learn to play some kind of sport. Then he laughed." Joel pursed his lips, eyes glistening. "Imagine that."

Rian placed a hand on his cheek. "That's so wrong."

"Yeah." He pulled in a deep breath, let it out slowly. "Happened all the time, things like that. But you get over it, you know? You have to."

Rian said, "Maybe that's why you started lifting weights?"

"Maybe," he said, eyes on the ceiling.

"To prove something to yourself, and to him. And look at you now, probably twice as big as your dad." That got a smile.

"Not hardly," he said.

"To me you are. And you're better looking, too." She poked him in the ribs. He protested, weakly, and she tickled him some more, then slid a hand down to his legs, then up, caressing him through his shorts.

He said, "Girrrrl."

She kept kneading, locking eyes with him. "Joel, you know I love you, right?"

He smiled dreamily and let her do as she pleased. "We're gonna have a problem with that money," he said. "You have any plans?"

"Yes. I plan to keep it. Spend it. Save it. Whatever. You like it when I do this?"

He shut his eyes. "You know the answer to that." He moaned. "Your mother, she probably already has the police looking for us."

"I know. I'm not worried as long as I'm with you." She scooted down, unzipped his shorts, and freed him. He was rock solid, shorts and briefs around his knees.

"Rian," he said, "right here?" He glanced around, craning his neck toward the other huts barely visible behind the distant buttonwoods.

"There's nothing to be nervous about, big boy." She took him in her fist, gently at first, then harder, Joel groaning, arching his back. She said, "Do me a favor?"

"Huh . . . yeah?" His voice thick, his breathing shallow.

She was stroking vigorously now, but pausing every few seconds. "Promise me tomorrow we check out of here? Go someplace where nobody knows where we are?"

"Yeah. . . . Okay, oh that feels good."

She said, "I've been thinking California sounds nice. We go

to Cancun, maybe even Acapulco . . . then up to California, far away, like start a new life?"

"Yeah. . . ." His chest rising and falling fast.

When she unsnapped her shorts, he looked up, his face and neck sweaty. She shed her clothes, dropped them on the porch. She swung a leg over and straddled him. Joel on his elbows, the hammock swaying threateningly, she eased him inside, and they began.

The hoot and shrieks of macaws in the jungle, the tick-tick-tick of bugs in the bushes, the murmur of the river.

They finished with heaves, making noises from deep down, Rian collapsing forward onto him, both of them drenched in sweat. Hearts still pounding. Their breath slowly, slowly returning to normal.

After a moment, he said, "Rian? How much money's in the briefcase?"

She blew air on his stomach. "Last time I counted, I wasn't too sure."

He said, "Damn. You had to show the lady just how much you don't like her, huh?"

Rian lay down beside him. "I love my mother. She's my mother, she raised me. I only have one mother. I just don't *like* her. Who she is. You understand? It sounds ridiculous, I know, but I don't know how else to explain it."

He nodded, gazing at the ceiling. "Yeah, I understand. I feel the same way about my father sometimes." Then he said, "So Rian? How much money is in that briefcase?"

She licked sweat off his nipple, rested her cheek on his chest. "I counted fast the other night in the hotel bathroom when you were sleeping, so I may be off. Not by much though."

"And?"

"Three hundred and fifty thousand. Give or take a hundred. That's how much."

He breathed in sharply. A cool breeze gusted across the porch and she felt him shiver. She closed her eyes and listened as his heart started galloping again, racing away at three hundred and fifty thousand beats a minute.

1.

MILES BEGAN SEARCHING for Rian Gilmore around noon Tuesday, driving his father's car, the day hotter than Africa. He had the air on and the windows down to let out the smell of Aqua Velva or Old Spice that reminded him of his dad, the sad sweetness still clinging to the seats.

Miles had dropped Lani off at the new babysitter, the lady agreeing to watch Lani until six. Prodded by guilt, he kissed Lani and promised to take her for ice cream later. Then he fled the scene before she could start to cry. In his pocket he had a pen and the sheet of paper with names Isabelle Gilmore had given him, and on the passenger seat a yellow legal pad for jotting down information. He felt a little self-conscious, a grown man trying to play detective.

He cruised over the swing bridge and down Queen Street aiming for Barrack Road. He yawned, stretched his legs, arched his back, tired in a good way. This morning he'd woken up too early for his liking. Five-thirty, night table phone ringing like no tomorrow. He picks up, Sammy says, "There's a brown girl in the ring, tra-la-la-la-la . . . Show me your motion." Then hangs up. So Miles swung out of bed, laced running shoes in the dark, and was at the gate when Sammy rolled up in his car. Sammy came out with a stopwatch, a *Ring* magazine under his arm, said, "Morning . . . go," pressed the stopwatch and Miles took off, on a slow four-mile run. Sammy parked himself on the front steps with the magazine, in case Lani woke up. After that it was nonstop: Miles making scrambled eggs for Lani, heading to Sammy's old gym on Slaughterhouse Road, and working on the heavy bag, the mitts, the speed bag and push-ups and sit-ups, while Lani skipped rope and played with her dolls in the middle of the sweat-stained ring canvas. Miles trained hard, back so soon in that dank gym, the unpainted wooden walls, ancient plumbing exposed and dripping, the bare cement floor. The only thing missing was Toby; Sammy said he'd gone by Toby's house twice yesterday but Toby was missing in action. Miles trained for two hours until, at last, a rubdown. Miles lying naked on the table except for a towel over his butt, Sammy kneading out the muscular kinks.

Miles's first stop was Gomez and Sons on Barrack Road. He parked in front of the barbershop and went in. Efrain Gomez's shop looked the same it did when Miles was a boy and came for haircuts with his father, the pile of old magazines on the side tables, the wide, peeling mirrors, the cracked leatherette couch. Miles had stopped coming here as a teen because Mr. Gomez didn't cut hair in young styles that well—fades, tapes, Caesars—so he became known as an old man's barber. Right now, an old man was waiting his turn on the couch, reading a tattered *Miami Herald,* while Mr. Gomez worked on another senior citizen with a trimmer.

Mr. Gomez said, "Morning there, Young Miles. You looking good." He switched off the trimmer, came and slapped Miles on the shoulder. "How you feeling?"

"Not too dusty. Banged up, but I'll survive."

"The seventh round, hear you almost had him the seventh."

Not wanting to go over all this pain again, Miles said, "Tell me about it. Alicia home, Mr. Gomez?"

"Alicia? She's upstairs. Still looking for a job, another part-time. I tell her, Alicia, working in your old man's shop not good 'nuff for you? She can't see the pride and honor in this. Thirty-one years, this shop, all the relationships, the families I cut hair for . . ." Mr. Gomez shook his head. "See if you can talk to her, Miles. Hell, the girl only works three days a week, not like I'm asking too much. Anyhow, she's upstairs." He pulled back his head, looked at Miles. "Can't do much for those bruises but you could do with a little trim. Got time?"

Miles said he didn't but maybe later in the week?

Mr. Gomez said, "You heard about the murder Sunday up in Corozal? Somebody shot up Salvador Escalante, the former minister, and his son Ray. Ray's dead."

"I heard about that. They're the ones that used to be kinda shady?"

"Used to be? Kinda?" Efrain Gomez shook his head. "Boy, it's a wonder this didn't happen before."

Miles thanked Mr. Gomez, for what exactly he didn't know, maybe just out of respect, and went through a side door and up the back stairs to the verandah. The door was open but he stopped and peered in before he entered. The sight almost knocked the wind out of him it was so unexpectedly sweet: Alicia, sitting on the sofa, rolling up stockings, her legs stretched out, skirt drawn high on her lean brown thighs, a flash of white panties. Holding his breath, Miles stepped back and rapped on the outside wall.

"Come in, Miles."

Miles hesitated, then walked in. "You saw me?"

Alicia stood up and smoothed out her skirt. "You saw *me?*"

Miles nodded. "Sorry." He sat on the plastic-covered settee. Alicia sat down on the sofa. He looked around the spartan living room, the old black-and-white photos on the wall of Mr. Gomez and Alicia's mother several years before she died. The silence was uncomfortable. "Listen, Alicia. I want to apologize."

She sat there looking way too attractive in her gray skirt and white blouse, long hair brushed out, pretty enough without makeup. He couldn't look at her anymore or he'd be distracted. He launched into his apology, eyes on the floor. He kept the part about the job vague, saying only that he would be busy in the afternoons helping his promoter's friend, and emphasizing the fact that he was sorry.

She said, "Let me ask you. You didn't have this job you wouldn't have bothered to come here, speak to me?"

"I knew you'd think that."

"How perceptive of you. Anybody would think that. You're fortunate I like Lani a lot. She's a lovely little girl and she deserves more of your time."

A dagger in the heart. He didn't respond. Couldn't.

"Apology accepted," Alicia said. "What time you want to bring her?"

"Hey, I really, really appreciate this. Maybe we can go out tomorrow night, you know, have–"

"Miles, hush. Don't bother. You're not speaking to a child. What time?"

Miles said, "In the afternoon, about one 'o clock? That good?" Feeling like a rotten user and admiring the class she was showing.

"I'll be here. Even if I get something part-time I won't begin this week. So. Are you okay, health-wise?"

He wished people would quit asking that. At the same time he was tempted to say he was feeling bruised, exhausted, just a little, gain some sympathy from her. He settled for he was feeling fine.

She stood up. "I have to go. I have a one o'clock."

He was being dismissed, and that was appropriate, because what else did he want? Where women were concerned Miles could never say that he knew his intentions.

"Thank you, Alicia," he said, and he kissed her fast on the cheek, Alicia accepting with a patient smile, soft skin smelling so pleasant he knew it would linger in his mind the rest of the day.

Second stop, New World Gym, where Joel Tablada worked, according to Isabelle Gilmore's info sheet.

Miles drove down Freetown Road, narrowly missing bicycles, trying in vain to avoid potholes. At the traffic circle he had to mash the brakes for a Mexican truck barreling through the stop sign, a taxi hard on its tail. He drove past Palotti High School, the all-girls Catholic that was one of the centers of his teenage life, and headed up the Northern Highway, the gym right there at mile two, a two-story square building that resembled a fort.

Inside was hardcore–fast music pounding, full-length mirrors, treadmills and stair steppers, gleaming chrome free weights–like a typical American gym except the a/c was off, louvered windows were open, and three ceiling fans were furiously throwing warm air around the room. The young lady at the desk told him that Joel Tablada had taken a leave of absence. Sorry, she didn't know when he was returning. Snapping her gum as she spoke. Miles told her the place looked great, like a gym in the States, and she said, "Uh-huh." Miles left his name and phone number on one of the gym's business cards, asked her to please give this to Joel if he stopped by. The young lady said, "Uh-huh." Miles didn't have much faith. He got her name anyway, jotted it down on his legal pad.

He risked his neck through the traffic circle again and drove south over the Belcan Bridge, going to his third stop, a barbershop on Central American Boulevard called Get the Edge. The boulevard turned into a washboard road and Miles took it slow, passing clapboard houses and high-grass lots. A black woman walking a plank over an open drain turned to look at him. A group of boys lounging on bicycles in front of a small tortilla shop broke off conversation and watched him park.

Get the Edge turned out to be a rinky-dink downstairs shop. According to Isabelle Gilmore's info sheet, this was the place where Joel Tablada came for his weekly trim, his hangout of sorts. If Miles had driven a couple of miles south he'd have hit the port, and that was all he knew about this area, most of it still under weeds when he had left Belize.

There were two barbers working, young black guys in sharp blue smocks that clashed with the beat-up appearance of the place. Two men sat waiting, chatting with the barbers, reggae blaring from a boom box on a shelf above a sink. The waiting area consisted of a low table piled high with a mess of magazines–*Ebony, Jet, Sports Illustrated*–and kitchen chairs, some wooden and graffiti scarred, others with foam pushing out of tears in the seats. Everyone in there was black, which in itself didn't make Miles feel self-conscious–hell, this was Belize, and black, white, brown, or mestizo, Belizeans in the city had the same accent, ate the same foods, shared the same culture, not like black and white in the States. What did make Miles self-conscious was everybody going silent when he walked in and took a seat.

He flipped through an October 2001 *Sports Illustrated,* glancing up occasionally after the talking resumed.

One of the barbers was watching him. "Yo, what's up, chief. You dat boxer? Miles Young your name, right?"

"Yeah," Miles said. "What's up. Long wait?"

The barber smiled. "I know I recognized you."

Everybody was looking at him. He could smell marijuana coming from either next door or the backyard, heard the clatter of dominoes on a table.

"I'll fix you up directly," the barber said. "Just give me a couple minutes." The barber said to one of the guys waiting, "Yeah, man, Cudo, so what di man say?"

Cudo, his hair nappy because he was beginning to grow dreadlocks, started to recount an argument he and his cousin had gotten into with some Chinese shopkeeper on Freetown, and how he or maybe it was his cousin, Miles couldn't follow it easily, slapped the man's glasses off his face, and right there with the marijuana smoke, loud music, men slamming dominoes in the heat of a workday, Miles recalled places like this from his youth and began feeling tense. Trouble lurked in joints like this, where men sat idle too long, talked too much.

Miles opened the top two buttons of his shirt, the place sweltering, the creaking standing fan in a corner not up to the job. A fly kept buzzing by his face and in his ear, amplifying the heat.

One *Sports Illustrated* later, the barber was ready for Miles. He flapped hair off the cape as Miles sat in the chair. "So how you take it?"

Miles said, "Number two on the sides, the top with scissors, pretty low."

"Righteous," the barber said. He wrapped the cape round Miles, took up clippers and set to work.

When Miles figured enough time had passed, he said, "Guy comes here sometimes I need to talk to. Wonder if you seen him."

The barber buzzed the clippers behind an ear. "Who dat?"

"Guy works at the gym, a trainer. Name is Joel Tablada."

Miles watched the barber nod in the mirror and glance at the other barber, who had finished with his customer and was reading in the chair. Miles's barber said nothing for a while, then he asked, "Joel? You know Joel?"

"No, actually," Miles said. "Just looking for somebody might want to be my strength and conditioning coach. I hear he's got some knowledge, and I could always use an edge, you know how that goes. Get the edge."

The barber's blank look told Miles he didn't get it. He said, "I hear you, man," then silence except for the clippers buzzing. He turned to the other barber. "Rico, when last you see pretty boy Joel?"

Rico looked up from his magazine and said, " 'Bout two weeks ago. How 'bout you, Cudo?"

Cudo, obviously just there for the company, said, "Boy, I can't tell you the last time I see dat man. Maybe he gone up top, like Chicago or something."

"Yeah, could be," the barber said.

Miles said, "I don't know about that. I hear the man was in town just last Friday. Somebody I know saw him with his girlfriend, you know the girl? Nice-looking young lady, can't remember her name. Know who I'm talking about?"

The barber cut off the clippers and gave Miles another blank look in the mirror. Didn't nod or shake his head or say a word. Picked up the scissors and started on the top.

"Rian Gilmore," Miles said, "that's it. Anyway, so nobody seen the dude lately, huh?"

The barber said, "Sorry, man."

His haircut half done, Miles thought he needed to stir the waters. "I hear how Joel and this girl might've run off together, eloped. Man, I hope that's not the case. I'd really like to talk to him. Anyway . . ." trying to sound real nonchalant.

The barber paused, scissors in midair, Miles's hair bunched between fingers. "I wouldn't know anything 'bout dat, chief." After a moment, he started cutting again.

"No, I understand," Miles said. "Just want to find him fast, me being in training for another fight and all, and his father being who he is, if he did run off with this girl, he could be anywhere, so I have to ask as many people as possible without actually contacting the old man."

Now, let's see where that took him.

Cudo walked out the shop fast, Miles saw that in the mirror. Saw Rico raise his eyes from the page and look at him. Really look at him.

"What you know about Marlon Tablada, chief?" the barber asked.

Miles took his time, into the game now. "Used to be a police inspector, back in the day."

The barber smiled. "You said something like, he being who he is." Cutting hair, waiting maybe for Miles to explain.

"A man of influence," Miles said.

Rico leaned back in his chair and laughed.

Smiling, Miles swiveled his head in that direction. "You don't think so?"

Rico went back to the magazine, tittering and shaking his head.

"You don't think so?" Miles said to his barber.

"Never heard it like that before. People got some other names for him, yeah, but 'man of influence' . . . I like that one."

Two guys stepped into the room, one of them wearing a do-rag, the other showing stringy muscles in a tight tank top. Cudo came in behind them. They looked at Miles. One of them nodded with Rico, saying, "Yo, Rico Rock." Rico said, "Game done?" Do-rag said for now, 'til he got more cash, looking at Miles.

Miles smelled the spliff only after they sat and started passing it around. He felt self-conscious, all eyes boring into the back of his head.

"So the man looking for Joel," Do-rag said loudly.

"That's what he said." Cudo handed the spliff to Rico.

"Called Marlon Tablada a man of influence," Rico said. He pinched the weed and took two deep hits, passed it along.

The other barber set down scissors and comb, took a couple of pumps over Miles's head. He watched Miles in the mirror and said, "You didn't come here for a cut, right, chief?" He said, "No, you want to find Joel. See, you shoulda said dat from the start when you come in, 'cause now it's time for my herb break which means to say it's time I stop cutting hair."

Miles stared at the flop of hair hanging over the left side of his forehead, the top of his head looking like a half-trimmed lawn. "You saying you're finished?"

The barber sat down among his boys, sucked on the spliff, eased back and released the smoke languidly. "Just occurred to me. You got your own personal hair stylist on Barrack Road. You don't need my services."

Rico said, "You with her all the time. You don't think we see you around?"

Miles thinking, shit, Belize was a small place infuckingdeed, too small.

The barber said, "I don't got no information for you and the haircut is finished. Usually I charge twelve. Under the circumstances, I'll take ten."

Miles looked at them in the mirror, all watching him, clearly amused. He reached over and picked up the scissors. Canted his head, sizing up how he was going to do this, then . . . a snip-snip here, a snip-snip there and the deed was done. Alicia would probably fix the damage. He undid the cape from around his neck and folded it neatly over the armrest, all the men watching him, Miles being as cool as he could while figuring what to do next.

He walked over to the barber, looked him in the eye. "Under the circumstances I'd give you the ten but I think the cut is worth, to tell you the truth, about four." He took out his wallet, slipped a five out and flipped it on the chair next to the barber. "Keep the change," he said and walked out the shop.

He walked fast, didn't look back, hearing the clatter and shouts of the domino game in the backyard and the men in the shop bursting out with laughter.

He drove to his next stop with his half-assed haircut, thinking what the hell are you getting yourself into? You're getting too old for that shit. But, hey, all that money for just one week, and more if he found the girl, and then the fight . . . He stepped on the gas to Dee Castillo's Grocery, as if speed, arriving there faster, could prevent him from changing his mind.

He was sweating, mostly from the humidity but a little from the tension. Still, he liked that back there he hadn't gotten angry. Fifteen years ago or so, before boxing, things would've gone differently–glares, words exchanged, maybe a punch or two. He had changed. Boxing had made him smarter, more cautious, thoughtful of the future. It was too easy to get hurt, derail a career. Some things in Belize hadn't changed, but he had, and he took comfort in this maturity that kept him out of trouble.

He parked in front of Dee Castillo's on Douglas Jones Street. A shirtless black boy filling a bucket at a city pipe trotted over as he got out of the car. "Mawning, sah, you have a shilling to give me?" Miles handed him a quarter and went into the grocery. The shop was cramped and dimly lit, burlap bags of flour piled high against a pillar, shelves behind the counter stocked with canned goods, a deep freezer in the center of the shop, the kind of shop where as a boy Miles used to buy cheap candy or cold soft drinks.

He bought a bottle of Fanta from the woman behind the counter, asked her if Laura Castillo was around. The woman walked over to the register to make change and returned with a young lady in tow.

Laura Castillo was small and fragile, wore glasses, and was pretty in a nerdy kind of way. Miles introduced himself, said he was a friend of Isabelle Gilmore and was helping her look for her daughter. He said, "I assume you heard she's disappeared?"

Laura said, "Mrs. Gilmore called me already. She didn't tell you? I told her already, I don't know where Rian is." Her small, high-pitched voice suited her well.

Miles said, "You know, it must have slipped my mind. I'm talking to a lot of people and I know you'll probably think it's frustrating answering the same questions again, but can you imagine how Mrs. Gilmore feels? A couple minutes, that's all I need. You might know something Mrs. Gilmore didn't ask about, who knows? Anywhere private we can talk?"

She lifted the counter flap and grudgingly beckoned him to come in. She led him to an office in the back, past white buckets of lard, burlap bags of rice stacked high on the bare cement floor, Miles going back twenty years with the images, the dusty odors.

In the office she sat behind a huge desk messy with receipts, pens, a calculator, Laura so petite she resembled a little girl playing store manager. She was studying his face, the bruises, his hair.

"I'm a boxer," he said, touching the welted cheekbone. "Hazards of the profession."

"And your hairstyle?" She must have seen a hurt expression on his face because she added, "Sorry."

He said, "Long story," smiling.

"With a sad ending?"

He liked that, the girl had a sense of humor, which would make his job easier. "Kind of. As I said, I don't want to keep you. Main thing I want to know is, did Rian ever tell you, give you any indication she might be going away soon, a trip, a short break, anything like that?"

"No. Maybe one day to Paris, a wish like that. But soon? No."

"How about Joel?"

"What about him?"

"Nice guy?"

She shrugged. "I guess. I don't know him that well."

"Rian and him, how long they been going out?"

"I don't know, six months maybe?"

"You and Rian are close, isn't that true? Would you say you're close?"

Laura sighed. "Yes, but she has other friends besides me, just like I have other friends. They could probably help much more than me." She swiveled the chair from side to side.

"I understand that. For some reason, though, it looks like Rian's mother thinks you and Rian were especially close. Like she didn't give me any other names to work with."

Laura looked away. "Well, that's stupid."

That took Miles aback. He said, "So Rian's other friends, you know them?"

"Some of them."

Miles nodded, tapped his feet, playing casual. "You think you could give me their names, phone numbers, maybe I could talk to them?"

She pursed her lips, thinking about it.

Miles said, "Look, they won't know I talked to you. I'll ask them the same things I asked you." He put the legal pad on the desk, set a pen on top of it and nudged it toward her. "I'd really appreciate it, Laura."

She picked up the pen, clicked the point in and out a few times then wrote three names, three numbers. She slid everything back to him. He read the names, looked up and said, "Thanks a lot," and stood up. "That's it. Now I'm out of your hair for—"

Wait a minute.

He reread the second name. He slowly sat down. "Alicia

Gomez?" He checked the phone number. "This the same Alicia Gomez that lives on Barrack Road, the barber's daughter?"

"Yes. You know her?"

"Matter of fact I do. She's got to be like five or six years older than Rian, though, right?"

"Yes. Alicia does her hair sometimes. That's how they became friends. Plus Alicia used to go to St. Catherine, like us."

Yes, Belize was small, Miles thought, and maybe you ought to be grateful. He said, "Tell me something. I went to a barber this morning that supposedly cuts Joel's hair. Why doesn't Alicia do that, cut his hair, you know?" Miles felt stupid the instant after he spoke. Had no idea why he asked that question, acting like a rank amateur detective shooting in the dark.

Laura looked at him. "I don't know. Joel likes his hair a certain way, I think. Could be, too, that Alicia only cuts women's hair? I don't know for sure. Hey, I have to get back to work."

"All right," Miles said, rising again. Then he remembered. "Oh, one more thing," flipping fast through the legal pad, finding the photo of Joel and Rian tucked between the pages. "You know where this was taken?"

Recognition flickered behind her eyes. Then she shook her head and pursed her lips. "No, sorry."

Miles wasn't buying it. "You don't know where that is?"

"Yes . . . I mean, no, I don't know, is what I'm saying."

Miles gazed at her and smiled. "Sure?"

"Yes." She folded her arms. "I really have to get back to work."

Miles stuck the photo between the pages, reached out to shake her hand. "Laura, thanks for your time, okay?" Her handshake was limp and not surprisingly her palms were damp.

He walked out into the glare of the street, feeling good. He was pretty sure she was lying. Either she'd seen the photo before or knew where it was taken, and the person who maybe could enlighten him about that was, sweet surprise, Alicia. He drove home for lunch, thinking this detective gig wasn't that tough after all. Seconds later he thought, Or maybe it was suspiciously too easy.

8.

HARRY ROLLE SHOWED up at the Makal River Ecolodge with a wild-haired friend and a gun.

What happened was, Rian and Joel were eating lunch under the open-air, thatched-roof dining hut, huge hot plates of stewed chicken with rice and beans, boiled yam and roast corn, a country meal, when they saw the white Nissan Pathfinder swerve into the gravel parking lot west of the compound. The hut was filled with suntanned Americans and Europeans, everyone tucking in, the air busy with amiable conversation. Birds twittered in the jungle humidity and you could still hear the river above the clinking of knives and forks. The resort was peaceful, as it was meant to be, so when the Pathfinder pulled in a little too fast, kicking up pebbles, lurching to a halt, and Harry Rolle and a Tarzan-looking dude stepped out slamming their doors, everyone looked up, and Joel said, "Oh, shit."

Rian asked, "Who's that?"

Joel's face was set hard. Rian asked again, "Who's that?" And in the instant before he answered, she knew.

Harry Rolle looked exactly as Joel had described him, a wiry, sharp-nosed guy with dirty blond hair that bounced when he moved. He was sauntering so as to come off hard. He walks like that as a front for his insecurities, Joel had said to Rian once. Compensate for all those times his father had slapped him on the head in public, insulted him in front of his friends when he was a kid. The same as Joel's father had done to him when Joel was a kid and he and Harry were friends—if only because old man Rolle and Marlon Tablada did business together. Joel discovered in bits and pieces over the years exactly what kind of business, but by that time his mother and father were divorced, he was living with his mom, and he and Harry seldom crossed paths.

Joel watched Harry treading over the lawn. "What's he doing here?" His friend right behind, a stocky dude with Mayan features and long knotty black hair. They strolled into the hut, scanning the faces. Harry saw Joel and broke into a grin of perfect small teeth. He was almost handsome, Rian could see that up close, the pimples on his chin and fuzzy goatee making him look like a teenager.

"Hey, big man," Harry said, sitting down on the bench across from Joel. Rian had to scoot over to make room, thinking, how damn rude.

Joel said, "Hey, what's going on, Harry?"

"Chicken, rice and beans, sweet yam, yum-yum. They feed you good here, man." He looked around. "This place is nice, man. No wonder you wanted to come here." He turned to his friend, who was hanging back. "See if you can buy two beers, Beto," handing Beto some crumpled bills. Beto strolled down the aisle between the tables and out to the kitchen house.

Joel said, "Harry, this is my girlfriend, Rian."

Harry turned to Rian. "Oh, sorry. Didn't mean to ignore you. Pleased to meet you, sister." He shook her hand—pretty hard. "So you enjoying yourself?" Before she could respond, he was saying to Joel, "So what you do for fun around here? Gone down to the river yet?" Harry looked American but his heavy patois accent gave him away.

Joel said he hadn't, they were just relaxing, really, a little vacation before they started looking for a place to live, but Harry's eyes had glazed over a long time ago.

Rian could see this guy was hyper, the kind who had given his teachers hell without realizing it.

"Not much to do?" Joel asked him. "Just came to shout me up?"

"Yeah, a little surprise. Long time since we talked, brother." Harry punched him on the arm.

"True, true."

"I see your old man all the time, but you? You're scarce, man." He threw his attention on Rian. "You Isabelle Gilmore's daughter?" Rian said unfortunately, and Harry said, "See, I know your pa, too, but I don't think I ever seen your pretty face before. Man, where's fucking Beto with those beers?" Knees pumping, moving his head to some groove only he heard. "You have a brother, Danny, right?"

Rian nodded.

"I thought so. Older than me. How old're you?"

Rian hesitated. "Seventeen."

Harry looked at her, then spun around to Joel and cackled. "Big man, biiiig maaaann." Guests turned to look at him.

"How old are you?" Rian asked, even though she knew he was a couple of years younger than Joel, about twenty-two.

"Guess," Harry said.

Rian said with a straight face, "Seventeen."

The smile dropped off Harry's lips, and he studied her,

trying to decide whether she was serious or was telling him something.

"Twenty-three," he said.

Twenty-three going on twelve, Rian thought. "Really?" she said, acting all surprised, overdoing it so he'd get the message.

"Yeah, really." He turned to Joel. "Saucy young thing. That's how you like them, huh?"

Joel put down his fork. "Easy there, Harry."

Harry grinned. "Yeah, finally," he said as Beto came back with the beers, flip-flops slapping against his heels. He set four open Belikins on the table and Harry grabbed one. They touched bottles and drank deep. Harry wiped his mouth with the back of his hand and said, "Now that's what I'm talking about." Beto stood there, staring at Rian. When she raised her head and stared back, he caught himself and looked away, nodding to what Harry was saying.

"Three miles downriver, the sweetest swimming spot. Takes like twenty minutes by canoe. What you say? Your girl will enjoy it," Harry said, talking about Rian like she wasn't there. He downed the last of his beer, picked up another full bottle and belched loudly into the side of his fist.

Right there, Rian lost her appetite. And the food was so delicious, too.

"Let's go," Harry said. "What else you have to do, right?"

Joel forked a last piece of yam into his mouth, patted his lips with a napkin. He nodded as he chewed. "Sounds nice, but I don't know. Like I said, we just wanted to take it easy."

"You could kick back on the canoe, boss, let the river do the work."

Joel looked at Rian. "You want to?"

"Whatever." She wanted to add, as long we have our own canoe.

"Okay then," Joel said.

Harry slapped the table. "Now we're talking. Cool. Beto, go rent two canoes and four paddles." Harry gave him more crumpled bills. As Beto was walking away, Harry bellowed, "And tell them we don't need no life vests like no mothafuckin' soft Americans."

Heads turned their way again, and Rian just wanted to get out of there as quickly as possible.

They slow-paddled up the river in the two canoes, Joel and Rian in one, Harry and Beto in the other, sipping beers in the heat of the day. The water was green and cool, flowing swiftly over pebbles in the shallow areas and where the river narrowed. The banks rose to about fifteen feet on either side, the high water mark showing in a long dark line in the earth just below the bases of the trees.

In some spots overhanging trees gave shade and it was soothing to break from paddling and listen to the river gurgling, birds in the jungle and a light breeze rustling the leaves. Harry and Beto were way ahead, talking loudly, occasionally flipping a bottle into the water.

Assholes. Rian could understand that Joel felt beholden to Harry and so agreed to go canoeing, and she also wanted to see the river, but after this they were going to say they had other things planned even if they didn't.

They came to a higher bank where cows and a mangy dog looked down at them, the dog barking as they glided by. Rian noticed a narrow trail snaking up the steep bank and disappearing beyond mango trees. Far up ahead, Harry and Beto were pushing their canoe, the water less than knee-deep.

A thick tree branch hung low over the river, the water light green and clear, the swimming spot. Harry and Beto hauled the canoe halfway up the sandy bank and waited for Rian and Joel. When they grounded their canoe, Harry said, "Is this sweet or is this fucking sweet?" He peeled off his shirt, heeled off his basketball shoes, and that's when Rian saw the gun in his waistband, pressed into the small of his back. He spread his shirt on the bow and dropped wallet, cell phone, and keys on it. Then he pulled out the gun, a stainless steel pistol, Joel and Rian staring as he cranked back the slide and emptied a round into his palm. He pushed a button and out came the magazine. He placed everything on his shirt, balled it up and lodged it in the bow of the canoe, Rian unable to take her eyes off the shirt.

Harry and Beto splashed into the river and swam out to the middle, whooping and hollering how it was cold like a bitch, then racing with sloppy strokes and shouts of laughter.

Rian slipped into the water, self-conscious in her bikini. Joel joined her and they dog-paddled out till the water reached their shoulders, the sun brilliant on the river, the jungle on the far bank a dusty green. Harry and Beto had swum out to the overhanging branch, and as one would try to climb up, the other would shove him off, their yelps and laughter echoing off the banks.

Rian ducked her head under, came up and wiped hair out of her eyes to see that Joel's expression hadn't changed–looking uncomfortable, like someone who didn't want to be there. She said, "Babe, what's bothering you?"

He shook his head.

"Babe?"

He said, "Funny you should ask me that. You don't know?"

"You're worrying about the money," she said. "You're afraid maybe they might find out if they hang around long enough."

"You're not worried?"

"Yeah, but you don't see me *acting* worried."

"What're you trying to say?"

"Babe," she said, drawing nearer, "we have to behave normal, don't you understand? We have to make it seem like we're having a good time, we don't do this every day, come to a resort. Act different, like we have something to hide, and we'll look suspicious."

Joel said, "I know," distracted, watching Harry dive off the tree.

"Something else worrying you?" She tilted her head at the canoes. "That gun?"

He nodded. "You know me too good."

"You really don't like him, this Harry, and I think I see why now. He could do with some Ritalin, looks that way to me."

"It's not just that, the gun. It's . . . Remember how we heard on the radio that they killed Ray Escalante on Sunday and shot the old man Salvador, too, the ex-minister? Yeah, well, listen to what Harry told me yesterday when I went to get the car. I wasn't going to bring it up."

Rian found that she was holding her breath, and she let it out, feeling dizzy and a little nervous.

"He was kind of boasting," Joel said, "like it was something to be proud of. Said how that evening police paid him a visit, told him they wanted to talk to him at the station in San Ignacio, and his pa said no way, they're not arresting him so if they wanted to talk to him, they're going to do it right there at the house. That's what they did, and the way Harry made it sound, he could be involved." Joel eyed Harry scooting up the branch. "Think he can hear me?"

"No, they're making too much noise."

"The thing is you never know with Harry. He's always tried hard to be a badass, from way back, acting like Mr. Tough Guy. Maybe he was telling me this story to show me how dangerous he is. All the time he's talking to me? He's kind of smiling."

A loud splash, and Rian flinched. Harry and Beto were wrestling now, water flying.

Joel said, "Maybe I should tell you later. I don't want them to hear me."

"Joel, they can't hear you. They're far away. Besides, they're too busy being childish. You said he was kind of smiling?"

"Yeah, he was sitting there in the car, the one I borrowed? And he starts telling me about how Ray Escalante got offed. That's how he said it, *offed*."

"Would you stop looking over there, please? So what else did he say?"

"Okay," Joel said, dropping his voice even lower. "Ray Escalante, okay, before he got killed, everybody says he was the one behind the family's drug business. I'm telling you what I've heard here, Harry didn't tell me this part. Remember how old man Escalante, when he was minister, he got arrested in the States, served, like, four years? Okay, when he came back, people said he found Jesus and went into like seclusion in that big mansion of a house the family has in Corozal. He hardly came out of the house, and the only people allowed inside the gates were family members and, like, religious people, Jehovah's Witnesses, that kind. Apparently, the old man likes discussing religion with them. You know how they said on the radio a white man is the suspect in the shootings? According to Harry"–Joel glanced at Harry and Beto wrestling on the branch–"what happened was two white guys in white shirts and ties came to the Escalantes' house on bicycles, Mormons, you know? The workers let the Mormons through the gates and upstairs to the back verandah where the old man hangs out. Well, Ray was there with his father, chilling out, since everybody knows he doesn't work. The white guys, the fake Mormons, walked up there, and according to the police they took their guns out of their satchels and bam, bam, bam, bam shot Ray two times and the old man two times, then they walked out, got on their bikes, and rode off. No one heard a thing, so they must have used silencers. It was a maid that found the Escalantes bleeding on the verandah. Now the police are searching for two white guys, and one of them, guess who people said he resembles?"

Rian casually turned her head toward Harry Rolle, then back to Joel.

Joel nodded. "Pleased as punch they came to question him. Is that sick or what?" He looked at Harry, who was swaying off a vine.

"But you know why I think he's full of shit if he wants me to think he did it?"

"Why?"

"Old man Salvador didn't die, remember? He's in a hospital in Guatemala and they think he might pull through. Harry knows that and doesn't seem scared that Salvador could identify him one day. Either he didn't do it or he's just stupid. He might act stupid sometimes but he's not stupid, and I don't really think he has the balls to do something like that anyway."

"You could be wrong."

"Yeah. I could be."

They watched Harry catapult off the vine, Beto reaching for it now.

A long moment passed, Rian and Joel not moving.

Rian said, "I feel cold."

"The water's freezing, I know."

"It's not the water," Rian said, and she appreciated that Joel seemed to understand that the cold was coming from inside her.

Back at the resort, they hung out at the dining hut, Rian trying to relax in a sling chair that hung from the beams while the others sat at a table playing cards with one of the workers from the kitchen. They were drinking beer, though Joel hated both cards and beer, going along only to be sociable. After the beer, he'd promised Rian they'd split, make the excuse that they had some business to tend to at the library in San Ignacio, something Harry would find boring so he wouldn't want to tag along.

Whenever she checked to see how far into the beer Joel was, she'd catch Beto looking at her legs and she'd let the chair slowly rotate away to give him her back. A couple of times Harry got calls on his cell phone and he talked for a while, cursing and laughing like chatting with a friend, then hung up and dived back into the poker game.

When Joel was almost finished with the beer, another call came in and Harry said, "Yo, talk to me," and then, "Oh, hi," and began explaining that he was at the Makal River Ecolodge, just hanging out, his tone even and formal. He spoke for a while, saying "yes" or "no" and "uh-huh, uh-huh." Eventually he walked out of the hut, still talking, some distance away. The others waited for him. Joel finished the beer and exchanged a nod with Rian: *Ready?*

Harry came back and sat down, straddling the bench, not turning around to continue the game. He set the phone on the table.

Beto said, "You in? Want a card?"

Harry looked up. "Oh. Yeah. Hit me." Beto dealt him. Harry turned to Rian. "Listen," he said, "my pa wants to talk to you."

Rian said, "Pardon? To me?"

Harry sniffed, nodding.

"Why?" Her mind racing, getting ahead of her.

Harry shrugged. "Don't know. He just asked me if you're there, the Gilmore girl, I said yes, and he's like, I want to speak to her, the sooner the better. I don't really question him. I think we should go now though. I'll take you and then bring you back, you and Joel."

He was talking to her as if she had already agreed. Rian and Joel looked at each other. She could feel the color leaving her face, actually feel it. What did Arthur Rolle want with her? She didn't even know him. But her mother did. . . . Rian thought, Play it cool. Act like you have nothing to hide. She heard herself say, "We could go now, sure, as long as it's quick. We're not doing anything right now, but I want to come back in time for the sunset dinner they're having. And I prefer if we go in separate cars." She looked at Joel. "Okay?"

Joel nodded and put the beer bottle to his lips to drink, then examined it, realizing it was empty, probably feeling as nervous as Rian.

9.

"ALICIA'S NOT HOME yet," Efrain Gomez said on the phone, "but I'll tell her to call you when she gets in."

Miles thought about it. "It's okay. I might not be home. Why don't I come around this evening, tell her. Around six, six-thirty. Think she might be back by then?"

"Oh yes. I'll tell her you're coming by so she keeps her butt home."

"Thanks, Mr. Gomez." Putting the phone down, Miles turned to Lani. "Come on, quit playing with your peas and eat."

"But I don't like them," she said, pouting. "I want a Gummy Worm."

"Not till you eat your lunch, all of it."

"But I don't like it. I like Gummy Worms."

Miles shook his head and sat at the table. He took up her tiny fork and ate some of her peas and carrots, going, "Mmm, mmm, mmm." Lani smiled at that, it never failed. Miles asked, "You want some? It's dee-licious," and she nodded, grinning. He fed her a forkful, and that's how Lani Young's lunch went for yet another day, Daddy coaxing, daughter manipulating him into feeding her.

Feeding her with one hand, he read the names and numbers he'd gotten from Laura Castillo and punched some digits into the portable. Someone picked up right away. "Isaacs' residence."

Miles squinted at Laura's handwriting and said, "May I speak to . . . Nic . . . Nicolette, please?"

A woman's voice said, "Nicolette's not home, she's at work. If I could take a message?"

Miles asked if there was any way to get in touch with her at work. The woman said she could give him Nicolette's work number but it wouldn't help him much since she was in the sky. After a pause, she said that Nicolette was a stewardess with American Airlines and was on a flight to Houston. If Miles left his name and number and what the call was about, Nicolette might return it. Miles said he guessed that would have to do and gave her his information. He called the other name on the short list, a Marie Zaldivar. More of the same: A girl answered, told Miles that her mother was at work. She could give Miles the work number but he'd have to leave a message because she was a teacher at St. Catherine and would maybe be in class. Miles left his name and number with the girl.

So. Rian Gilmore's closest friends were all older than her. What did that mean? She was mature for her age? Maybe that explained why she was dating somebody much older. Maybe that explained nothing. Miles was no investigator; all he wanted right now was for his daughter to eat her vegetables. Let someone else worry about Rian Gilmore's motivation. He was too tired.

After lunch Lani took a cup of milk and sat in front of the TV, *Dora the Explorer* on Nickelodeon. Miles stretched out on the carpet beside her, waiting for a cuddle. It came when the milk was finished and her eyes were at half-mast.

At least there was something in life that he could predict. After his wife left, Lani would wake up in the middle of the night crying, and Miles would bring her to his bed, sing softly to her, *London Bridge, My Bonny,* whatever popped into his head at three a.m., until she fell asleep. This went on intermittently for a couple of weeks. Lani became overly sensitive and often broke into tears over the smallest of things, asking for her mother as she cried. Miles spent a lot of hours holding her, and holding on for better days. Then Lani's sadness faded as naturally as it had come. She asked for her mother less and seemed to accept that she was away on a very long trip, she'd be back one day, they just had to be patient. *In how many fingers, Dad?*

In more fingers than you have, baby.

Now, Lani seldom asked for Mommy, and Miles didn't know whether that made him sad or just plain relieved.

Miles took Lani to the babysitter at five p.m., then drove to another one of Joel's hangouts to spread word that he was looking for him. Cat's Lounge was really an apartment downstairs in a wooden house on a dirt street in the poorer part of King's Park. The apartment was renovated to vaguely resemble a club, zoning laws being no obstacle. The interior walls had been knocked down to make room for a couple of pool tables, the bar counter, the few metal tables and chairs, and the jukebox in one corner.

When Miles walked in the air was smoky and loud hip-hop was pumping, about a dozen guys playing cards or pool and drinking Belikins. Miles ordered a Fanta from the bar man, a light-skinned black guy with green eyes. He asked Miles was this his first time in here, and when Miles replied it was, he said then it was on the house. He shook Miles's hand and said his name was Ray but they called him Cat, and pointed at his eyes.

Cat's eyes–it was true. Miles said, "I'm looking for somebody they tell me comes here a lot. I'm hoping you might know where I can find him." Straight out with the truth: He'd learned a lesson this morning. "Joel Tablada, seen him lately?"

"Joel," Ray the Cat said, "Joel, man, been days since I seen him." He called out to a group sitting at one table, "Anybody know where Joel is?"

A couple guys looked up, shook their heads, went back to the cards. One guy said, "Who wants to know?"

Ray tilted his chin at Miles. "Man here."

The cardplayer nodded at Miles. Then his face broke into a grin. "Oh, shit. Look out, Miles. You dat?" The guy, a little older than a teenager, jumped up and came over to Miles. "Eric," he said, patting his chest. "You don't remember me? Eric from Cleghorn Street. Bones is my brother."

"Bones the mechanic? Guy that went to St. John's?"

"Yeah, man, yeah. Used to be in your class." Eric pumped Miles's hand.

Miles said, "Oh, hell, how you doing? When I left here you were, what, this high, seven years old or so?"

Eric chuckled. "I used to see you come 'round the house all the time. I watched some of your fights on TV and my brother used to say that's my man right there."

Miles said, "How's Bones?"

"Still here. He got a shop on Plues Street, got five kids, too. The man's fat now. They still call him Bones, though." They grinned. Eric said, "So you looking for Joel? You know, now and again I see him here, but lately . . ." His lips turned down as he shook his head. "You friends with Joel?"

Miles said actually he wasn't and pulled out the story about looking for a personal trainer.

Eric said, "Let me ask these boys. Come with me."

As they were going, Ray the Cat called out, "Hey, hold up. Sign this for me?" Holding out a Dewar's White Label coaster and a pen.

Miles signed his name. Ray said, "Thanks, my man. I *knew* you looked familiar." He thumbtacked the coaster to a corkboard between invoices and a poster of a buxom black woman arched back in a bikini advertising Guinness Extra Stout. He tapped three other coasters on the board saying, "Snoop Dogg, Tupac, Marion Jones. All of them came to Belize. Now the local boy is among the big names." He pointed at Miles.

Miles shook a lot of hands as Eric took him around to the card games and the pool tables, everyone looking genuinely pleased to meet Miles, a couple of them recounting fights they'd seen, but nobody knew where Joel Tablada was.

"Let's go outside," Eric said.

They went through a side door and into the backyard. Some guys were sitting on the steps, beers at their feet. Eric introduced Miles to the crowd, the guys getting up to bump fists or shake hands, showing some love, except for one of them. He sat leaning against the railing and just nodded, sleepy-eyed.

Miles recognized him, the sinewy guy in the tank top from the barbershop.

"Me and Miles go way back," Eric said. "Miles used to hang out with Bones." Eric looked proud, standing there grinning. He said, "Anybody know where Joel is? Miles looking for the man."

Nobody knew, they hadn't seen him for about a week. Miles scanned the faces. Everybody seemed comfortable with their response, nobody glancing down or looking away. Only the guy in the tank top flashed a trickster's smile and said, "You still on that trip, boss?" He picked up his bottle and strolled past Miles into the bar, smiling all the way.

"You know Stick?" Eric asked Miles.

"Not really."

Eric got the message and left that alone. The sound of a toilet flushing caught Miles's attention, and he noticed a tiny cinderblock shed for the first time, someone jiggling the door from the inside, having trouble getting out. Eventually, the door opened and a man lurched out. It was Toby, unshaven and disheveled, looking nothing like the cut-man who had been in Miles's corner on Sunday. Toby paused, took his measure and walked over to the steps, listing to starboard. He grabbed the railing for support. "Okay then, which one of you's buying the next round?"

Eric said, "Next round? Better g'wan with that shit."

A couple of the guys chuckled. Toby shook his head, looked at them one by one, saying, "You got me covered? How you? You my man?"

Then he saw Miles, and Miles said, "Hey, Toby."

Toby exploded into a cough. He palmed his mouth, turned his face, his shoulders heaving as he coughed. "Oh shit," he sputtered. He shook his head and beat his chest. He spat. "Man, you frightened me. What you doing here?"

Miles smiled uneasily. "Two months down the drain, eh?"

Toby stared at him with unfocused, red eyes. "Don't do me like that. Of all the people, you the one I always think might understand me."

Miles looked down and toed a pebble. "Yeah, well . . ."

"Miles, you disappointed? Think how I must feel." Toby walked off, a hitch in his step. He turned around. "Don't judge me. We all got–" He coughed, seemed to lose his train of thought. He sucked in a breath. "We all got to lose some time, right?" He went inside.

Miles stood there mildly embarrassed, everybody looking at him.

Eric said, "Toby . . . that's right, he used to be your trainer. I forgot about that."

"My cut-man," Miles said, gazing at the empty doorway. "He's my cut-man. And a damn good one." He looked at Eric. "Used to be an even better boxer. He was a gifted middleweight, believe it or not." He felt that he had to defend Toby. He wanted to say, hey, that's not the real Toby; I know the real man and he's dependable and hardworking and has a golden heart. He wanted to say all this and hope it was true, but he realized that they knew another man, one he might hardly recognize.

"What happened to him?" Eric asked.

Miles was already moving toward the door. "Life," he said, walking back into the smoky room.

An hour and a half later, they sat in the car with all the windows down, drinking cold bottled water. They could see people filtering in and out of Cat's about a half block away down the dirt street.

"Sammy didn't even tell me you had a fight coming up," Toby said, "so I know I'm out of the loop. I mean, how else I'm supposed to take that?"

"Sammy told me he can't get in touch with you," Miles said. "Called you three or four times, no dice. Went by your house yesterday, nada. That's how he figured something was up."

Toby shook his head and looked off in the distance. "Fucking Sammy. Never had faith in me, always thinking the worst. Can't cut me a break, you see?"

"You blaming Sammy now? You the one picked up the bottle and drank. Can't stop yourself? Then get some help. Sammy's been telling you that for years. I have to agree. You're letting me down, Toby."

Toby lowered his head and put a hand over his eyes. "You don't understand," he said, "you just don't understand." Then quietly he began to sob.

Miles felt sorry for him, truly did. But he knew there was nothing he could do anymore for Toby short of driving him to rehab. Sammy had said once, "Toby doesn't really drink anymore, the boy swallows," and Miles had laughed, but he didn't feel like laughing now. Toby no longer had the control to enjoy one or two beers; when he drank he binged, and his sprees lasted for days. He couldn't hold down a job longer than three or four months. He got by on the good graces of friends like Sammy, and a forgiving landlady who had known him since he was a boy and was like an aunt to him. All this Sammy had told Miles.

Now Toby dried his eyes with the front of his shirt and looked off down the street. He said, "Sometimes I feel like just yesterday I was fighting at the Blue Ball Room in Atlantic City, my whole career ahead of me, and then I wake up one morning and I'm forty-two years old and got nothing to account for all the years."

Maybe it was one of the saddest things Miles had heard, maybe a version of every man's tale. He didn't know how to respond without sounding trite or patronizing or spouting psychobabble. So he told the truth. "Sometimes I feel the same way, believe me."

Toby wiped his nose on his sleeve. "Life is slipping by and I never achieved any one of my dreams, not a single one."

Miles said, "Listen. You're telling me a story I *lived*. I ever been a world champ? I look rich to you? I dedicated my adulthood to something that won't see me through, left me without any professional skills for the real world or whatever you want to call it. But I ain't gonna cry, Toby. I refuse. You have to strive to be positive, it's a skill you learn. You get knocked down in the ring, what do you do? You get up. You fucking pick yourself up and steel yourself. Me? I pick myself up every time just thinking about my daughter. The most precious thing in my life. Maybe a year ago, you know, I'd have said my family meaning my wife, but then she left, just like that. Shit, I don't even think she knows why . . . but that's okay. It's not for me to try and figure out someone else's head. I've got to keep my mind healthy. Like they say, don't worry about your opponent, fight *your* fight, and when the shit gets tough you bear down, roll with the punches. Sounds corny, right? But it gets me by, and that's all I care about. Think about the most meaningful things in your life, the things you want to be known for. Focus on that. Help yourself, Toby."

Toby nodded, his eyes slick and shiny. "I know, I know . . ." He took a deep breath and shuddered. He dropped his head on the headrest and shut his eyes. He opened them after a while and just stared at the ceiling. He stayed quiet for a long time. Miles played the radio, slow reggae. After a few minutes, he turned it off.

"So," Toby said, "you're finally fighting Wahed."

"Yeah. In three weeks."

"Three weeks. I think you could do it." Toby rolled his head to the side and looked at Miles. "What you doing in a bar if you serious about this fight?"

Miles told him about the job of finding Rian Gilmore and Joel Tablada.

Toby was quiet a long time. Then he said, "Marlon Tablada. You fucking with Marlon Tablada?"

"No. I'm looking for his son."

"No, you're fucking around with the father. You don't know who he is?" Miles said he did. Toby said, "No, you don't. Because you'd know that he owns this bar."

"What? What about that guy in there, Ray?"

Toby snorted. "Ray just runs this place. If a one-legged man named Pete worked the bar, they'd call the place Peg-leg Pete's. Fuck, Miles, you coming to Tablada's club you should know something about him. This guy, man, this guy's a major league asshole. Only reason I come here is because it's within walking distance from me. Tablada, Miles, the man is as crooked as they come, ruthless with a capital dick. So you prepared to tell him why you're looking for his son?"

"I want his son to be my training and conditioning coach, that's all he has to know."

"This lady Gilmore, she told you to come here?"

"Yeah. But maybe she didn't know Tablada owns this joint." As soon as he said it, he didn't believe it.

Toby said, "Or maybe she didn't quite give a fuck about your health, sending you into the hornet's nest like this."

Miles pondered that. It was clear to him that Isabelle Gilmore was working some sharper angle. Concealing her relationship with Tablada, but giving him leads that put him in the heart of Tablada's turf. What was that all about?

"Check this out, Miles." Toby jerked a thumb down the street. A blue Land Rover had pulled up in front of Cat's and guys were milling around it. "That's a Tablada Security Company vehicle. Notice how everybody's out there to greet it? Tablada isn't in there, case you want to know. Nah, the security guy, the driver, he used to hang out at Cat's. The way it works, Tablada's smart, he hires all these guys, street guys, pays them good, makes them halfway legit. Basically, he's got a crew that does whatever rough-house shit he has in mind, or security for this or that business. Everybody, all of them you see there, either they work for him or want to work for him. Street informants, he's got plenty of those. And the way I hear it, if you prove yourself, he might hire you, put you in one of those funky-ass blue uniforms you see that driver wearing over there. Hey, Miles, you want to get me a beer, please?"

"No. So let me ask you, guy in there called Stick, slim dude looks like a welterweight, he works for Tablada? Or Eric, you know, the mechanic's brother, how about him?"

Toby stared at Miles. "No, just like that, huh? Me and you go way back and just one goddamn beer?"

Miles drank off his water and started the car. "You went deaf and I didn't know about it? I wasted my breath talking to you. Let me get my ass home."

"All right, all right . . ."

"You want to pour your life down the drain go ahead, but I don't have the time to listen to your self-pitying bullshit when I've got more constructive things to do, feel me?"

"Okay, okay, cool down. I hear you, damn." Toby sighed. "What did you ask me?"

"Stick. Eric."

Toby said, "Yeah, yeah, they kind of work for Tablada. Unofficially anyway. Part of the street crew, in other words." Toby drank some water and wiped his mouth on his sleeve. "I'm just tired, Miles. Just tired of life. Maybe I should go home and sleep. You think you could take me home?"

"Gladly. You look like you could use your bed."

"Can't argue with that," Toby said, "but you, honestly, you don't look too hot yourself. Like, what's going on with your hair?"

Miles examined the botched haircut in the rearview. He tamped down the prickly parts. "I got outnumbered at the barbershop," he said. "Four against one."

"What?"

"Ask Stick. He'll probably be happy to tell you about it. You still live on Baymen Avenue?"

10.

MILES SAT IN Toby's messy living room and phoned the babysitter to say he was running late, could she keep Lani another hour? The lady agreed but didn't sound too happy. Miles was glad he'd be seeing Alicia that evening. He preferred her in every way.

He stayed a few minutes talking to Toby about nothing special, staying mainly to make sure he fell asleep, stretched out on a ratty brown couch, one shoe on. Miles positioned the standing fan so that it blew directly on Toby. Then he left quietly, quickly, before the scene made him really depressed.

He headed toward Princess Margaret Drive with the twilight gathering. He fiddled with the radio, passing through Mexican music, the hiss and crackle of static, before giving up and settling on silence to smooth out the evening. In front of him, a blue Land Rover was going slowly, too slowly, the driver obviously mistaking the day for Sunday. At the corner of Baymen and Princess Margaret the driver stopped too long, facing the sea view, not looking left or right. Just sitting there, pissing Miles off. Miles considered swerving around to pass when another Land Rover drew up behind him, stopping inches from his bumper. There were two men inside, and they were smiling. At which point Miles realized what was going down.

He sat cool and decided to let the situation ride. No need to panic. Let's see what Tablada's boys had in mind. The head Land Rover turned right, and Miles did, too. He could have turned left, but he was heading into town and didn't see the need to change his route just yet, especially being as curious as he was. They escorted him along Princess Margaret Drive in a slow-moving sandwich, the sea breeze easing the tension in the back of his neck. They drove to where the street changed into Barrack Road, then passed the outdoor restaurant where he and Sammy ate that morning. He should have turned right at the corner to go to Alicia's, but he didn't want to expose her to any of this.

They passed the town clock and bore deeper into the city, turning right on Hyde's Lane, Miles simply following the Rover. He breathed deeply and slowly to keep calm, checked the other Rover in the rearview. Two black men, the driver in uniform. The procession rolled on. A left on North Front Street, then over the swing bridge. Other cars began honking, unable to pass on narrow, one-way Albert Street. They rolled past Independence Park, the corner where Miles could have turned left toward home. But he had no intention of drawing them anywhere close to his house. Not that he doubted they already knew where he lived. There were other side streets coming up in case he needed to bail out, but that was Plan B. Stores were closing now, shutters rolling down with a bang and a puff of dust. People crowded the sidewalks, heading home after the day's work.

He passed all the side streets, trying to figure out what these boys' intentions were. They came to the V at the end of Albert, and the lead Rover took the right lane. Miles faked left, just for the hell of it, and the rear Rover bumped him. His car jerked and he swung into the right lane. Then the lead Rover stopped abruptly in the middle of the street, blocking him. Miles waited. Several seconds passed. The rear Rover inched up to his bumper and tapped it. "Let's do this then," Miles said. He turned off the ignition, pocketed the keys, and slowly got out of the car.

It was almost dark. A few people were in the street, and some men were hanging around in front of a clapboard shop with a lighted Coke sign. Miles walked toward the lead vehicle. Before he was even close, the driver poked his head out the window and said, "Get back in your car."

Miles stopped halfway. "Come again?"

"Get back in your car. Somebody wants to talk to you."

"I don't usually carry on conversations parked in the middle of the road. Tell this somebody they want to talk to me, meet me on the side. And I don't have all day." Miles turned around.

A man was strolling toward him. In the lamppost light Miles could see he was a dandy, sporting a white guayabera, dark slacks, hair cropped low in gentle waves and parted at the right; built slim like a blade. His dress shoes clacked on the street as he approached.

"Young Miles Young," he said, extending a hand. "Well, I be sugared, you're back in town."

Slowly, Miles recognized Marlon Tablada. The man had not aged, still sharp-featured and handsome, with a sly one-sided smile.

"Mr. Tablada," Miles said, shaking his hand, wondering why in the hell he felt compelled to say *Mister*. Tablada's extra-hard grip was like a challenge, and he stared into your eyes like he was saying, how's that for a fucking vise. Miles said, "Can I help you with something?"

Tablada cocked his head and looked at Miles. "Can *you* help *me* with something?" He laughed softly. "I'm about to ask you the very same question, my brother."

They were standing in the middle of the street and a car came up, braked, then moved around them. Another one followed, the driver touching the horn. Tablada turned around and glared. The man behind the wheel drove off wide right, muttering and shaking his head.

Tablada turned back to Miles, looking cool and amused. "I hear you're asking about my son. That true?"

Miles said it was, and he made sure he held eye contact. The boxer in him had already sized up Tablada physically. Height, weight, arm reach—the man had him beat in all departments, but Miles had age on his side.

A smile twitched along Tablada's pencil-thin moustache. "Why are you asking for Joel?"

Miles hesitated—damn it, and Tablada said, "We need to talk. That's why I followed you."

"You could've simply told me."

"I'm telling you now."

"A phone call or something, instead of all this drama through town."

Tablada smiled. "Merely a demonstration of how determined I am to talk to you. Come on," holding out a palm toward the side of the street, "let's have a drink, kick back, and chat." Tablada walked away. Two houses down on the right he opened a wrought-iron gate and looked back at Miles. "You coming?"

A quick glance around told Miles this was decidedly Tablada's neighborhood. Three blue Land Rovers parked on the side of the street. A couple of blue uniforms sipping soft drinks at the chicken-screen window of the shop, three more hanging around by a low-slung BMW with gleaming rims, and everybody looking at Miles. He took his time parking his car on the side of the street.

Tablada's house was concrete downstairs, where he kept an office–TABLADA SECURITY on a shingle over an iron-grille door–and wood upstairs. The building was narrow, a hundred feet long, and on either side stood tall concrete fences with broken bottles embedded in the tops. They went upstairs, met a heavy iron-grille door that Tablada unlocked, then a steel door, then they were in the house.

It was definitely like no other old house he'd ever entered in that part of Belize. The interior didn't match the exterior of this neighborhood of old wooden houses with zinc roofs and chicken coops in the yards. For one, it was cooled by central air, in a country where even window units were a luxury. For another, the open floor plan came straight out of *Better Homes and Gardens*; Tablada had gutted the innards of the old colonial style and replaced it top to bottom with trendy America. A polished pickled pine floor, Oriental rugs here and there, a sumptuous leather sofa and club chairs, and contemporary furniture with hard angles.

A forty-inch plasma TV on the wall stared at Miles as he sat down, sinking into a club chair, checking out the DVD player and high-end stereo on shelves built into the wall, the surround-sound speakers affixed in every corner.

"I'm taking a beer," Tablada said. He pointed at Miles. "What's your taste?"

"Water's fine."

Tablada opened a walnut cabinet on the outside of the kitchen counter, slid out a shelf of a small built-in refrigerator stocked with frosty tumblers and imported beers of all kinds. He grabbed a bottle of Red Stripe and a tall glass.

Miles maintained a lazy expression, trying to show he wasn't too impressed. Tablada brought him a glass of iced water and sat in the opposite club chair with his beer.

"Back in town," Tablada said, "the man, the myth, the legend." He raised his glass in salute and took a neat sip. Set the beer down on the chair arm and held it there. "I'm sure Belizeans everywhere are happy to have you back, but after that fight Sunday, you don't think it's time to hang it up?"

"Maybe," Miles said. "You might be right."

Tablada smirked. "I know I'm right." He watched Miles, eyes traveling from head to foot. "So why you looking for my son?"

Miles was ready. "For my training."

"Oh? How's that?"

"I need a good strength and conditioning coach. Your son, everybody tells me he's the man that can help me."

"Everybody's telling you that? Like who?"

Miles shrugged. "People at the gym. Sammy Wade's Boxing Gym, the New World Gym."

"So you know Joel."

"No. But I've seen him around." Miles lied smoothly. "Seen him working with people, gym members, I'm thinking, yeah, this guy knows his stuff. I ask around, everybody's telling me he's the man to contact. Only now when I decide to do it, I can't find him. Something I should know about why you're asking me up here, trailing me through town?"

Tablada raised his glass, tapping it with a huge silver ring on his finger, smiling. "So who sent you?"

Miles put on a frown. "Who sent me? My trainer, me. I don't understand the question. Listen, you have a problem with me inquiring about your son, I'm doing something you don't like, tell me and I won't do it anymore, but I'm just looking for your son 'cause I'm interested in hiring him, that's it. To tell you the truth, I'm thinking maybe I should forget about it, the amount of suspicion my interest seems to be raising. I'd like to talk to Joel but maybe it's for the best I look elsewhere."

Tablada said, "Maybe."

Miles nodded. "Well, then. There you go." He sat up as if getting ready to leave. "Don't understand it, but hey." He gulped down some water, reached over and set the glass on a coffee table. He stood up. "Thanks, I guess. You saved me a couple thousand. I have a decent paying bout in a few weeks and I'd have plunked down some solid change for a little edge, but I'm saving money so maybe I shouldn't be too disappointed."

Tablada looked at him. "Another fight?"

"Yeah. Up in Miami. Kind of fell into my lap. Against a former champ, too. Funny how things work out sometimes. Anyway, I'm gone." He half-turned to the door. "Like I said, I didn't mean to cause a commotion."

"Wait," Tabalda said. "Sit down." He stretched a palm toward the empty chair. "Maybe I came on too strong."

Miles sat down, liking the switch, how talk of money had hooked him.

"So you're fighting again," Tablada said. "How old are you now?"

"Thirty-five."

"Getting up there. Boxing is a young man's game and you think you need an edge."

"Exactly."

"And you're ready to pay for it, same way you pay your trainer and sparring partners and nutritionist and such."

"I don't have a nutritionist. The rest yes."

"And you talking about how much?"

"Well . . . that depends. Which is why I need to talk to Joel. I still really don't understand what the problem is."

Tablada sat back and considered Miles. "My son is unavailable at the moment. Went on a little vacation with his young lady. But maybe you already know this."

Miles said, "This is the first time I'm hearing it," his voice so flat he almost believed himself.

"Me and Joel aren't too close," Tablada said. "It didn't work out with me and his mother. You have any kids?"

"A daughter. Three and a half years old."

"Then you know how hard parenting can be. You've got to be a good father or kids, they can stray. When I lived with Joel I raised that boy with a stern hand. He knew his place, you better believe it. From when he was a baby, reaching for cookies or something on a counter and he shouldn't have it, his hands got slapped fast. Work to do 'round the house, he better be first in line. When he was about thirteen, getting a little flab, I used to shame him, so he hauled his ass out the house, go running. Boxer like you could relate. Boy dropped, like, twenty pounds that summer. And you should see him now." Tablada puffed out his chest, reared back his shoulders. "Boy's buff. And that's because he learned discipline early. Takes after his old man in that he's handsome as a devil." Tablada winked, flashing his sly smile. "Good boy, nice fellow everybody always says. Except now, he's in love, so I hardly see him. Got himself a beautiful young lady from a well-to-do family, and from what I gather talking to people, this girl loves him back something fierce. But we have a problem. Girl's mother disapproves. Her daughter going 'round with a common black boy like Joel Tablada? No, can't have that, that's unacceptable. But what's she going to do? Can't forbid kids nowadays to knock it off, can you? Jack and Jill like that special privacy at the hilltop, you better believe they'll be climbing that hill again tomorrow. Now, what you do, what you think as a certain kind of mother, is to contact the boy's father and ask him to try and convince his son that the relationship won't work. Two people from the different sides of town, literally, southside black boy, northside Caribbean Shores white girl. What could be more offensive to the prejudiced mind?" Tablada blew out an exaggerated breath, eyes on Miles. "The problem as I see it, I want to know what's wrong for a boy, now that he's a man, to reach up on that counter for that sweet vanilla cookie if he's tall enough, doesn't need a stool to reach and won't fall off?"

That threw Miles for a second. Then he couldn't help it. He said, "What if somebody hides the cookies?"

Tablada smiled. "You could try that. But what's to stop the boy from looking and finding them."

"Finding them and eating them, you mean."

"Or taking them into his favorite hiding place to enjoy them in peace and quiet."

Miles leaned forward. "What are we talking about here?"

Tablada's ring clinked against the beer glass. "You tell me."

"All I want to know is where I can find your son."

"He might be eating cookies."

Miles put up his palms and sat back. "I'm not getting anywhere. Look, it's okay. Let's just forget it."

Tablada said, "When I asked you earlier about how much money, what I really shoulda asked is how much money is Isabelle Gilmore paying you. That's what I shoulda asked."

Trying hard not to look away, Miles focused on a mole above Tablada's left eyebrow. He was tired of the game, the barbershop this morning, the slow-speed chase, the barely masked hostility from Tablada and his crew, and the certainty, growing by the minute, that Isabelle Gilmore was using him in some larger scheme. He was getting wary, and wanted out soon.

But—and wasn't there always a "but"?—he had six thousand dollars total to gain if he found the girl, or got information that led to her. But maybe that was just the lure to keep him playing? Of course it was. Pushing some energy into his voice, Miles said, "Hey, believe what you want to believe," and stood up. "I've got to go now. Thanks for the water."

Tablada said, "You know the way out."

Miles said, "I certainly do," going toward the door.

"Top lock . . . no, the other way . . . yeah, that's it."

Miles opened the door, looked back, Tablada sitting there in the same position. Miles closed the door, the grille one behind that, and went down the stairs.

On the way to his car he spied a crew hanging around the BMW on the corner. When he reached halfway down the street, someone hollered, "Ricardo Garcia!" Calling out the Mexican boxer's name, fucking with Miles.

Miles looked over his shoulder. They were all leaning against the BMW, watching him. He stopped to inspect his bumper where the Land Rover had nudged it. No scratches, no dents. He could hear the crew talking louder, laughing, openly having fun at his expense. He drove off feeling a little pissed, just a little.

11.

MARLON TABLADA STOOD at the living room window and watched the boxer driving away. He drained the beer and stood there a minute.

He rinsed out his glass in the sink and wiped down the counter, taking time to fold the rag neatly and gather his thoughts. Then he plucked the phone off the wall and dialed. He said, "*Marta, hola. Es Señor Marlon. Como estás, mi amor?... Bien, bien...si, la señora, por favor.*"

He waited a few seconds. Then he leaned against the counter, put a smile in his voice and said, "Hello, Isabelle, how we doing this fine evening?" He nodded, listening. "Oh, sorry to hear, sorry to hear...Well, maybe I can help with your situation after all." He laughed. "No, I wouldn't describe it as kindness of my heart, it's simply that, shall we say, the conditions have changed....Well, a little talk with a certain prizefighter is why....Pardon?...No, but it has convinced me that you're resorting to desperate measures. He can't find out anything that I can....Yes, maybe I can, it depends....We should talk.... Tonight?"–glancing at his watch, deep into the act–"Tonight's fine....Alright, sevenish on the dot then....Goodbye, Isabelle." Smiled as he hit the off button, set down the phone.

He stood leaning against the counter and folded his arms, staring into the middle distance, seeing her in her house putting down the phone, contriving already to outwit him. Because that's how she was.

He knew Isabelle too well, and if she thought she was slick, he was slicker. How much was she paying the boxer? A few thousand, he hoped. For leads that would probably be fruitless. How much would she cough up for someone she thought knew where her daughter was, or had the contacts and experience to find out? Someone like him?

Everything comes down to money. Her dollars had to be sizeable, or he would walk, saying, "Look, I'll see what I can do, ask around, but with all I have on my plate, I'm too busy to commit to something like this. I'm sure you understand."

Joel had said twenty thousand. *Dad, we're going to take off with twenty g's.* His son felt obliged to tell him, but that didn't mean he believed it. Could be less, but was likely more. Washing cash was the Gilmores' business. You mean to say, twenty grand was all the girl could scrape up? On any given border run that he accompanied Isabelle on, she carried ten times that in her briefcase. *He* knew; he'd glimpsed the dough countless times. So how much would Isabelle part with to recover her daughter and her money in one stroke? He'd soon see.

Joel would have to understand. If the money was right, Joel would have to elope some other time. Sorry, son. Business always takes precedence over youthful pleasures, foolhardy adventures. You'll grow up, you'll learn that somehow. Money is always thicker than blood.

Isabelle put down the phone and gazed out the bedroom window at the darkening sea. A good wind was blowing and she could hear the waves crashing against the pier in front of the house.

"Who was that?" Manny said behind her.

She listened to the waves, enjoying the moment, how things were falling into place. "Guess," she said.

"Umm . . . Miles? No, that couldn't have been him. I give up, who."

"Marlon Tablada," she said, turning to face Manny, who was sprawled naked in her bed. "And isn't it just wonderful that he might be able to help me now? How considerate of him."

"Your plan worked, love."

"Appears so, doesn't it. And I have you to thank."

"Not me. Miles."

"You're the one who suggested him."

"Okay, that part, yes. Come on, take off that robe and get back in bed."

She slipped it off and eased in next to him, her arm going high in order to reach over his stomach. "He said he talked to Miles. Obviously, he didn't believe him."

"Tablada's pretty sharp. Used to be a cop, remember."

"Uh-huh, and I'm sharper." She nipped his shoulder. He flinched and rolled onto his side with a grunt.

"I do believe you are," he said.

"Smoked out and he doesn't even know it." She held him tight as he stroked her hair with his meaty hand. The breeze lifted the curtains over them.

After a minute he said, "I can feel your heart. It's beating fast."

"Yes," she said and turned over on her back. "I'm a little scared." She stared at the ceiling. "Sometimes I think about Rian and I can't believe my own daughter did this to me. Maybe we haven't been getting along of late, but to put me in jeopardy like this? I don't know when she comes back whether I should hug her or give her a good slap. But I worry about her, I do. Is she using protection, has she gone hog wild, drinking, doing drugs, not taking care of herself? Silly mother's stuff. Things that have nothing to do with the money. I want her home. And she better have all the money, by the way."

"She'll be back," Manny said, trailing a finger down her stomach. "Tablada will show his hand, I'm pretty sure."

"I'm so furious with her yet I want her back home. Not like me at all. So you think I'll get the money back?"

"You will, you will."

"Arthur Rolle keeps calling. He's left about five messages already and he sent one of his goons around. Any day now he'll turn up on my doorstep himself. I know he wants his money, but I can't talk to him. Not yet. What do I say? Sorry, my daughter borrowed it?"

Manny whispered, "Babe? Isabelle?"

She turned. "Yes?" His eyes were wide, looking at something across the room. She peered over his shoulder.

Her husband was standing in the center of the room staring at them.

"Jesus Christ!" Isabelle bounced up, clutching a pillow over her breasts. Manny wrapped the sheet tightly around his body.

Nate Gilmore stood watching, perplexed. His white hair was tousled, bread crumbs littered his shirt, and his fly was open. He said, "What are you kids doing?" He stepped toward them and stopped, looking more puzzled, like he had lost his way.

Isabelle bounded off the bed, saying, "Nate, hon, let's go back to the TV room." She threw on her robe. "I thought I locked the door, Jesus."

Nate shuffled around to face her. "Want to go skinny-dipping?"

She took him by the shoulder. "No, Nate, let's go watch some TV. I'll put *My Fair Lady* on again." She guided him to the door.

He said, "I saw that man in the bed." He swiveled his head to look at Manny wrapped like a mummy. "Who is he? What is he doing here?"

Isabelle said, "Walk, hon, walk," gently pushing him out. He leaned back and applied the brakes at the doorway.

"I think we should call the police," he said.

She put her shoulder into it and got him into the hallway. She slammed the door shut. She took his hand and walked him to the TV room. Sat him down in front of a table of tea and biscuits. She raised her voice toward the other room, "*Marta, ven aquí!*"

A toilet flushed down the hall and Marta came rushing out of the bathroom. Isabelle lit into her. Told her all she had to do was watch Mr. Gilmore until the evening shift nurse came and if she couldn't do that properly, then she better speak up so somebody else could be found to perform the duties this house required. *Ay dios!*

She stormed back to the bedroom. She fell back against the locked door and put her face in her hands. "Oh. My. God."

"I think I just had a heart attack," Manny said. He sat in a chair by the dresser, fully clothed, buttons askew, one sock on.

Isabelle sat on the bed, a palm at her cheek, shaking her head.

They sat in tense silence, listening for sounds in the house. The breeze puffed into the room. Darkness thickened.

After some time, Isabelle said, "You know what? I'm horny."

Manny smirked, glanced at his watch. "Perverse, but I'm sitting here feeling the same way. I still got some time." He stood up and started undressing.

Isabelle said, "One quick question. When are you planning on telling Miles there's no fight?"

Manny tossed his pants over the back of the chair. "When it's all over, I suppose. Miles has been around, he knows how boxing is. This isn't the first drug test Wahed failed. Hey, that's how things shook out. Nobody's fault but cokehead Wahed's. He signed the contract, he should've tried to stay clean. I certainly can't apologize for that." He came to Isabelle and put his hand on her shoulder. He pushed her back onto the bed, then wisely rolled his weight to the side. "Don't you worry about a thing, love dove. Miles will know when it's all over."

She swung a leg over him and pulled herself on top. "That'll be soon. I don't know how long this will last. . . . Oh, boy . . ." She moaned.

"No, I meant he'll know after we find Rian, the—"

"Shhh." She dropped fingers over his lips, rocked her hips. "Shhh."

12.

RIAN HAD TO figure something, and fast. She was in hotter water than she thought and it seemed she was on her own. Because Joel was no good right now, freezing up, saying, I don't know, babe, I don't know, when she asked him, What're we gonna do?

She finally answered her own question. She told him: We pack our bags. Put some of the money in amongst the clothes. Leave first thing in the morning Wednesday. Fucking crack of dawn—that's exactly how she said it, grab his attention. Go to the Castillos' farm like they'd planned for emergencies, she said, wait till her birthday to get married, Friday, just two days away. And if they couldn't find a justice of the peace, or if they had to leave quickly, then they would leave, forget about marrying for now. But they agreed on something: If they had to split up now to avoid anyone, they'd meet up at the farm, wait at least a day for the other one to show up. They had to get out of the country eventually, and leaving Belize as soon as possible would be the smartest thing.

So they packed, hid some of the money in her travel bag, in pockets and folds of jeans and pants and shirts and shorts, and then sat breathing fast, staring at each other in the cabana. The night music of crickets and toads filled the air, and her mind was abuzz.

* * *

"You look like your mother," Arthur Rolle had said that afternoon.

Last thing Rian wanted to hear.

"You have her eyes," he said. "Come on in, have a seat. Don't be bashful."

He was eating spaghetti at a little table in front of the TV, CNN turned way up. He looked far older than when she'd last seen him, his hair mostly white, skin mottled from too much sun. "Eat yet?"

"Actually, I did a couple hours ago."

"How about you, Joel? Man, you get any bigger you're gonna bust that shirt. Pretty soon you're gonna get your clothes tailored." Joel said, thanks, he'd eaten as well. Arthur Rolle said to his son, "Hey, boy, turn that set down."

Harry hopped to, clicked it off with the remote.

"Jesus," the old man said, fork hitting the plate, "turn it *down*, not turn it *off*." He smiled at Rian. "Simple instructions." He twirled a forkful of spaghetti and pushed it into his mouth. He chewed, nodding at Rian. "Sure you don't want some? It's lip-smacking stupendous. We've got mounds."

"No, thanks." Beginning to feel a little disgusted watching him eat, talking with his mouth full, she threw a glance at Joel. He was sitting ramrod straight and still, like there was a bomb under the seat. Harry lounged in a futon near a corner, staring at the TV, bored and sullen like a teenager in his father's presence.

"I got this great cook," Arthur said. "She makes anything, Mexican, American, Indian, Italian, ask Harry. When my wife was here, God rest her soul, she said, Arthur, this girl's going to be fantastic, she listens well, we should keep her. I did. Twenty-two years she's been with us. I've been in this hot, forsaken, backward, beautiful country for twenty-two years and couldn't have found anyone better. Now I hear Francis Ford Coppola, you know Francis Ford Coppola? Big-time, Mr. Big-deal, big-ego director? Owns this resort in Mountain Pine Ridge and is complaining about the locals, hear that, the locals"–his voice went into hoity-toity mode–"says they're so ignorant about fine cuisine. Know what he was referring to? The staff couldn't make a pepperoni pizza the way he likes it. I read that in a magazine. Pizza, for Christ's sake." Arthur Rolle grimaced and went back to his plate, pushing spaghetti onto his fork with a thumb and scooping it into his mouth. He nodded at them as he chewed as if they were in agreement that the food was lip-smacking stupendous.

Rian smiled at him ever so sweetly; at the same time, her palms were sweating a river.

Arthur Rolle dabbed his lips with a napkin, lifted the table out of the way, and sat back, stretching out his legs. He looked at Rian, sucking food from between his teeth. "Coppola comes here, the middle of the bush, expecting Manhattan bistros and Miami Beach spas. In a third-world country, wants that overnight and he's calling people ignorant? What a man like that doesn't know, ignoramus that he is, these things take time in a place like Belize. One has to foster trust, develop relationships. Twenty-two years I've been here, and you know who befriended me, one of the first people? Your father, that's who. I remember, here we were, two Americans with no money in this jungle paradise. But talk about freedom! You could create your own opportunities here if you were ambitious enough. And," he lifted a finger, "if you had the connections. Your father did. Nate led me down the path of the wheel-greasing righteousness.

Introduced me to the power brokers, the politicians, it was a real education. Associations, you see, friendships. Before you know, me and Nate, we were both doing pretty good, and we kept doing business for years and years. Now, it's me and your mother. Rian . . . I said that right, it's 'Rian'?"

She nodded.

"Where's your mother?"

"My mother?"

"Yes. Where is she? On vacation somewhere? For days I've been trying to get in touch with her. Left a million messages, she hasn't called back, which isn't like her at all. She okay?"

"She's at home, as far as I know."

Arthur nodded. "Rian, we're like family, your parents and me. And you, too, Joel. Me and your father, we've been doing business for so long. Family has to stick together," he held up two crossed fingers, "keep that bond, that trust." He shook his head, a sadness coming over his face. "But, ahh, now, now we're having family problems. Harry, close that door for me."

Harry came alive, jumped up and closed the door to the hallway.

"Listen to me, Rian," Arthur said. "It's an integrity problem our family's having. And wouldn't you know it, it's because of money. The root of all evil, they say. But I say the *lack* of money's the root of all evil, and we've witnessed some evil stuff recently. You know what I'm talking about, dear?"

"No." Her voice was a croak. She cleared her throat. "No, I don't."

"Ever heard of Salvador Escalante?"

"Um, the one who used to be a minister?"

"Yes. The former government minister. Still among the living, but barely. Not doing too well. He was shot Sunday morning, he and his son Ray. Ray passed on, for better or for worse. Salvador, what can I tell you about Salvador. He's in the import-export business like me, we've been associates, go way back, but he lost the trust of someone we do business with, a very demanding Mexican gentleman, let's just call him El Padron. Rian, the way our business works, you have El Padron, and El Padron helps supply people like me and the Escalantes with products to sell and we pay him on a certain day, just like any business, and everybody's happy till the next month, nothing complicated about it. What was happening, our friend Salvador was in arrears. Padding El Padron's accounts receivable month after month, El Padron telling him, *Que pasó? Quiero mi dinero.* Been going on for months, you understand what I'm saying, Rian?"

"Yes." She sounded frail.

"Finally the day comes when one big bill is way past due and El Padron is long past sick and tired and he thinks to himself: This man is cheating me. Must think I'm a fool. So what he does, he sends somebody across the border to collect. Only problem is, and I hate to sound dramatic, but this is very important you understand, very important. The kind of business we're in, people sometimes collect in blood. When money for whatever reason does not change hands like it should, pain is the price we pay. The Escalante family? They're in pain at this very minute. That is the kind of business we're in. Which is where you come in."

"Pardon?"

Arthur pointed at her. "Your family. This is where you come in. What does somebody like Salvador Escalante have in common with somebody like me that could put me in harm's way? Know what? We have the same personal banker. And that's your mother, Rian. I want you to listen to me closely. I need to speak to your mother about a certain transaction we need to complete, meaning, my dear, she owes me a very large sum of money. Some of that I owe a certain man with little patience, our friend El Padron I just told you about. So it's kind of awkward that I can't contact your mother. I sent one of my people to your house. No luck. Your mother wasn't there, apparently. Hasn't been seen for a couple days. So I need you to contact her for me." He fixed her with a stare and said nothing for a long time.

Rian got nervous and said, "Yes . . . ?"

"Something is going on with you and Joel here, I don't know what. But you came here, borrowed my son's car, being all secretive, and we helped you. Are you in trouble? Doing something you shouldn't be doing?" He cocked his head, gave her a look. "Is it something I should know? I can find out if I really want to. You believe that?"

Rian nodded.

"Listen, sweetheart, we shouldn't be keeping secrets from each other. Isn't that right? We deal straight with one another, it's the best policy. So considering I'm deciding not to probe into your business for the time being and you have my son's car, it's my turn to ask that you do something for us, keep it all level. You agree with my reasoning?"

Rian nodded.

"Good. Maybe if Salvador had gotten hold of Isabelle when he needed to, Ray would be alive today. Because from what Rosa Escalante, Ray's wife, is telling me, your mother also owed the Escalantes an amount of cash that they needed to pay El Padron. Now listen to me: You will get in touch with your mother for me. She'll call me on the phone, we square things away, and we'll be one happy family again. If by tomorrow night, though, I still have no word from Isabelle…" He shrugged, showed both palms. "Let me put it this way: One of my people will pay you and Joel a visit and stay with you until you've reached your mother and explained exactly what I need her to do. Unless she's acting stupid, everyone will keep their health. You understand everything I'm telling you here?"

Rian nodded. "Yes."

"Did what I say frighten you?"

She thought about the most respectful response. "Yes. A bit."

"You're a clever girl. I assure you this is very serious business."

"I understand."

"That's good. I don't typically get young people involved in my business affairs, but in this case, due to the urgency of the matter, I have to make an exception. No one is clean in our business, dear. Your family, whether Isabelle cares to admit it or not, *is* in our kind of business. No need to go into the details, just so long as you take this message to your mother and remember for future reference." He raised a bony finger. "Your family has been protected. Protected because it's on the financial side of things. The darker elements of our trade are what people like me and the Escalantes and Joel's father face as a matter of routine, while the Gilmores see none of it." He settled back, nodded. "We all know the risks, but nobody can save anybody else from the consequences. So, I'll say it again. I need to hear from your mother by tomorrow night."

He stood up. He walked over and put a palm on her back and gave it a circular rub. "You're a nice young lady," he said quietly. "Thanks for coming."

Passing his son on the way out of the room, he said to him, "Make sure you fill the Nissan with gas, and when you come back I have errands for you. You've been pissing around with Beto enough for today." At the door he turned. "Take care, Joel. Say hello to Marlon for me."

13.

MARLON TABLADA STOOD on the Gilmores' verandah, enjoying the night breeze, the waves washing up against the seawall. He heard the sliding glass door open behind him and turned to see Isabelle. He glanced at his watch. Hell, she'd kept him waiting for close to an hour.

It wasn't her style to apologize, so he didn't mind pointing it out. Like his time was hers to waste. He said, "You said seven on the dot, this is more like eight."

"And good evening to you, too, Marlon."

Tablada offered a little smile. "How you doing, Isabelle?"

She stood beside him, both hands on the balustrade, and looked out at the sea. "I'm waiting for you to tell me it's going well. Waiting for you to say you've made a few calls and can help me find my daughter. That's what I hope this visit's about."

"Maybe it is, maybe it is. I do have some information. Don't know if it's worth anything."

"Oh?"

"How much is it worth to you?"

She gazed at him lazily. "Depends on what 'it' is." She turned back to stare at the sea. "But we're not going to play this game, are we? You wouldn't come here for that. You know something and you want to tell me, so why don't you just do that?"

"Actually, there's something I *don't* know."

"And what would that be?"

"Why you want to break up my son and your daughter so badly."

She stared at him. "It shouldn't be too hard to figure out. Rian is seventeen years old. Seventeen. Your boy should know better. *You* should know better."

He said, "Well, I'm just wondering, asking myself if this is about class and all that, Joel being black and not anything close to rich and Rian being white and a little on the aristocratic side."

Isabelle folded her arms. "You don't even believe what you're saying."

"I'm just wondering, that's all. I mean, because if that's the case then maybe I should say good night, because if there's anything I don't like it's prejudice and class consciousness and harassing a young couple because we don't agree with their kind of love, that sort of thing."

She shook her head. "My husband always used to say you can be full of shit, and to think I'd defend you." She walked off, saying, "What are you drinking?"

"Beer's good." He smiled.

She poked her head inside and bellowed, "Rosa, *dos cervezas y vasos*."

She led Tablada to a long teak table under the overhang, where they sat. Marta came out after a minute and poured their beers. "Cheers," Tablada said.

"*Salud*." Isabelle took a sip and set down the glass. "She is in Belize and you came to tell me where."

"Say what?"

"That's what you came to tell me."

Tablada leaned back in the chair and looked at her. "Now

why'd you presume that? Why couldn't this be two old friends sitting down together to assess a situation, something like that."

"Because I know you better. Because we're not really friends, and we're both okay with that."

He pointed at her. "See, there you go again with that class consciousness thing." He put on a sad face. "Why can't we be friends?"

Isabelle sighed heavily, getting impatient. He liked that. He took a long drink, wiped the corners of his lips with thumb and forefinger. He said, "I believe I can find them, Joel and Rian."

"What I need you to say, Marlon, is I *know* where they are and I *will* bring Rian back."

"Okay," he said. Dragging it out, smiling.

"You need to say that, or we're wasting each other's time. I have someone looking already. I believe he'll find her."

"Sure he will," Tablada said. "One has-been boxer equals an eagle-eye investigator. I admire your logic."

"So you want me to pay you to bring back my daughter. Why don't you just say that?"

"Okay." Leaning toward her confidentially. "I know where she is and I'll bring her back at a certain fee for my time and trouble, which is why I'm here, to talk business."

"I should pay you instead of Miles Young because you can bring back Rian by tomorrow afternoon. That's what you're saying?"

"Tomorrow afternoon it is."

"Great," Isabelle said. "Now that we're getting somewhere, I'm going to tell you why, since you know where Rian is, it's in your best interest to bring her back." She locked eyes with him. "For a very small fee."

Tablada lifted an eyebrow. "Small? What does that mean?"

"Oh, more than enough to cover your gas. Say two hundred."

Tablada let loose a bark of laughter, shaking his head. "You must be outta your mind. How much you paying the boxer?"

"Irrelevant."

"Irrelevant? What you're paying him you're gonna pay me." He was ticked now. "Plus a few hundred more because I will bring the results you desire. You forget who you're talking to? I do this for you, I'll have informants to pay off, my employees who'll help me, not just gas. Look, don't bullshit me."

She was quite calm. "Want to know why it's also in your best interest to forget about how much you'll be paid for this?"

He gestured. "Go ahead."

"Because Rian and Joel stole a substantial amount of money from me, and a lot of that money belongs to Arthur Rolle. Arthur needs this money by tomorrow night. He doesn't know it's stolen. Not yet. Now: If you don't accept this job with the conditions I've laid out, I'll be speaking to Arthur. I'll be giving him the reasons for my delay, which he'll no doubt convey to his friend in Mexico, the most esteemed El Padron. What I'll tell Arthur is that your twenty-five-year-old son and my young impressionable seventeen-year-old daughter have his money, and Marlon Tablada knows all about it, knows where they are, but refuses to get them. You need to ask yourself, knowing Arthur's influence with El Padron, knowing their extreme tendencies, if you're comfortable with all this. You following me? You must tell me tonight. Are you going to get my daughter and if so when will you be back? Tell me now or we have nothing else to talk about. You and I, that is. Perhaps you'll be speaking to Arthur Rolle next. Your choice."

Tablada picked up his beer and drank. He put the glass down a fraction too hard, thinking, this woman is the origin of bitch, the meaning of bitch. Felt his neck getting hot. Wanted to let his hand fly across the table, back-hand her like he hadn't bitch-slapped somebody in so long. But he sat quiet, composing himself, trying to be cool and easy. He stared at her hard, stared through her. Yeah, she'd set him up good. Let him show his cards by revealing what he knew, then trumped him with the threat of Arthur Rolle and the mad Mexican who no sane person would ever care to fuck with.

He said, "I can't believe you're doing this to me. After all the years your husband and I did business, you got no loyalty, and that's a downright shame." He wagged a finger at her. "One of these days, one of these days, you're gonna need a friend to watch your back. Just keep on burning your bridges, see what happens."

"Oh, please, stop. Spare me the goddamn lecture. You came here to make some money off my misfortune. You use me, I use you, we all have ulterior motives. The only reason you're here's that you saw Miles Young going around asking questions and you figured there's money to be made. If I hadn't hired Miles, whose ulterior motive, by the way, is that he wants to fight again, if I hadn't hired him you wouldn't be sitting here drinking my beer and trying to insult me with your self-righteousness." She leaned in. "Yes or no? Do we have an agreement or not?"

Tablada sat in a long silence. Then he raised his hands in surrender. "All right, Isabelle," he said. "You got me."

Isabelle turned her face toward the darkness, the sounds of the sea. "The reason I'm being so hard is I suspected all along you knew where they were but weren't telling me. I simply don't have the patience for games anymore."

"So you're going to put me in the line of fire. You realize it's El Padron had Ray Escalante knocked off? And how come that sits fine with you, threatening to turn me over to him like I did something wrong?"

"It's my health we're talking about as well. You're doing something wrong by not doing something right, which is finding Rian, getting that money, and ceasing this nonsense of thinking you can shake me down. Marlon, you have until tomorrow afternoon."

Tablada pursed his lips, thinking that was not a problem, but he had to ask something. "How much–"

"You don't need to know how much money. I just know that when it gets back into my hands, every dollar must be accounted for. As long as I can give Arthur what's his, he and I'll be fine. Any shortfall after that, that's between me and Rian."

Tablada said, "One more question. The boxer. Who's telling him he's fired, me or you? I can't have him still looking, getting in my way."

"You do what you need to do," Isabelle said. "Let me talk to Miles."

14.

ALICIA SAT IN the swing watching Lani play in the yard, half-lit by the streetlights. Miles sat beside her, wanting to sit closer but respecting the distance that had come between them since the fight. In silence they watched the shapes of pelicans standing on pilings far out on the dark water. On the swing between them was the photo of Rian and Joel posing in front of the cabin, the photo Miles had shown Laura Castillo. Downstairs Lani played with a skipping rope, getting her legs tangled.

"The rope's too long, hon," Alicia called to her. "Wrap the ends around your hands."

Lani stopped to figure this out.

"Or you can play hopscotch instead," Alica said, Miles stealing a glance at her, the soft skin of her throat, her strong chin, the wind moving the curls by her ear.

On the walkway to the gate, Alicia had drawn a hopscotch grid with sidewalk chalk, and Lani walked over and contemplated it. She looked up at Miles. "Daddy, please, you can play hockscotch with me?"

Miles said, "In a minute, sweets. Why don't you start. I'll come down in a little bit."

Lani tossed her bottle cap on a square and hopped into the game, stepping on the lines with glee.

"See what you've got me into now?" Miles said to Alicia.

"Good. She needs to be with her dad."

Miles leaned back and picked up the photo of Rian and Joel.

Alicia took the photo from him, stared at it. "So this is what you wanted to talk to me about?"

Sounding disappointed.

She said, "To answer the question you asked over the phone, yeah, I'm pretty sure this is where Rian would go. It's desolate, nothing around for miles. Only horses. And a watch-man that lives in a little house on the farm. The only reason we'd all go there was to ride the horses. Laura's father didn't mind if we stayed overnight, long as we cleaned up the cabin afterwards."

"And to think," Miles said, "if I'd talked to you first, I might have saved myself some trouble. You pretty sure about this?"

"Yup. And didn't you tell me Laura was being kind of evasive when you talked to her? That place is your best bet, Miles."

"I'll drive up there tomorrow morning. Maybe you could give me directions?" He stood up, touched his hair. "Right now, though, think you could fix this geek look?"

Alicia shook her head, grinning. "Why? I think it looks quite cute."

"Hey, come on now."

"Daddy!"

Miles spun around. Lani was sprawled on her stomach on the pavement, chin up, bawling. Miles ran through the house and down the front steps. By the time he got there she was standing up, sobbing and pointing to a raw scrape on her knee.

Miles said, "Oh, poor baby, oh baby, you'll be okay, it's not too bad," even though he hadn't inspected it yet, talking out of instinct to calm her. "Come here," he said and picked her up, Lani sniffling on his shoulder. He carried her upstairs and in the living room met Alicia holding a bottle of hydrogen peroxide, cotton swabs, and Band Aids. He laid Lani on the sofa and Alicia took over, cooing to Lani, soothing her as she cleaned her knee, gently pressed on a bandage. Like a mommy.

Miles watched her, feeling reassured by it, and it pleased him that she'd felt comfortable enough in his house to trek into his bathroom, rummage in his messy cabinet for first-aid supplies.

The phone rang. Miles tried to ignore it but it kept ringing. He took the call in the hallway.

"Hello, Miles," Isabelle Gilmore said. Miles returned the greeting, and she said, "I'm calling to thank you so very much for your hard work. I appreciate your efforts in trying to locate my daughter but after some consideration I think I'd be best served if we called off our search. I have good reason to believe I'll be in touch with Rian soon. But, again, I want to thank you."

Miles said, "So you're saying my services are no longer required?"

"You got it in one, Miles."

"Okay, but we had an agreement. Three thousand up front, three more if . . . Look here, Isabelle, I believe I know where they are."

"Do you?"

"I'm about ninety-nine percent positive. I'll go out tomorrow morning like I planned and deliver them."

"Why don't you tell me where they are?"

Miles snorted. "And you'll pay me."

"Miles, if you do know, tell me. You gained this information while you were still under my employ, it's the ethical thing to forward this information to me."

"For three thousand, sure."

"You don't know where they are."

"Do you want to find out? Tomorrow morning. I find them like we agreed, you pay me like we agreed. Or would you rather hope she *contacts* you?"

"I'd rather you say you understand that you're no longer needed. Don't force this issue, Miles. I want you to listen to me, okay? Because of me, you have three thousand dollars in the bank and a comeback fight in Miami. You should understand that and be grateful for that much. Now, if you know where they are, you need to tell me."

Miles pulled the phone down to his chest and looked up at the ceiling, shaking his head. He said, "The fight I was preparing for but taking time away from, not to mention my own daughter here needs my time, then to have you fire me when I'm this close? For that I should be grateful? I will see this job through, Isabelle, and I will get paid in full. Do you still need all of that money your daughter took? Maybe *she'll* pay me after I find her tomorrow."

"Miles, are you threatening me?" Sounding almost amused.

He didn't answer.

Isabelle said, "This conversation is over. For the last time, you are not needed anymore. And I will not pay you any more than you've already been paid. Goodbye, Miles."

He put down the receiver and stood there a moment. He returned to the living room. Lani had calmed down, resting her head on Alicia's lap. Alicia said, "What was that all about?"

"About the job, searching for Rian Gilmore. That was her

mother on the phone just now. My services are no longer re-quired."

"They find her? She back home?"

"No, nothing like that. Just that she has good reason to believe they'll be in contact with Rian soon. So she thinks. Fine with me."

Alicia stared at him. "You don't look fine."

"I'm a little..." He shook his head. "A little pissed off. I mean, I could say I got paid regardless. I could've made more if I'd found that girl but I'll get to train more, so . . . But I don't like this lady's way of doing business."

"She hurt your pride?"

Miles didn't say anything to that. Because he knew it was true. Miles was thinking, Alicia sure cuts to the chase. He was thinking who the fuck does Isabelle Gilmore think I am, going back on her word, then demanding the information? Thinking something didn't smell right about this from the start. He told himself to forget about it.

He sat with them, snapped on the TV, found *SpongeBob Squarepants* for Lani. No one said anything for a long time and Miles began to feel better, at peace, as if somehow this small moment might mean the start of something for the three of them, that with this Rian Gilmore thing over he could focus on his daughter and restore some of the happiness he'd lost when his wife left.

He said to Alicia, "Want to have supper with us?"

"I better not," she said, "my dad's probably going to be wait-ing. Your haircut, remember?"

Miles nodded. "Okay. I'll get the scissors." He stood up, looking down at her tanned shoulders, the thin arc of her eye-brows, finding her exceedingly attractive as she stroked his daughter's hair. He said, "Afterwards, after supper I mean, you could come back, we could have a drink, maybe—"

"No, Miles," she said. A patient smile.

"Okay, okay," he said. "I'll go get the scissors."

"You do that."

Oddly, it felt encouraging to be rejected so handily.

He awoke in the dark to a faint banging noise from downstairs. The digital on the nightstand read 5:04, almost time for him to get up for his run. A strong breeze was blowing through the open windows and he stumbled out of bed and looked out at the sea. The water, what he could see of it, was choppy; it was going to rain any minute. But, hey, he'd better run.

A minute later, Sammy called and said, "Morning, time to get cracking." Miles dressed into his shorts and running shoes so that he could be out the gate as soon as Sammy arrived. He traipsed down to the kitchen and poured a glass of O.J. for a sugar boost, still hearing the banging. He unlocked the back door and stood at the top of the stairs overlooking the back-yard. Already it was drizzling.

The side door to the garage was flung open and in the wind the door was smacking the wall. Strange, he always kept that door locked. He went down to check it out. Everything in the garage seemed in order—the car, the garden tools hanging on the wall, the lawn mower in a corner—until he flicked on the light. The car's rear tires were flat. A closer look and he saw why: They'd been slashed. Then he saw the hood wasn't shut properly. He lifted it. The battery was gone.

He came outside and looked around, over the fence into the

neighbor's yard, behind the rain water cistern, without knowing exactly what he was looking for.

Just behind the neighbor's far picket fence, he saw someone walking down the alley.

Miles trotted into the front yard, out the gate onto Southern Foreshore, and down to the head of the alley. The asphalt was slick, the smell of rain fresh in the air. The man was about fifty yards away and was carrying something with both hands. He stopped at the empty lot halfway down the alley and pitched what looked like a brick into the weeds. Miles knew it was his battery. He started jogging toward the guy, not exactly sure what he planned to do when he got there.

The guy must have heard Miles because he glanced over his shoulder, then kept on walking, only faster. Miles said, "Hey." Recognizing something about the guy's movement even in the darkness, his physique.

The guy kept walking, deaf.

"Hey," Miles said. Louder this time. Then it came to him. "Hey, Stick."

Stick broke into a trot and Miles gave chase, still not sure what he had in mind. The chase didn't last long, Stick spun around, something in his hand. Miles stopped. "What you doing in my yard, man?"

Stick lunged at him, slashing the air with a knife. "Fuck with me, come fuck with me," he said, swinging wildly.

Miles stepped back, scared, saying, "Easy, easy," instinctively putting his hands up in a boxing defense, left hand and foot forward, body angled, knees bent. Thinking he'd better back off, let this asshole run. Thinking just don't get hurt. Then Stick charged, right hand leading, and Miles timed him, ready after a long morning yesterday hitting Sammy's mitts, training for a southpaw, nailed him flush in the mouth with a right, Stick's head snapping back, but he came forward again. Miles had planted his left foot outside of Stick's right, just as it should be, and this time he connected with a left downstairs and a right up top, Stick stumbling backward. But Miles knew instantly he was cut, on the left arm. He reached for Stick's right wrist, Stick holding the knife tight, and that's when it got wild, boxing out the door, a streetfight now. Miles held the arm with both hands, Stick hit Miles on the side of the head with his free hand, the two of them losing balance and falling to the ground. They grappled in the street, Miles gripping Stick's wrist, Stick clenching that knife and still hitting Miles behind his head, his neck, his head again. They struggled to their feet, breathing hard, and Miles locked Stick's knife arm under his, Stick half-behind him when Miles flung back an elbow and cracked him in the forehead and did it again, but losing his hold on the knife arm, realizing it a second too late and catching the blade as it sprang up toward his face. He released immediately, feeling the pain, spun around and let fists fly, terrified, knocking Stick on his ass. Stick scuffed up to his feet, the knife lost somewhere in the dark. Miles stepped forward, Stick backed up, then he turned and ran. Miles chased him but the younger man was too fast, opening a gap between them. Miles stopped, watched him flee, past the streetlamps down to the end of the alley, then slowing to a jog before he stopped, maybe to show he wasn't scared. He looked across the distance at Miles, the two of them saying nothing, breathing hard. Finally, Stick jogged off down Regent Street and out of sight.

Miles knew there was something wrong with his hand. He knew he was cut on the forearm, too, but didn't want to look. He turned to go back and when the breeze hit him cold he realized he was sweating, a light rain falling. He walked under a streetlight and lifted his left hand. Covered in blood, all the way down to his elbow.

Half of his index finger was missing, sliced off clean.

He said, "Fuck," but it didn't sound like his voice, and confusion and nausea swept over him. He started shivering. He breathed deep and told himself to chill, just chill out. He walked, then stopped at the edge of the light. Picked something off the street. No, that was a stone. Tossed it, picked up something else. That was it.

He walked home bleeding in the rain, cupping the severed half of his finger in his palm. One foot in front of the other: concentrating on that to keep panic at bay, one foot in front of the other.

He fumbled with the gate and made it up the steps and into the hallway without getting too much blood on the floor. In the bathroom he put the shower on full blast and stuck his arm into the spray. Blood swirled thickly down the drain. He could hear his heart pounding inside his head and he thought, All right, what're you gonna do now, Miles.

Get a towel, hold it tight to the finger, wrap the loose end round your hand. Then go to the kitchen, put the half-finger in a bowl of ice.

So he did all that, but he felt like he was moving in slow motion, his thoughts spinning but his body doing tai chi in a fog. And when he stood there in the kitchen holding the towel, dripping blood on the linoleum—tip, tip, tip, the sound hypnotic—staring at his severed finger wedged in ice cubes looking so surreal, he went weak in the knees. He heard Sammy pulling up in front of the gate and walked out to meet him.

"Oh, shit, oh my God," Sammy said. "Miles, you all right?"

"Yeah, I guess." Miles dropped his butt onto a step, began telling Sammy what happened, saying they should go to the hospital. He ended with, "Lani, we have to wake her up."

Sammy said, "Okay, okay" going up the stairs, his *The Ring* magazine falling from under his arm onto the steps. Miles watched the pages flutter in the breeze then settle, the rain pelting it–tip, tip, tip–until it flattened and lay soaked and gray. Somehow, watching it became very important to Miles. He stared and stared, then he broke from the trance and said to himself, "Move, boy."

He got the bowl with the finger from the kitchen and was coming out the door when Sammy walked into the hallway holding Lani's hand, Lani wearing a *Dora the Explorer* nightgown and tennis shoes. Lani looked at Miles, looked at the bloody towel, and screamed.

Miles dropped the bowl, the bowl shattered, ice cubes and ceramic flying across the floor. He'd heard terror in that scream. It seemed to have come from a gaping black hole inside him.

"Miles." Sammy pointed to the floor, just as Lani came running to Miles.

"No," Miles said too late, seeing her step on the finger as she frantically reached for him. Miles stooped down and embraced her with one arm, saying "It's okay, it's okay, baby," knowing that he was talking to himself, trying to quell his worries. Because he knew his boxing career was really over now.

Sammy pulled Lani off him long enough for him to walk

over to the baseboard and pluck the finger from among the ice cubes and pieces of dish. He straightened, smiling like a fool, desperately wanting to calm his daughter, but knowing in his bones that it would take far longer to calm himself, give himself a sensible reason why this had happened, knowing that every time he looked at his hand he'd think of bad decisions he'd made and would want to hurt someone, out of bitterness alone.

15.

WAKING UP EARLY in the morning to go to the bathroom across the clearing was what saved Rian, no doubt about it, and if she believed in a god, she would have thanked him.

Actually, it was the rum and Cokes that saved her. When they had returned from their visit with Arthur Rolle and stuffed more of the money into her travel bag, she said to Joel, "Hand me the bottle of rum, please," meaning the complimentary bottle of Caribbean White that came with the cabana. If Joel couldn't find any fresh ideas about how to get around the fix they were in, if all he could do was sit and mope and say negative crap like, "Maybe we should just better go back home," then she'd give him something that might rinse away his annoying pessimism. She said could he go and get a couple Cokes from the bar, please, and a bucket of ice? But he said he didn't want to drink, and she said, okay, for me then, and handed him a twenty.

He had one anyway, a weak mix, to please her, while she sucked the first two down. The quick buzz felt sweet, mellowed her so that his brooding didn't get on her nerves as much. She drank maybe five, stiff ones too, stumbled over their bags and crawled into bed with him where he was curled up, already asleep.

She awoke in the half-light of dawn hearing birds, the river burbling in the distance, her bladder about to pop.

Joel was snoring softly, the sheet twisted around his legs. She slipped on her Tevas and headed out across the dew-wet grass to the restrooms. Her head felt achy, her vision was a bit hazy, and her mouth dry like cotton.

She gulped palmfuls of water from the bathroom tap, splashed it over her face, and let it run down the front of her shirt. Swished out her mouth, wishing she'd brought toothpaste and toothbrush. All the while she stood bent over the sink, one thought poked at her, needled her, demanding to be considered.

Was it her fault? Somebody killed Ray Escalante, a drug dealer, a bad son of a bitch, everybody always said so, and that was *her* fault? How could she be held responsible for choices he made in his life, or that her mother made?

Because you stole that money, that's why.

Rian couldn't escape that fact. She stole the money and that had led to Ray Escalante's death and to keep on running was going to lead to . . . ? This was nagging her. Her mother's life could be in danger because of her? She didn't want to believe it but it was probably true. "Oh my god, oh my god," she said and put her head under the running faucet. This wasn't what she had planned. Somebody was dead because of her. Okay, maybe that part wasn't entirely true. She looked at herself in the mirror, hair wet and dripping, eyes puffy. She said, "Stop thinking about it."

The sound of a car outside caught her attention. Rian dried her face and neck with paper towels. She cracked open the door and looked across the clearing to the rocky two-track that ran past the dining hut and ended at the office. About three seconds later a blue Land Rover came grinding up the track, headlights on. Brake lights flashed and the Land Rover stopped at the side of the track, midway between the restrooms and the resort office. There were three people inside. They got out, three men.

Harry, Beto, and Marlon Tablada. Standing there looking around.

Not good.

She closed the door, locked it quickly. She shut her eyes, leaned against the sink. When she opened her eyes again she wanted to be back in bed at home, waking up, realizing that all of this was just a stupid dream.

But they were out there, talking. She could hear them. She went to the window, opened the glass louvers a couple of inches. They stood in a circle, talking, occasionally glancing toward the cabanas beyond the clearing. They'd come for her and Joel and the money, she knew that much. She tried to guess the distance between them and the restroom. About fifty yards maybe? If she went out the door on the men's side, ran, she could make it, tell Joel then . . . then what?

They'd see her. How could they not? Maybe if she went around the side, on the jungle trail? They'd still spot her but she'd be close to the cabana by then.

Rian chose her best option. She got down on her stomach and crawled under the half-wall to the men's side, the cement floor doing a number on her elbows and knees. Someone was showering in one of the stalls, clothes hanging over the door. She hurried past and slipped out the door, closing it fast. She sprinted into the bush and found the trail a few yards in. She followed it in a wide curve to where it came out at the edge of the clearing. She stopped to catch her breath, hands on knees. Before she stepped out into the open she looked to the right. About a hundred yards away, the three of them stood talking. She was sweating, collecting her courage. She took another deep breath and stepped out into the clearing, turning her face away from them. She marched toward the cabana, fighting the urge to run, telling herself it was still too dark for them to spot her.

She sped up. Another glance. They were strolling across the green now, looking off to the side. She strode past cabanas, towels hanging over porch rails, muddy boots on steps, everything quiet inside. Her legs wanted to run, her heart was hammering. After what felt like an eternity, she came to the stand of bamboo that hid her cabana, then she ran, she flew. She raced up the steps, banged through the screen door. Joel was asleep. She said, "They're here, they're here."

Joel jerked awake, saying, "Huh? Huh?" sitting up, rubbing his eyes. "But I don't like sardines."

Rian said, "What?" She didn't have time to wait for him to come around. She snatched up the travel bag, threw it on the bed, pulled the briefcase from behind the headboard, unlocked it and dumped the rest of the cash into the travel bag, a block of hundreds bouncing off the bed onto the floor. She picked it up, shoved it in, the overstuffed bag not wanting to close. Bag in hand she turned to Joel. He was asleep again, on his side, a pillow over his face. And this moment told her a truth she'd always known about him. She standing there with a bag ready to run, while he slept, pillow over his head like he was hiding from the facts, oblivious to the action. Joel the timid, Joel the ostrich.

Rian turned and ran out the door and down the steps, none of those three in sight yet. She took the only route open to her, through the bush behind the cabana and down to the riverbank. If she followed the river she knew she'd come to the canoe dock, and if there was a canoe with a paddle then she'd go out on the water, maybe cross to the other side or head a few miles downriver, anywhere, as long as it was far from the resort.

She walked into the jungle, hugging the heavy bag, high grass swatting her legs. The land began sloping and she slipped on her butt, pushed herself up, struggling with the bag. Rian moved deeper into the tangle, downward, tripping through the undergrowth. It was damp, rough going. The air was still and humid. She was parched. Her little vacation was over and now she was really on the run.

Harry led the way. "It's that one," he said, pointing to a cabana they were approaching. "No wait, that's not it. Farther back. I think … yeah, must be."

Tablada had patience today. Let the kid feel important. Showing the way to the money. He was goddamn lucky his father had gone easy on him. Probably used the same psychology Tablada used on his people: If they were valuable enough, you give them an opportunity to redeem themselves. If they couldn't, then they had no reason to cry when you sent their asses packing.

"Right under your big nose," Arthur had said to Harry when Tablada told him everything. "That girl was sitting right here. In my fuckin' house," he said to Tablada. "Boy, do I feel like a fool." Then he said to Harry, "You're going with Marlon this morning. You're going to bring that girl back here." He turned to Tablada. "You hear me, Marlon. That girl comes back here immediately. With my money. After I get my money, only after, then maybe she can call Mommy to come and get her. Then Isabelle and me, we'll have a little sit-down."

Tablada said, "I'm telling you, Arthur, she tried to shift the responsibility for this on me. My son comes to me, Dad, give me advice, where can I go for some privacy, said it like that. So I helped him, but if I knew they had money belonging to you, I'd have taken care of this a long time ago, Arthur."

The old man put up a hand. "No, I understand. You made a wise decision driving here this morning. There I was, complaining it's not even daylight and why the hell are you coming to my house, but you brought good news."

"I didn't like it," Tablada said. "I know it's my son involved, but accountability comes first and foremost, and the truth, which is why I had to come to you with all this. No way I'd keep this in the dark like Isabelle wanted." Then Tablada showed his most hangdog expression—man, that little acting had taken a lot out of him, but sometimes a man had to do what a man had to do. He'd weighed his choices, and the conclusion he'd come to: Better to side with Arthur Rolle than have Isabelle use him like a flunky, dictate terms to him, blackmail him. Who'd she think she was playing? Thinking that because his son was involved he'd kowtow. He'd give her something she'd never expect. This was business; she should know that. And it was bad business to play hardball with him. Okay, so his idea of a finder's fee from Isabelle was dead. Fair enough, but his good terms with Arthur Rolle lived on, and who in their business had more pull than Arthur?

Then Arthur said, "Don't worry, we'll get this mess cleared up pretty soon. We'll take care of little Rian so Isabelle will be eternally grateful. How much money did she say the girl took?"

"She wouldn't say, but she wants it back so bad it's got to be a lot more than just pocket money, if you know what I'm saying."

"Good. I love it. She owes me one eighty. If there's more,

we'll be deducting an inconvenience tax, a dishonesty penalty, and a little nonrefundable serves-your-ass-right fee. You understand me, Marlon?"

"I certainly do."

"I owe you for this, Marlon, don't fret yourself." Arthur stood up, the meeting finished. "People don't know how to discipline their kids anymore, what the fuck?"

Tablada knew how to do that, don't you worry. As for Arthur—well, you only had to look at his boy Harry swaggering up ahead now in those baggy hip-hop jeans halfway down his ass to know Arthur hadn't slapped the immaturity out of him yet.

Tablada looked around, noticing how everything was quiet, too quiet. Not that he expected a trap; he just didn't want to attract attention in case the matter got hairy. *I owe you for this, Marlon.* Yessir, that was the icing on the cake.

They came to a stand of bamboo and Harry stopped, looking lost. Then he smiled, "Yeah, right behind here, that's it."

Tablada walked up and dropped a stiff arm in front of his chest. "Wait. Before we go any farther. When we get in there, let me do the talking. I want this done quickly and quietly so we don't alarm the guests. We get to where either one of them's refusing to go, I'll give you a signal, like a nod, got that?"

Harry shrugged. "Yeah. Whatever."

"I nod, that means you and Beto secure the girl. By which I mean put your hands on her. Hold her so she can't go anywhere. Let me take care of my son. Got me?"

Harry looked away. "Whatever you say, big chief."

Tablada smiled at the kid, looked at Beto. Beto shifted from one foot to the next, glanced away.

"I'm glad you agree," Tablada said. "Follow me." He moved up front and advanced on the cabana. He imagined Harry making faces behind his back like the little kid he was.

They stomped up the stairs, across the porch, the girl's bikini and Joel's trunks hanging over the railing. Tablada peered through the screen—Joel asleep on one bed, the other rumpled, empty. The girl wasn't there. He opened the door and walked in, Harry and Beto following. Tablada stood by the bed and looked at his son. Harry and Beto stood off to one side. In here it was cool, smelled faintly like liquor.

Tablada said, "Boy." He nudged Joel's shoulders with a finger. "Boy, wake up."

Joel groaned, moved the pillow off his head. He opened his eyes, started blinking. Puzzlement crept over his face. He sat up fast. "What happened . . . Dad, what you doing here?" He saw Harry and Beto, rubbed his eyes and turned back to Tablada. "What's going on?"

Tablada crossed his arms and watched him reach for his jeans on the nightstand and struggle into them. "Where's your girl, Joel?"

Joel said, "What?" Looking around. He picked up a T-shirt, slipped it on.

Tablada waited while the boy tried to come up with a lie.

"She's not here," Joel said.

"Hell, boy, I can see that. So where's she?"

Joel shook his head. "I don't know. She went to the bathroom maybe? It's across the way. I don't know, Dad. What's going on? Why're you all here?"

"Don't act like you don't know."

Joel frowned. "But you're the one told me about this place,

to come here. You knew we were coming here. What're you talking about? You knew Rian's age."

"You're off the subject and stalling, son, you're wasting my time here, and I'm in a bit of a hurry. Again, where's the girl?"

Joel looked at Harry as if Harry could help. Tablada noticed that Harry and Beto had glanced twice at something on the floor, so he took a backward step and sat on the other bed to get a wider view of the room, see what was so interesting about the floor. Elbows on knees, hands together, he said to Joel, "I'm waiting, tick-tock, tick-tock, any day now," and saw them peeking out from the sheet hanging off Joel's bed, dollar bills, a tidy stack of fifties it looked like, with a paper band around it.

"I don't know, Dad. I was sleeping."

Tablada nodded to himself. "Fair enough," he said. "But clearly she ain't here, so it's up to you to tell me where she coulda gone. She and the money." Tablada decided to bluff. "We saw her just now, Joel, five minutes ago. She wouldn't stop. In a big hurry. Isn't that right, Harry?" Again, he caught Harry eyeing the floor.

"Yeah," Harry said. "That's right," looking all shifty now.

Staring at Joel, Tablada said, "Do me a favor there, Harry. Pick that thing up off the floor."

Harry said, "What?"

"That something by the bed," Tablada still staring at Joel.

Harry and Beto exchanged a glance, then Harry picked up the stack of bills. He held it a few seconds, looking at Tablada, before he slowly raised his arm and put the money out, making Tablada stand up and reach for it. Tablada ignored what that meant, for now. He slapped the bills against his palm, tested its heft. Flipped through the corners, all fifties, about, oh, four thousand here. Then he looked up and said to Joel, "Seems that someone left this room in a hurry," and knew that the boy was about to cave. He'd seen that rabbit-in-the-headlights expression many times when he cornered him with something. "Don't even think of telling me you don't know where the rest of this money is. You get two choices. One: You tell us where your girl is taking it. Two: I rip you apart until you start talking. Take your pick, and I don't have all day."

Joel turned his face to the side, his jaw clenched, and looked at the floor. "You know I told you, Rian brought some money with her, like about twenty thousand–"

"I'm not referring to no supposed twenty thousand. We're talking about a *lot* more. Rian's got it, it's not hers, and one of the owners sent me to retrieve it and bring the little thief Rian back to face the consequences, so why don't you fucking tell me right now. Where'd she go, boy?"

Joel said, with a steely gaze. "I don't know what you're talking about."

The slap happened so fast even Tablada didn't expect it, his hand bouncing loudly off Joel's face, Joel's head snapping to the right. Joel touched his cheek and looked shocked, eyes welling. "You crazy!" A shriek. He sprang to his feet, making fists.

Tablada reared back as Joel came forward. What the hell? This boy actually thinking of testing his old man? Tablada squared his body, just in case. Eyes on Joel, he said, "Harry, Beto, go outside and search the premises for that girl. She can't have gone far."

They stood motionless.

Tablada turned his head slightly and said, "You hear what I said? Go. Scour the place."

They looked at each other, then Harry spun around and shouldered his way out the door. Beto trailed him.

Tablada listened to them going down the steps, he and his son glaring at each other. Tablada said, "You want to hit me?"

Joel said nothing. He looked ready to start crying any second, big man like him.

"The money still here?"

Joel said, "I don't know."

"You know where she kept it?"

Joel nodded.

"Okay, where? A suitcase, knapsack, what?"

"A briefcase."

"Okay," Tablada said, looking at the bag on the floor, towels on the rumpled bed, "is it still here?"

Joel exhaled loudly. "I have to see."

"Then see, goddamit."

Joel walked wide around him, curving his shoulders in, insecure all over again like when he was a teenager, and just seeing that made Tablada want to smack him again. Act like a coward you get treated like one.

Joel kneeled on the messy bed and peered in the space between it and the wall. He got off the bed, lifted the sheets and checked underneath. He shrugged. "Looks like she took it."

Tablada took in the room, walking over to check both spots and under the bed. He lifted the towels and there it was, a black briefcase. A Samsonite he recognized as being Isabelle Gilmore's. He flipped it open. Empty. Of course.

He said to Joel, "You gonna tell me where she went with the money?"

Joel shook his head. "I told you, I don't know where she is."

"Notice you're not answering my question. The question I'm asking is where is she going at this minute."

"I said–"

Tablada slapped him.

"No!" Joel said, raising an arm to ward off another blow. "Stop it or I'll fucking, I'll fucking–"

"What. Or you'll what, you sissy." Tablada lifted his hand to slap that face again but this time Joel struck first, popped Tablada in the mouth. But it had no snap to it. The boy was obviously scared.

But to be hit by your *son?* Disrespected by your own boy? That Tablada was absolutely not going to accept. He wiped his lips, examined his fingertips. He said, "You lost your mind? Oh Joel, you've gone and lost your mind," and he went after his son to teach him a lesson he evidently failed to learn before, one he'd never forget.

Outside in the bush at the edge of the jungle, Harry turned to Beto and said, "Shit, you hear that?"

Beto said, "Fuck yeah," the two of them turning around to look up at the cabana. It sounded like they were breaking down walls in there.

Harry pictured Joel being tossed up against a wall, but that didn't make any sense since he was the bigger, stronger man– but then, getting slapped by your father in front of people and just swallowing it didn't make sense either. Harry said, "See how dude got bitch-slapped and didn't do nothin'?"

Beto said, "Yeah. Muscled-up but soft."

"Man, if it was me, I'd ... man, I don't know what I'd do. I'd ..." But he let that drop. Beto knew him too good. Beto had seen his father cuff him and him just stand there and take it, lots of times. But that was then. Anyway. Harry gestured. "Come on, let's go." His eyes roamed the jungle all around him, the cabanas at the edge of the clearing, a thin fog low over the grass, the day heating up. "Only way she coulda gone," he said, pointing into the thick of the jungle. "Couldn't come 'round those trees there or we woulda seen her. So she must've gone this way down to the river."

He started in, going down a slope. When he looked back, Beto was still standing in the high bush. "Let's go," Harry said.

Beto jerked a thumb over his shoulder. "Maybe we should go back, see what's happening. Shit, that's a racket they making, man."

"Let's go, let's go," Harry said.

Beto stood there. "The man said scour the place, like that means I should better go one direction you the next, we search all about."

"Fuck *scour*. Which way else would she go?" Harry throwing his palms up. He couldn't believe Beto was second-guessing him, taking asshole Marlon's instructions more seriously than his. Beto was his buddy, sure, but technically his employee, too. He squinted at the murk between the trees, down to where the land sloped to the river. "This is the way she went," Harry said, "this is the way we're going." He watched Beto hard, the guy he knew from seven years old, the dude he partied with, who knew him better than anybody, but no way was he going to let friendship take priority over business, and like his pa always said, this was pure, cool, calculated business. He was going to find Rian Gilmore *and* his old man's money.

They tripped and crashed through the bush. Harry said, "I

think she went down to the riverbank, might follow it out to the canoe dock." He swiped at branches, knotty vines. "Maybe she took a canoe, too."

Low vines tripped them repeatedly. Dry branches scratched their faces, their arms. They pushed on, making a big noise. Going down the slope, trying to lean back and slow the descent, Harry slipped, right on his ass. Hauled himself up quick, embarrassed. Beto took a tumble soon after. They would've laughed at each other, but not today, the stress was too high. They were breathing hard when they came to flat land down by the river. Harry pointed in the direction of the dock and that's where they went, double-timing it.

The river was smooth and mellow, burbling over the rocks near the far bank, a bird screeching in a tree overhead. And no sign of Rian.

Then at the docks, nothing either, except the padlocked shack that stored paddles and life vests, and canoes on a wooden rack. Harry watched the river, green and mysterious, running west with its secrets . . . Carrying Rian Gilmore where? He checked out the canoes—didn't know how many should be there so he didn't count but he thought, okay, if she took one, how's she gonna paddle it?

Beto spat into the river. "What now?"

Harry said, "Wait. I'm thinking." Although he'd already made up his mind, he wanted to make Beto wait for an answer, make sure there was no mistaking who was in charge. Plus, Harry thought he looked cool in the process, not impulsive like his pa always said but—what's the word?—*measured?* Something like that.

"We're turning back," he said, staring at the river. "Turn

back, find out where that bitch is, see if Joel knows, and then–we take it from there."

They returned by going up the two-track and across the re-sort grounds, their arms and shoulders scratched bloody. The day was getting hotter, the sun rising behind them. Harry could hear voices inside the cabanas, people moving about. A man came down the steps of one cabana in flip-flops and a towel around his neck. Harry flashed him a grin, trying to act calm.

The second they turned the corner at the bamboo trees, he knew something was wrong. A low moaning–he could hear it coming from the cabana.

Beto said, "What the fuck?"

They slowed down, listening hard.

Somebody in the cabana coughed. More moaning. Harry stopped at the foot of the stairs, and Beto said, "What hap-pened, you think–"

"–Joel might've whipped old boy's ass?" Harry reached be-hind and pulled his Smith & Wesson from his waistband.

Beto said, "Yo, dawg, what you doing?"

"Getting my pa his money, what's it look like to you." Harry stepped quietly up the stairs.

Beto whispered behind. "You think the gat necessary?"

Harry reached the porch, jacked a round in the chamber. "Shut the fuck up, Beto." He wasn't taking any chances with muscle boy Joel. Probably fought like a girl but he had size. Well, a 9mm in your face said, Fuck your size. Would he shoot someone though? In the middle of a crowded resort? Man, the problems that would bring–cops, arrest, prison, who knows, some shame. Shame because like his pa said to him once the thing he was proud of, despite the rough business they were in, no one in the family had ever been convicted of anything. We take risks intelligently, he said. Harry thought, Be measured, and fitted the gun back in his boxer shorts. He looked through the screen door before he went in.

Tablada was standing in the middle of the room holding a bunched-up towel to the side of his face. A night table was overturned, one of the screens was busted, a lamp lay on the floor. Where was Joel? Then Harry saw him, in a heap between the beds, moaning.

Tablada said nothing when they walked in. After a moment he took a glass of water from the sill and poured it over Joel's face. Joel pushed up on hands and knees, coughing. Tablada hooked an arm under Joel's arm, hoisted him up, and flopped him backward on his bed.

"Damn," Harry said when he saw Joel's wrecked face. Nose misshapen and bloody, lip fat, one eye swollen shut, cheekbones puffy.

Tablada stood over him. "Come on now, wake up." He slapped his knee twice. "Wake up, wake up."

Beto said, "Shit . . . what happened?"

Tablada glared at him. "You blind?" He said to Joel, "Come on, son, show me some life."

Joel lifted his head a little, one eye open. "Leave me . . . leave me alone."

Tablada put his hand on Joel's arm. "Son, I coulda killed you, you know that. What's wrong with you? Why you acting like this?"

Joel rolled on his side, face turned to the screen.

"You brought this on yourself. Why couldn't you just cooperate? Don't let this girl get you in any more trouble. You in deep trouble here. This money, it don't belong to you, don't belong to her. The people who this money belong to, they won't play with you like I did, they're fucking killers. Your life got no value to them, boy. You think what happened here's rough, wait till they get hold of you. Come, Joel, tell me. Where'd the girl go?"

Tablada touched his face with the towel and examined the blood spots. He had scratches on his face and his bottom lip was cut. He dipped the towel in water left in the glass and pressed it against his face. He turned to Harry. "You didn't find the girl."

"No sign," Harry said. "She took off."

Tablada turned to Beto, and Beto said, "It's true. She ain't nowhere 'round here."

Tablada looked them up and down. "What happened to you out there?"

"Went in the bush, got scratched up," Harry said, "no big deal."

Tablada wasn't even listening, talking to Joel again, "Hey, last time before I really hurt your ass. Where did this girl go, Joel? Save your skin, boy."

Joel lay like a dead man. Tablada clenched and unclenched his right hand. Joel said something. Tablada said, "What? I can't hear you."

"Bamboo Bank Farm."

A smile passed over Tablada's face. "Good. That's a start. Where's this farm?" When Joel said nothing, he turned to Harry and Beto. "Know where that is?" They shook their heads. Tablada asked again, "This farm, Joel, where's it?"

Joel muttered something and Tablada stepped closer, cocked his head. "What? Speak up."

Joel coughed twice, his body jerking. He said, and this time everyone heard, "By Belmopan."

"Ah," Tablada said, nodding. He sat next to his son and watched him, Joel's shoulders moving as he breathed. Tablada reached out and squeezed Joel's upper arm. "Son, I'm sorry, okay?" He rubbed his shoulder, getting all gentle now. "You'll be okay. Everything's going to be all right. You did the right thing and I'm proud of you, okay? You just lay there a while, take it easy. You did real good."

Standing there watching, knowing what had just happened, Harry felt for a second like he was listening to his own father.

16.

MILES HAD DREAMS in the hospital bed. Sweaty, roiling, drug-induced dreams.

His father said to him, "You're wasting your life, smart boy like you boxing for a living."

His mother, who didn't resemble his mother, was sitting at the dining room table and smiled wistfully. "I want something better than this for you, you know that. Think about your future."

"But Ma," Miles said, "I'm good at it. You should've seen that right hook that knocked down Mr. Simmons. They carried me around the school, all the boys."

"Oh, I see, and that's something to be proud of?" his wife asked, taking the place of his mother at the table.

"It's not a matter of being proud, it's a matter of practicing a craft, the craft of boxing, mastering it. Right, Sammy? It gives my life purpose and meaning."

Sammy was in the room now, a white towel around his neck, a bottle of oil in his hand to give Miles a rubdown. Sammy said, "I've always said a man must follow his heart. Life is hard enough, and if fighting makes you happy then you got no other choice. And answer me this, what else do you know how to do? What marketable skills you have?"

"Shameful!" his father shouted.

Miles jumped up from his chair, wearing boxing trunks and

boxing shoes, and began shadowboxing around the room, bobbing and weaving, flicking loose jabs. Then he saw he had no hands and said, "I can't do this anymore, I can't," and he sank to the floor and broke down crying, and Alicia came from somewhere to hold him.

When he opened his eyes, he was in a large hospital room with beige walls, and he smelled medicine and saw the IV pouch hanging by the bed, a tube running to a tape over a vein at the back of his hand. His body felt sore like he'd boxed a brutal ten rounds, and for a moment he almost believed it, but after looking around the room, seeing the cobwebs in the high corners, the old black man in the bed next to his, the peeling wall paint, he knew he was in Karl Heushner Memorial because of the fight with Stick.

What time was it? He sat up, groaning with the effort, joints stiff. How long had he been here? His left hand was wrapped in a bandage so thick it resembled a white boxing glove. He swung his legs over the side of the bed and put his feet on the floor, the tiles cold. He sat there looking at his skinny toes, the faded, ill-fitting hospital gown. His memory was hazy. Sammy speeding through the dawn streets, Miles comforting Lani in the backseat. Sitting in a hard plastic chair in the emergency room, waiting for the doctor while a nurse took his blood pressure, another nurse sticking the vein in his hand and hooking him up to the IV. Then he couldn't remember much else, except a blur of dreams and the sweating.

Where was Lani? Who was taking care of her? Where was Sammy? He wanted to get out of here. He stood, steadied himself, began searching for his clothes. He found them in a drawstring plastic bag under the bed.

Alicia walked into the room. Miles had another question in the back of his mind, but he was a little scared about the answer.

"Miles?" Alicia said, her voice soft. "What're you doing?"

"I'm going home. Getting out and going home. Where's Lani?"

"With my dad. You can't go home, you just had . . . You need to stay in that bed until the doctor sees you." Hands on her hips, Alicia watched him.

Miles looked down at the bandaged hand. "Did . . ." But he couldn't finish, couldn't bring himself to face it.

Alicia said, "I'm sorry, Miles." She came closer and said, "I'm so sorry," and she hugged him. He let himself be hugged, Alicia saying, "They tried, they tried, but you know how things are here. Oh, Miles, they couldn't do it." She sobbed quietly into his neck, smoothing the back of his head with a hand. "The hospital, it doesn't have the proper equipment, and the surgeon, he's never had to do this before," and she continued to explain, but he wasn't listening anymore. Nodding, absorbing his loss, he stood quietly and let her try to comfort him. He exhaled heavily, turned away from her and picked up his bag of clothes.

"Miles? Please don't do this."

He shook his head, not at her, but because he was sick of disappointments and pissed about what had happened to him and confused. They obviously didn't know he was off the job. Isabelle had called him, told him herself, which meant she had good information and didn't need him, but obviously they didn't know about any of that, and who the hell *were they?* Who had sent Stick?

Only one person came to mind.

He sat on the bed and guided his legs into his bloodstained running shorts, fumbling with the IV tubes.

"A policeman's coming, Miles. To get your statement. I saw him outside at the nurse's station a minute ago. You can't go anywhere."

Miles looked at her. "Want to help me here?" He saw her expression and dropped the impatient tone. "Please?"

She untied the gown behind his neck. He stood and tried to put his shirt on, but the tubes prevented it. He pushed his bare feet into his running shoes, forgoing the socks. He sat shirtless. There were bloodstains on his shoes.

Alicia's eyes lifted toward the door and Miles turned to see a uniformed policeman there.

"Morning. Mr. Young?"

"Yeah, that's me," Miles said and watched the policeman come around to the side of the bed. A guy about his age. Alicia stepped aside. The cop stood in front of Miles and considered him, eyes lingering on the bandage. "I'm Inspector Swayze. I heard you had a violent encounter this morning?"

"That's right."

"Want to tell me about it?"

Miles thought, Not really. He cleared his throat, began telling the tale. The cop produced a small notebook and wrote in it a couple of times. Miles's tongue felt thick, his mouth tasted like sand. He pressed on with his story, wanting to be done with it. Then he noticed the inspector had put the notebook away.

The inspector interrupted. "This guy, this Stick, you saying he might work for Marlon Tablada? *The* Marlon Tablada?"

Right there Miles knew he'd started down the wrong road. "I think so. I'm pretty sure actually."

The cop made a little grunt. He and Miles watched each other.

"Like I said, I know where he hangs out."

The cop lowered his head to look into Miles's eyes. "Who? Mr. Tablada?"

"No. Stick. I know where he hangs out, maybe you find him there."

The cop straightened. He sniffed, pulled a hankie from a pocket, and wiped his nose saying, "You and Stick ever had a run-in?" Miles said no, and the cop nodded, examining the hankie. "Sure?" He folded the hankie meticulously.

"Of course," Miles said.

The cop sniffed again, tucked the hankie in his pocket and said, looking away, "So what would give him cause to do this, vandalize your car, why you suppose?"

Miles flicked a glance at Alicia, then said to the inspector, "That's why you're here. To investigate. I only know that it's him who messed with my car and did this to me," raising his bandaged hand. "And if you don't find that asshole, I'll do it myself."

Inspector Swayze scratched his chin, looking mildly amused. "We'll see what we can do."

"What?" Alicia stepped forward. "What do you mean you'll see?"

The inspector gazed down at her.

"You'll *see?* He just gave you who it was did this and where you can find him and that's the best you can do, you'll *see?*"

The cop regarded Alicia coolly. "And who are you, miss?"

"The woman who called the police." She gestured toward Miles. "The victim's girlfriend."

This last piece of info surprised Miles, but he was fine with it, liking how she was standing up for him.

The cop said, "Miss, that's all I can tell you at the moment.

We'll go by this place, Cat's Lounge, see if we can pick him up. Could be that he's lying low for a few days and we won't find him. That's how they usually do. In which case, we'll all have to be patient."

"You can go to Marlon Tablada," Miles said, "ask him where to find Stick."

The inspector gave that grunt again. "You're playing a dangerous game there, Mr. Young, associating a suspect with a man like Mr. Tablada. This man used to be a police officer. Owns the biggest security firm in Belize. This man is well respected, an upstanding citizen in this community, and I'd advise you should take caution about what you're saying. Let the police do their job, that's what I will insist upon until this thing is wrapped up. If you can be of any assistance, well, we'll be in touch."

So that was the size of it. Tablada's net was cast wide. And no police officer would come to find Stick anytime soon. Miles watched the inspector walk away. At the door he stopped and said, "I really suggest, Mr. Young, you sit tight until you hear from us. Take care of yourself now."

Miles lowered his head, closed his eyes, listening to the cop's footsteps down the corridor. "Yeah," he said, "sure." He nodded, coming to a realization. He stood up and stripped off the tape holding the IV tube to his hand. Then he sucked in a breath and pulled the needle out of the vein.

"What're you doing?" Alicia gripped his forearm.

Miles said, "Excuse me," and draped the dripping tube over the IV hook. He started putting on his shirt.

"Miles?"

"I'm getting outta here." He repositioned the gauze over the puncture and pressed down.

171

"But . . . Miles. Don't. You're going to have medication to take, you can't just walk out. Is this how you're going to take care of yourself? Please, don't do this."

"I *will* take care of myself. Starting with taking care of certain things myself, understand? You could help if you want, by picking up my prescription from the doctor. I'll buy the drugs later. What time you have?"

She looked askance, then glanced at her watch. "Nine fifteen. Why?"

"I've got to pay somebody a little visit, do my own investigation."

"What? You're in no shape. . . . That's crazy."

"No, no. Be honest with me," locking eyes with her. "You hear how that guy was talking. You think the police intends to find Stick? Be honest."

She stood quiet. She shook her head. "I don't know."

"Not good enough for me," he said. "Just so you understand," and he turned and walked out of the room.

Alicia drove him in her father's old Honda, the air blasting but hardly cooling the car. The sun was out again and the humidity was stifling. Miles dropped the visor down. His eyes ached, his finger throbbed. He rested his hand in his lap. After a mile, it started to drizzle and Alica put on the wipers, muttering how the day couldn't decide what it wanted to do. A minute later, the drizzle turned into rain that pelted the windshield. The streets were soggy and some cars had their headlights on. This whole morning was bewildering Miles. He said, "You have your cell with you?"

Eyes on the road, Alicia fished her phone out of her handbag. Miles took it and closed his eyes, trying to remember a number. His brain was full of cobwebs. The number came to him and his finger punched in the keys.

"Hey, Toby, how's it going? . . . It's Miles. . . . No, I'm okay. . . . No, I just left the hospital. . . . Toby, I'm fine, serious. Listen, I have a question. That guy Stick from Cat's, you know where he lives? Toby . . . Toby, I'll tell you all about it later, just tell me where Stick lives, please." Miles put a finger over his ear, frowning. "Uh-huh . . . uh-huh . . . Yeah, I'm familiar with the general area . . . right. So it's down that lane? . . . Uh-huh . . . one of those houses in there, okay . . . Got it. . . . No, just want to talk with him . . ." He listened for a while. "Of course, I will, don't worry. . . . Hey, partner, I got to go. . . . Thanks, we'll talk later, all right? I got to go, Toby. Take care."

He sat straight, breathing slow and easy, building resolve. He handed Alicia the phone, ignoring her glances. He said, "Go down Queen Street and bank left on New Road."

Alicia said, "That's not where you live. I'm taking you home."

"I'm not *going* home, I never said I was. Could you just go down Queen Street? Look, it's coming up on the left."

She turned her face his way, then back to the road. "No. I'm taking you home."

The car moved steadily in traffic, nearing the bridge they had to cross for him to get home. At the turn to Queen Street, Miles grasped the steering wheel and jerked it left. Alicia mashed the brakes, tires screeching, horns blaring behind them. "What the hell're you doing, Miles?"

"Listen to me," he said, lifting a finger, "you take me where I want to go or pull over so I can get the fuck out, but don't get in my way."

Alicia said, "But why, why do you want to go there and look for trouble? You could hurt yourself, you could–"

Miles spun away from her and opened the door, one foot out. Cars kept honking behind them.

"Okay, get in, get in."

Miles slammed the door and Alicia drove on and turned left on Queen. She pulled into a space by the post office and threw the shifter into park. They sat looking at each other, the engine running.

"Miles," she said, gripping the wheel hard, "I can't stop you, but all I want to know is why. You have your whole life ahead of you, a daughter who needs you, why do this?"

Miles swallowed. He was thirsty and headachy and wanted to go home, but something in him refused to sit back and accept this mess. He examined his bandaged hand and tried to clench it. "Alicia, let me tell you something," he said. "This morning a man trespassed on my property, damaged my car, assaulted me, sliced off half my finger. All of that for what? If Tablada had a problem with me looking for his son, all he had to do yesterday was say something. He didn't. Instead they come after me like this? It doesn't make sense. Now, I'm sitting here in a good deal of pain, missing half my finger, my daughter's terrified, and I don't know how to even begin explaining all this to her, and to top it off, I'm out thirty thousand dollars because I can't fight again. My boxing career is over, finished, done with, no use me trying to rehabilitate for the ring at my age. You hearing me?"

"I'm hearing you, Miles."

"Thirty thousand. I was looking to make thirty in a few weeks. You know how far that would've carried somebody like me who's got no real career outside of boxing? But today cost me more than that, it cost me some pride and me and my Lani's sense of security, not to mention a finger. So you got to understand me, I'm in no mood for peace. I want an answer. I want to know why Tablada came after me. And this asshole Stick is the man I need to talk to."

Pursing her lips, Alicia stared out the window. Cars streamed by, tires hissing on the wet street, rain beating down on the roof. "Okay," she said. "I'm not going to argue with you. I disagree, that's all."

Miles nodded. "That's allowed."

"Men," she said.

"I know. Can we go now?"

She put the car into drive and guided it into traffic. The sun was gone and it was raining harder now. They took a left on New Road and she said, "I'm waiting in the car until you get back if that's all right with you."

He said, "That's fine."

They crossed over Hyde's Lane and drove slowly through the narrow channel of cars parked on both sides of the street. They were approaching Douglas Jones and he said, "Take a right."

The car rattled over the bumps and potholes on Douglas Jones, Miles scanning for the lane Toby told him about. "Here. Park by the corner."

She drew up behind a truck and parked. Miles said, "Hey. Thanks, Alicia."

Alicia nodded, eyes straight ahead.

"For your concern I mean. I know you're being smart. Maybe I ought to listen but, I don't know, I can't. Like you said, men."

That provoked a smile. She tilted her head and watched him. "Be careful."

"I will."

"How long before I should start getting worried?"

He shrugged. "Say twenty minutes? Yeah, twenty."

"Come looking for you?"

"I guess." He pointed to the lane. "It's right down there, Toby said, down that one and then the first alley on the right, then behind one of the houses in a big dirt yard back there."

"Okay." She reached out with both hands, grabbed his face, and kissed him full on the lips. "Just so you understand."

He thought he blushed. He looked down at his seat. "That's one of the nicest things anybody—"

"Shh, shh," waving him away. "Go, go. Be safe."

17.

THE TAXI CRESTED the hill and rolled down the other side, plowed farmland spreading out to the east and west. Up the dirt road by the farm gate an old man stood watching the car approach. He leaned against a walking stick and watched the car pull up and Rian get out and pay the driver.

After the taxi turned around and drove up the road and over the hill, Rian stood holding the travel bag with two hands, she and the old watchman looking at each other. He hobbled over and stopped about five feet in front of her. He canted his head and said, "I can help you with something?"

"Um, I'm Rian. Rian Gilmore, didn't Laura tell you I was coming?"

"Laura Castillo? If I recall, her daddy didn't say anything like that to me. But maybe I wrote it down and forgot."

"Yes, my boyfriend, he was supposed to come with me but couldn't. But I was wondering if he already came by, he and some friends."

"He and some friends?" The watchman studied her.

"Yes, about four guys, in a Land Rover? They didn't come by?"

The watchman shook his head. "For the last hour, I been out here weeding and examining this ditch, see maybe I need to clean it, and I haven't seen nobody pass by in a Land Rover. But my eyes don't work too good, dear, so maybe I missed them. But hardly anybody come on this road, so I think I'd notice a Land Rover."

Rian breathed a sigh. She had decided to trust Joel. They'd started this together and they'd promised each other to meet up at the farm and they were going to get to the States together like they agreed. She wasn't bailing out on him, and she had to trust that he wouldn't fail her. But still, she had to take precautions, and she had a backup plan, just in case Joel did the stupid thing and led his father to the farm. She wasn't about to make anything easy for that man or the Rolles or her mother. She only wished–actually, she wasn't sure what she wished anymore. She'd decided it on the drive: She'd give Joel till six this evening to show up. If not, she was leaving Belize by herself. Thinking about all this, she said, "I'm so tired . . ."

The watchman said, "What's that?"

She shook her head. "Oh, nothing, nothing, just . . . So Laura didn't mention someone was coming?"

"I'm remembering something like that now, you know. I'm getting forgetful in my old age, you see me here. I know I must have wrote it down somewhere if that's what Mr. Castillo told me." He made a motion with his head. "Come with me. Let's get out of this heat. Can't tell you the last time I seen it so hot before."

Rian followed the old man to the tall iron and barbed-wire gate, about ten feet wide. He flipped a latch and pushed it open, the bottom scraping the dirt. Rian was having doubts about why she was even thinking of staying here, knowing they could be on their way at that very minute. But when the old man shut the gate and chained it and snapped a fat padlock through the latch, she exhaled, feeling a touch more secure. Hey, she needed to have faith.

The watchman's house was a few hundred feet down a weedy two-track. It was a small whitewashed limestone cottage with a thatch roof, and inside it was cool and dim and smelled delicious.

The watchman motioned to a bench against a wall. "Sit down. You eat yet? My wife is cooking some lunch."

"I'm starving," Rian said.

The wife was a rotund woman stirring a pot at a gas stove in the back. While the watchman rifled through papers tacked to a wall, the wife wiped her hands on her apron and came to the front. "Hello dear, how you doing?"

Rian said, "Oh, I'm fine," basking in the home-cooking smell and feeling all warm and comforted looking at the matronly, friendly faced lady.

The watchman came with a piece of paper. "Right here it says it. Rian Gilmore and fiancé Joel Tablada, the fourteenth of the month, expected to stay two or three nights. See, I did jot it down."

His wife looked at him with astonishment. "John Paul, what's wrong with you? I told you this morning I put fresh linen on the bed in the cabin and cleaned up the place for visitors and you said you're going to put the generator on, now you're telling me you forgot that already?"

John Paul gave his wife a blank expression. "I must have forgot, Nettie."

They giggled with each other before she waddled back to the pot bubbling on the stove.

They all sat at a small wooden table by a window for an

early lunch of split pea soup with smoked pigtail over white rice. A genuine Belizean country meal like the kind Rian's mother would never serve, one of those po' folks' meals that Rian loved because they were simple and tasty. She washed it down with a tall glass of Kool-Aid, the last time she had Kool-Aid being when she was about ten or eleven, back when her home life was predictable and secure, back when she was truly deep-down happy, before her father started slipping into Alzheimer's and her mother started her affairs.

She was sleepy after lunch and she said she'd better get to the farmhouse to take a nap. "Could you show me the way? I remember it was . . . that way?" pointing south. "Not too far from an old well, if I'm not mistaken. That well still there?"

John Paul said it was, but the cabin was this way, more southeast, just give him a minute and he'd show her. He got up to go outside.

Rian helped clear the table, gently placing the chipped plates and mismatched utensils in the sink. The linoleum in the kitchen was old and peeling, the counter and cupboards speckled with stains and knife scars, everything in the small house showing age. These were poor people, but Rian felt right at home.

Nettie touched her on the shoulder. "You coming for supper?"

Rian hesitated. "You're inviting me?"

"You like flour tortillas? I make them on a fire hearth out back."

"I didn't want to impose, but that's very nice of you. I'll gladly come."

Rian heard something and turned around. Through the open door she saw that John Paul had pulled up in a golf cart.

He walked in and put his hand on her travel bag before she could say don't touch. He said, "Whenever you're ready."

She reached out and took the bag from him. "It's okay, I can carry this."

John Paul shook out his hand. "What you carrying there, girl, gold bricks?"

"Something like that." Grinning stupidly.

John Paul drove them down the two-track, the golf cart bumping along, then straining to make a hill, then down to an expanse of green land and cows grazing in the distance or taking shade under trees, and the cabin beyond that on a rise. "Your eyes shutting down there," John Paul said. "Long day, eh?"

Rian nodded, smiling tiredly. Too tired to converse anymore, to even want to think about how she'd run through the bush that morning with her heavy bag, falling three times, sliding down to the riverbank. But those images kept popping into her head. How she waded in the river until she came to a resort canoe tied to a makeshift floating dock and found a paddle inside, untied the canoe, and pushed out. How she paddled downriver so fast it felt like her arms were going to fall off. Then, after the panic, floating along, ears perked for any sound—twigs snapping, bush rustling. How she found the trail that ran alongside a huge farmyard and wooden house behind a barbed-wire fence. How she hitched a ride to San Ignacio in the back of an old pickup truck, scrunched between coops of clucking, heaving, flapping chickens and the smell of chicken shit. How she persuaded a cab driver to bring her all the way out here.

After John Paul left the cabin and she was settled in, she sat on her bed staring at the walls and the spare furnishings and figured she'd better get to work hiding the money—minus the amount she had in Harry Rolle's car, shit, she'd forgotten about that.

Anyway. She shouldn't get too greedy. She had to stay focused. She didn't need an extravagant sum, only enough to take her to the States and live on for a couple of months until she found a job, started re-creating her life. With or without Joel. There. She wanted to believe in him, but who was she fooling? She felt it strong: He might betray her. But then in the next instant . . . she doubted he'd ever do that. And one moment she felt confident everything would be okay, the next she felt like a little girl playing hide-and-seek and everyone knowing where she was and amusing her by not rooting her out yet.

She removed her clothes from the bag, piling them on the bed. She took out a stack of hundreds, wrapped it in a shirt and stuck it under a pillow. The bag felt much lighter now. Make it hard for them, Rian, she kept telling herself. That was her plan if they found her. She liked how mature she was acting, taking things one at a time.

She walked across the field, heading for the cows under the trees. The field smelled rich and earthy and made her feel good, relaxed. She trudged up an overgrown path to the old well. She remembered from when she was here last that the well had run dry, had been dry for years. She slowed down, looked around to see if anyone was watching. No one, only cows and egrets in the distance. The rim of the well was made of huge stone blocks stacked precariously and cemented together. She placed a hand on top gently and peered in, chips of concrete falling into the darkness. She said, "Hello, hello." "Hello, hello," echoed up. A rope tied to a wooden crosspiece hung into the well and she pulled up the rope. A rusty metal pail appeared at the end of it. The pail was bone-dry. She set the bag of money into the pail, then took it out and dropped a sandal in the pail. She lowered the rope hand over hand and when it could go no farther, she shook it, listening for water. The sandal came out dry.

After she lowered the bag into the well, she walked to John Paul's house. She was nervous and thought conversation might ease her mind, and she liked being in that little house, smelling the food, relaxing in the cozy warmth that reminded her of her own house long ago when she used to call it home.

18.

THE CLOSER MILES got to Stick's place, the calmer he felt, like walking through a cheering crowd toward the ring, every cell in his body ready after weeks of hard training. Walking casually, feeling confident he'd win. Except there was no cheering crowd, the only sound being the rain hitting the broken and patchy asphalt and the tin roofs of the old wooden houses he walked past. And with a half-severed finger hurting bone deep, he didn't feel particularly fit.

The lane was narrow and dirty, trash piled by an overflowing garbage drum. The farther in he went, the shabbier the houses and fences were. He came to an alley, his shirt drenched, hair pasted to his skull. Despite the rain, the air was thick and stifling. He paused to get his bearings, marking how far he'd walked from Douglas Jones, and yeah, he recognized this area: Long Barracks, what you might call a Belizean ghetto. He'd been here before, he and his high-school buddies, scored some weed. Later, after he started boxing, he'd sneak back here when he broke training. In more ways than one, areas like this with their seedy allure were why he eventually left Belize.

He walked on, saw a shop ahead on the right, the wooden awning propped open by a stick, a man reading a magazine behind a chicken-wire screen. He ran under the awning for brief cover, thought of buying something to ease into a conversation but remembered he was wearing running shorts and didn't bring money. He and the shopkeeper exchanged nods. The man went back to reading, probably assuming Miles was looking for shelter.

Miles said, "Some serious rain, eh?"

The man looked up. "Nasty-ass weather. But it's still hot." He put down the magazine. "What you doing out here, chief?"

Miles took a second to decipher the guy's tone–suspicion? curiosity?–and decided to forget the small talk. "I'm looking for a dude lives somewhere around here, guy called Stick. You wouldn't know where he lives?"

The shopkeeper said, "In all this rain you come?" He chuckled. "You must really want to see Stick bad."

Miles worked up a smile. He had a mind to say he'd been taking a jog, got caught in the rain and so dropped by to see the dude, but he didn't really care if the shopkeeper believed he was a friend or not. "Yeah, me and Stick got things to discuss."

The shopkeeper's fingers drummed the counter behind jars of hard candies and chewing gum. "Tell Stick he owes me nine fifty for the three stouts from last night."

"All right. Will do."

"Behind here," the man pointing at the back wall of the shop. "Fourth house on the left, in a yard before the corner. Take the alley down, you'll see it."

"Thanks, man." Miles threw up a wave, ran into the rain.

"Nine fifty," the shopkeeper called.

Miles slowed to a trot when he came to the alley, then to a walk when he came to the yard. The rain had eased some and he could see a good distance without having to squint or wipe his eyes.

It was a dismal scene. A rotted picket fence with missing planks ran the length of the yard, the yard muddy from the rain. The houses were all ramshackle, on stilts, dark, unpainted. The fence had no gate; Miles walked in. A woman with high, bushy hair was brushing her teeth at a window, spitting water from a cup into the yard. Miles gave her a half nod, walked on with purpose. Under the other house two shirtless black boys were playing marbles. Nearing the fourth house, Miles began looking around for a heavy stick, a stout tree branch, some kind of weapon in case things escalated and a knife showed up for the party.

He passed around a wooden cistern of rainwater, searching the ground, no luck. He eyed the fence. No one was watching him as far as he could see so he ran up, grabbed the top of a paling with both hands, jacked one foot on the fence and pulled, wrenching the paling loose with hardly a squeak. He tested its heft. Not bad. Maybe a bit too long and unwieldy but it would do. He saw four nails sticking out of it and thought, What're you doing, Miles? Thought about it a second longer and continued on his way, just too pissed to be merciful.

He stopped behind Stick's house and considered. A light rain kept falling. He stepped up cautiously. It was a shack on stilts really, a square box with a rusting tin roof. The windows in the back and at the side were shut. Miles went under the house and started quietly up the stairs, holding the paling low like a baseball bat. The steps creaked and sagged and he was scared one would snap under him. Fuck it, Stick must be hearing him— Miles ran up and barged through the half-open door.

Nobody there. A bare mattress on the floor at one end of the single room. A boom box by the mattress, CDs stacked against the wall. A naked lightbulb hanging on a wire over a kerosene stove on a table. Sandals and expensive Adidas in a corner by a rough-hewn chest of drawers.

Miles backed out, stood on the top step, and gazed out into the rain. The guy had to be somewhere close, wouldn't just leave his door unlocked in this neighborhood. He heard a cough and saw the outhouse for the first time. It was under the heavy branches of an almond tree, about thirty feet from the steps. It was a shower stall plus outhouse, actually, a semi-transparent fiberglass roof over a rectangular room.

Miles came down the stairs. The stall door opened and out stepped Stick, fumbling with a towel around his waist, wearing flip-flops and a ladies shower cap. He looked up, saw Miles, and that was it. Dude went bug-eyed. He froze, watching Miles straight in the eye. Then he turned and ran. Sprinted under the al-mond tree, kicking off flip-flops, clutching the towel to his waist.

Miles dropped the paling and gave chase, no fear the guy would produce a blade now. Stick ducked through an opening in the fence and down the alley, Miles right after him. Stick hooked a right at another alley, arms flailing for balance, the towel flying off and catching wind like a parachute before it hit the ground. Miles pursued his naked ass down that alley, high corrugated zinc fences on both sides, a dog barking some-where, the rain starting up harder.

Stick was a speed demon, he was opening a distance. But the lane seemed endless and Miles was in decent shape, thinking as long as he kept up the chase the guy would tire and he'd catch him. Then like some desperate prisoner Stick threw a hand up on a fence post and launched himself over the sharp zinc into a backyard, how he didn't castrate himself Miles didn't know.

Miles jumped the fence carefully, still managing to scrape a knee, watching Stick dash around a house and through a gate and down another alley. Miles slipped, got up and kept going. He followed Stick down the alley and into a dirt yard, old houses in there, chickens clucking and fluttering out of the way, then under some trees and around another house where some kids were standing on a porch under an overhang, heads turning to watch the naked man being chased through their yard. As Miles was passing them, Stick skated onto his butt by a bank of chicken coops along a fence. With four long strides Miles got there as Stick was pushing himself up and kicked him back down with the flat of his foot. Stick bounded up, half-turned to face Miles, Stick's eyes wild, like some cornered cat. Miles took two quick steps in, slugged him hard in the jaw with his good hand. Stick staggered backward and fell crashing into an empty chicken coop, head cracking a length of the wood frame.

Out cold.

Miles stood over him. He could hear the kids behind him shrieking and shouting, one voice calling, "Ma come see dis!" The goddamn rain kept falling.

Stick opened his eyes, lifted his head and shoulders, then rolled onto an elbow. He lay there leaning on his elbow, legs half in a puddle, hips muddy. At Miles's mercy. Miles had wanted to hurt him so bad, but looking at his sorry state that feeling was gone now. Mostly gone anyway.

Miles waited until he thought Stick wasn't dazed anymore before he said, "Who sent you to my place this morning?"

Stick hawked up and spat a wad of blood. He spat again and passed the back of a hand across his lips.

"Who sent you? Who's the man you have to thank for this?"

Stick turned his head and slowly sat up, darting a glance at Miles, looking scared.

Miles said, "So how much Tablada pay you for this morning? Think it's worth an ass-whipping? 'Cause you dare get up I'll knock your ass flat again, make sure you get your money's worth. See this?" He crouched to show Stick his bandaged hand. "I'm talking to you, man. You did this. I'm thinking I need to return the favor. What you say?"

Stick stared at the ground, saying nothing.

"Why'd Tablada send you?"

Stick shook his head. "Tablada didn't send me, boss. It's the white lady."

Miles said, "Who?"

Stick flicked mud off his elbows and wiped rain from his face. "The rich one Tablada worked for sometimes. Live out by Caribbean Shores."

"Isabelle Gilmore?"

Stick looked off to the side. "Yeah."

Miles's head was spinning. Isabelle? That didn't make any sense. "Why?"

Stick shrugged. "I don't know, boss."

Miles wiped water from his face with his shirt. "How does she know you? Tablada tells you she got a job for you, you show up, like that?"

"Yo, I need some fucking clothes, yo."

Miles crouched and jabbed Stick's cheek with a finger. "Answer the question."

Stick pulled back his head. "Somebody come look for me, all right? Fuck."

"Tells you she wants to see you?"

"Yeah."

"Who?"

Stick spat more blood. "Dude works for she. I don't know his name, the gardener."

"So she tells you to come fuck with me she'll pay you what, fifty dollars?"

"Hundred. Disable your car, she said. Yo, I need some fuckin' *clothes*."

"Got paid yet?"

Stick shook his head.

"She had to make sure you did the job first, right?"

Stick nodded.

Miles straightened, nodding back. He said, "Listen up. I'll pass on a message, make sure you get your hundred. But I want you to understand something. If I so much as smell you around my house again, I'll call the police. Not for you. For me. So that somebody can pull me off your ass before I put you in a coma. And if I ever see you again, cross to the other side of the street, 'cause you come close to me, I'll jump in your face and beat the shit outta you for no reason other than you're an asshole."

Miles turned and walked off. The kids on the porch watched him. A little boy had come down into the yard, in the rain.

"This not finished yet," Stick shouted. "You got more than Tablada to worry 'bout, bitch. Arthur Rolle will crush you. Then El Padron will eat your ass."

Miles looked over his shoulder. Stick was standing hunched over, hands cupping his privates. Miles kept walking.

"Better watch your back from now on, mothafucka," Stick hollered.

Miles stopped. He turned around and said in a level voice, "You got the balls to be threatening me now?"

"Fuck you."

Miles pulled in a deep breath. Man, he was so tired. A part of him said, Ignore it, walk on. But his legs were already on their way over there. When he got closer he said, "No, fuck you," and ran up fast and delivered a chopping right hand. Stick dropped on his butt and rolled over to his side, holding his nose.

Miles spun back and saw the kids staring at him, a couple of them no older than Lani. He walked past, feeling their eyes heavy on him. He'd glimpsed fear in their eyes just now and felt ashamed of himself—confused about Isabelle Gilmore's motives, and damned ashamed.

Soaked and shivering in the car, he told Alicia, "One more stop, at Sammy's nephew, the lawyer," and he directed her there. She said nothing but kept looking at him.

Pete Leslie's office by the river was shrouded in rain. Miles walked into the air-conditioned front room, where the secretary was typing at the computer. She swiveled in her chair, pulled off her glasses, and studied Miles. "May I help you?"

Miles shivered. "I need to see Pete."

For a moment, she seemed unsure, watching him drip rain on the wood floor. "Do you have an appointment, Mr ... ?"

"No," Miles moving toward the office door. "Is he in there?"

She rose from the chair. "Sir, you can't go in ... sir?" and Miles walked in, Pete looking up from his desk, as Miles closed the door behind him.

Pete set his pen down, standing up, frowning. "Miles. How you doing, man? What's going on?" He scanned Miles: all wet, the blood on his shoes, the bandaged hand. "You all right, Miles?"

Miles nodded and tried to wipe water from his eyes. "I apologize for this unannounced visit but I might be in a little situation and I need some information I hope you can help me with."

Pete put up his hands. "Hey, anything, anything if I can. You sure you all right, you want a cup of coffee, something, tea? What happened to you, man?"

Miles sat down and shook his head. "I just need a moment." Pete sat down, looking at him with concern. Miles took a deep breath. He said, "Listen, this job I told you about?"

"The boxing match? The contract is fine, Miles, everything–"

"No no, not that. It's this Gilmore thing."

"Ah." With that Pete sat up straight.

"Well, this thing might run deeper than I expected, you see. You probably could help me. With some names."

"Okay. But let me ask you. This ... Gilmore thing. Doesn't have anything to do with that bandage on your hand there, does it?" When Miles only stared, Pete nodded, saying, "Okay, fine. Look here, Miles, just be careful. What names?"

"Arthur Rolle. El Padron."

Pete pursed his lips and nodded again. "Arthur Rolle, you've never heard of him?" Miles said no, and Pete continued. "Okay, then. Arthur Rolle is an American, lives out in Cayo. Remember I told you about Marlon Tablada, him being associated with people of questionable repute? Tablada is associated with Arthur Rolle, too. Old man Arthur Rolle's been acquitted twice on drug-trafficking charges, wears Teflon. And the fellow that was killed over the weekend, Ray Escalante, son of the ex-government minister? He was also one of Arthur Rolle's buddies, and Tablada's buddy. So Arthur Rolle, the Gilmores, the Escalantes, Tablada, they're all connected," Pete clasping his hands, "all one big happy family."

Miles thought, Yeah, and I'm right in the middle of a family feud.

"The head of this family is somebody we don't even know if he exists," Pete said. "That other name you asked me about."

"El Padron."

Pete nodded. "All of them, a friend in the police department tells me this, they all get their drugs or stolen cars or whatever through Mexico, through this one man whose name keeps popping up but no one has ever seen him, this guy they call El Padron. He might not even exist, but we do know for sure that across that border there is a force everybody over here respects. Belize police have traced dirty deals back to Mexico, but they get only so far and then, *poof.* Case disappears behind international red tape and whatnot and it's back to square one, and before you know it, old man Arthur Rolle is acquitted again. El Padron. Could be a syndicate, could be one man. Who knows?" Pete was staring at Miles. "You sure there isn't something else going on you'd want to tell me?"

"I'm fine, Pete. Really. I appreciate this." He felt a tad dizzy.

"Be very careful, Miles." Pete eyeing the bandage.

Miles nodded, smiling politely. He thanked Pete and turned to go. He was beginning to shiver noticeably from the a/c and he had to get out of there before Pete saw and mistook it for fear.

Which it probably was. Miles left quickly, jogging through the rain back to the car, working up the courage for what he was planning.

19.

THEY STOOD IN front of the locked gate staring at the padlock and chain. Across the road behind them the Land Rover sat idling. Harry Rolle sucked his teeth and spat into the high grass to the side. He lifted a part of the chain and let it drop with a clank against the gate. "Think a bullet could do it?"

Beto sniffed, hands on hips. "That or a Land Rover going forty, fifty miles an hour."

Harry glanced over his shoulder at the vehicle, the two heads inside. He looked at the gate again and said, "Asshole better watch how he talks to me, that's all I got to say."

"Tablada?"

"Any other asshole around here?" Harry shook his head at how thick Beto could be sometimes. "Go check that gate, go do this, do that, shit."

They walked back to the vehicle.

Tablada said, "It's locked?"

"Locked tight," Harry said.

Tablada drummed the steering wheel. Cicadas made their shrill sound in the heat. He turned to his son sitting in the backseat all sullen, his face a mess, blood spots on his T-shirt. His nose looked broken. Tablada hoped it wasn't–he didn't hit him *that* hard. He said to Joel, "Any way else into the place, boy?"

"No. Well, I don't think so."

"Make up your mind, which one?"

"I don't know about any other gate."

Harry said, "Maybe we could, like, ram the gate open, you know?"

Tablada said, "Oh really? You think so, genius? And you the one gonna pay for my paint job?"

Harry stepped back, like he'd been slapped. "Just trying to help. But since you could figure this out yourself . . ." He bowed and waved Tablada through.

Tablada swung the door open and sauntered over to the gate, gravel crunching underfoot.

Harry and Beto watched him. Harry peeked at Joel. "You all right there, man?"

Joel nodded, eyes on the floor.

"Sorry, big man. I wish none of this ever happened, you know?"

"Me, too," Joel said.

"But you shoulda come clean with my old man, you and your girl. You brought this on yourself. You know that, right? I mean, fuck, you shoulda just told him, that's all you had to do. Like just now, you had us driving all over the place wasting time before you suddenly remembered where this fucking farm was. That's not cool, man."

Tablada returned, went around to the back, and opened the door. From under one of the rear bench seats he pulled a long bolt cutter. He said to the back of Joel's head, "The watchman, you ever seen him armed?"

Joel said no. Tablada shut the door and walked back to the gate. He picked up the chain and put the bolt cutter over a link. He pressed down hard, harder, the link snapped, and he held onto the gate, breathing hard. He pushed open the gate. Walking back he said to Harry and Beto, "You girls getting in or you're gonna stand there and look pretty?"

They jumped in and Tablada threw the Land Rover into gear, turned left sharply and sped toward the gate, shouting, "Open fucking sesame!"

Nettie was teaching Rian how to make flour tortillas, the two of them crouching in the backyard over a fire hearth in the ground.

Nettie said. "You slap it flat like this first, see," tossing it from hand to hand. Rian repeated the movement, tongue pressed between her lips. Her tortilla was misshapen and she wasn't getting the rhythm. Nettie touched her wrist, showed her again, real patient. Rian was enjoying herself. A cool wind picked up from the west, feeling like rain. John Paul came and stood at the back door and watched them. Banks of clouds covered the sun, a pleasant time to be outside.

They all heard it at the same time, the engine coming up the track, and Rian lifted her head, then looked at John Paul.

He was already halfway through the house. Nettie dusted off her apron and stood and followed him. Rian came late to the front door, John Paul standing there with an ancient shotgun, Nettie behind him. A vehicle had just flown by on the two-track. Rian glimpsed the back of it, a Land Rover.

John Paul said, "Your friends?"

Rian's mouth went dry. She said, "Yes . . . no, they're not my friends."

John Paul studied her. "You in some kind of trouble, girl?"

Rian said, "Okay, look." She sighed and said, "It's like this," both of them waiting. "These guys, they want something I have."

"What? What do you have?"

"Money."

"They want to steal your money?"

"No, it's not like that. What I mean, I thought it was my mother's, I didn't know it belonged to someone else."

John Paul and Nettie just stared at her.

Rian sighed. "I ran away," she said, and then before she could second-guess herself she launched into a version of how she and Joel left, that they wanted to get married, go to the States, saying all this quickly and leaving out whose money they'd taken and how much.

John Paul said, "Somebody in that jeep owns the money?"

"Yes."

"You have the money in that bag," he said, like he knew all along.

"It's at the cabin."

John Paul shook his head. "I don't want no trouble here, understand. I think you better go and give that person his money. I don't want nobody here that shouldn't be on Mr. Castillo's property. After that, I think maybe you better leave. Sorry, pet, but I don't want no trouble."

Rian had to sit down under the weight of the stress, ponder her choices. Fuck you, Joel, fuck you, fuck you. He had let her down. Why wasn't she shocked? It was her fault for trusting him. God, she was stupid. What real choices did she have now? She'd left everything at the cabin: her passport, the money under the pillow. She didn't think they'd be here so quickly, barge onto the farm like this. Goddamn Joel. She could run, but . . . to where? Maybe she'd better face them, tell them she'd spent the money, then tell Laura, Hey, could we go to your farm so I could get some cash I accidentally left in your well? Yeah, right.

You can't keep running forever, she understood that now. Especially when your own boyfriend will help to hunt you down.

She stood up. "You're right. I better give them the money." But even as she was saying this, she didn't believe it, and a part of her was trying to cook up a plan.

John Paul motioned to the golf cart. "Take that. Tell them I know they're here, and if you don't come back in half an hour I'm calling the police."

"All right," Rian said. "Listen," catching Nettie's eyes. "I didn't mean to trouble you like this. I never figured wanting to be with somebody you love could bring so much strife."

And she found herself appropriately teary-eyed.

Riding in the cart to the cabin, she thought that what she said was such crap. Because, to be honest, really honest, she didn't think she loved Joel. She was in *like* with him, in *lust* with him, yeah, but the true, deep marrying kind of love? No, it wasn't there. But that was okay, since her leaving home wasn't really about love anyway, it was about escaping unhappiness, finding some freedom, and getting far away from her mother's manipulative ways. Then she thought about the tears she put on for Nettie and had to admit there was just enough of her mother in her to ensure that she survived. God, she was scared.

20.

"THIRTY THOUSAND," MILES said. "That's all I want."

"Oh? That's all?" Alicia shook her head and gazed out the car window. Trees and lampposts flashed by as they sped along the Western Highway.

"I'm due that money. That's the way I see it. Look at this, look at it," holding up his bandaged hand, the other hand on the wheel. "Isabelle Gilmore cost me my finger, cost me a fight and thirty grand. It's called justice, Alicia."

Alicia folded her arms, stared at him. "It's called robbery. You're planning to rob that girl of her mother's money, is what it is."

If anybody else had said it, he would've been instantly pissed, but here Alicia was taking time away from helping in the barbershop to show him the way to the farm. So Miles stayed cool, focused on one thing: compensation.

Alicia said, "I'm worried, Miles, to tell you the truth."

"Don't be, everything'll be all right, you'll see."

She made a face. "You don't know that. I'm worried about Marlon Tablada."

"You think I'm in over my head."

"I didn't say that. Not exactly. But what if Tablada has his crew there, what if he's armed or something. He used to be a police officer, don't forget. Jesus, Miles, I'm getting anxious just talking about this."

Miles nodded. He wasn't in doubt, because he had finally seen everything clearly. Came to him like something he'd forgotten. One second he was at home, tossing back half a Percocet with a swallow of water, confused and his finger aflame, the next he was staring into space, realizing that it had been nothing but a ruse: Isabelle had used him to draw Tablada out because Tablada knew where Rian was. Sometimes all you needed was a quiet moment to interpret the obvious. The barbershop, Cat's Lounge, the slow-speed chase—who did they all have in common? Tablada. He couldn't ignore the coincidence that the day Tablada met with him, Isabelle fired him. And why did Isabelle resort to such a roundabout method? Because Isabelle and Tablada were on the outs but she knew some of his leads? Or maybe Tablada was charging her too much so she wanted to show him she had someone else on the case, entice him to lower the price. Whatever the reason, going to all that trouble probably meant Isabelle Gilmore, the money launderer, was missing much more than ten thousand. When you're that rich, you don't involve strangers in your affairs to recover a measly ten thousand. And Tablada must have suspected as much, too, which is why he wasn't helping. Because he was holding out for a chunk of cash.

Miles saw this logic like he was seeing the answer to a math problem. How in the hell could he not figure the design before? Running about, asking questions in places full of Tablada's people—that had been a game so that word would reach Tablada. And when Miles told Isabelle that he'd uncovered a lead, she panicked, contacted Stick to make sure Miles kept his ass at home. Jesus, Miles was embarrassed he took so long to reason this out. He sat at home a few minutes feeling like a fool before he knew what he had to do. So he had dragged himself out of the house, taken Lani to Alicia's father, and now he was on his way, feeling justified. Justification worked wonders on a man's sense of purpose.

They were approaching the turn to Belmopan and Miles slowed down. He wanted to tell Alicia to relax, be positive, all that, but he was feeling edgy himself. The more he thought about this mess, the closer he got to the farm, the more he saw that she was right. Things could get out of hand pretty easily. He gripped the wheel hard as they came around a curve doing sixty.

"Slow down, please."

Miles let up off the gas a fraction.

"How are you feeling?"

"Percocet is very, very nice. Dulls the pain, got me feeling just a little drunk, life is sweet."

"And here you are behind the wheel. Lovely." Alicia said, "I'm worried, Miles. What if Tablada is at the farm already, what if..." She shook her head. "I don't know about this."

He gave the journey a second thought. Then the moment was gone. He would not accept the situation.

He watched the road twisting ahead. It was time to get paid.

Rian stopped the golf cart well short of the farmhouse. She sat holding the wheel, staring at the unoccupied Land Rover parked by the porch. Her palms were perspiring, her underarms. It was starting to feel like the most complicated day of her life.

She was thinking, just wondering–what if she gave them the money? Just said, Here it is, and climb into their vehicle with them and go home? Maybe she and her mother could patch up their relationship. Maybe now her mother would sit down and admit her jealousies and resentments toward her and quit trying to control her daughter's life and . . . what utter bullshit.

The problem was, her mother put no value in honesty. She'd always preferred appearances, the façade that concealed whatever scheme she was brewing. And how she manipulated people. As long as money was the end result and she maintained her lifestyle, she was happy. Rian sat there thinking, she loved her mother, her mother loved her, but it was all so twisted with deception and greed and control and resentments that it would take years of therapy to untangle.

She got off the golf cart and looked toward the well, wondering. She decided she'd have a long talk with her mother.

In about twenty years.

She walked along the dirt path to the cabin. A light was on in the living room and she could see heads moving about inside. She stepped quietly onto the porch. Put a hand on the doorknob. Thought about fleeing, turning on her heels and running, far, far till the past just disappeared. Then she braced herself and turned the knob.

Standing in the center of the room, Marlon Tablada smiled. They had turned the place upside down. Kitchen utensils on the floor, pots, pans, kettle, Tupperware containers, plastic cups, and broken coffee mugs. The cupboards were open and canned foods were piled on the counter and in the sink. The fridge was open, too. Every drawer, nook, and cranny had been searched.

"Good afternoon there," Tablada said.

Rian couldn't even fake a sarcastic smile. "What do you want?"

Tablada flinched. "What do I want? You enjoy playing games? Look around, does it look like I came here to play games?" He came toward her, glass crunching under his boots. "You gonna tell me where it is or you want me to continue and tear this motherfucka up?"

Out of the bedroom came Harry Rolle and Beto, Harry carrying a pillowcase filled with something. He mocked a show of surprise when he saw her. "Well, look what the cat brought in."

Rian said, "It's 'dragged.' Look what the cat dragged in. Jesus. Where's Joel?"

They said nothing.

"Where is Joel?" She marched past them into the bedroom. Her clothes were strewn across the floor, the mattress flipped on its side against the wall. They'd found her bunch of hundreds. She went back outside. "Where's he?"

Harry sneered. "How about pussy dragged in?"

"You're a child and you need to grow up," Rian said.

"Pussy like your boyfriend."

Tablada said, "Careful there, okay?" He walked to the bathroom door and rapped with the back of his hand. "Let's finish up in there, boy."

A few seconds later, Joel slouched out, clutching a damp towel to his face.

"Jesus, Joel," Rian said. She looked at them. "What happened to him? What did you do to him?" She moved to go to him but Tablada put a straight arm out and stopped her. "No time for this right now. First thing, go sit down," tilting his head at the tattered sofa by the window. "You hear me?" His eyes widened. "Sit the fuck down."

If Rian was nervous before, she was full-blown terrified now. The man looked to be on the brink of a rage, the place wrecked, and Joel had been pummeled, no doubt about it, his face all bruised, blood caked around his nostrils. He stood touching his face with the towel, trying not to look at her.

"Who sent you to come for me?" Rian asked Tablada. "My mother?" She turned to Harry. "Your father?"

"Take a seat, girl," Tablada said.

"Please, Rian," Joel said, sounding meeker than usual.

"Or else what? They're gonna beat me up, too?" She jutted out her chin at Tablada, not budging. She was scared all right, but at the same time she wanted to fly at someone and scratch or kick or slap, anything to hurt them, show they weren't getting the best of her. Instead, slowly, she sat down, folded her arms, and stared back at Tablada.

He said, "I'll ask you a couple simple questions, you give me a couple simple answers, how 'bout that?" He came to stand a few feet in front of her. "First, where's the money?"

"I don't know what you're talking about."

Tablada said, "Hell, you see now. I'm about to lose my patience. Know what I'm fixing to do now, right?" He took a big step toward her, a tight smile pasted on his face, eyes hard and gleaming.

She didn't doubt that he wanted to hit her, a man like him, known for his easy brutality. She swung her glare on Joel. "You've been talking to him some more?"

Joel wouldn't meet her eyes.

Tablada standing over her, Rian tipped her head back to look at his face. "The money's in the car."

Tablada said, "See how easy that was? What car?"

"She's lying," Harry said, watching Joel. "Look me in my eyes, Joel, tell me she's not lying." He turned to Tablada. "I see it all over his face."

Harry reminded Rian of a tattletale kid, a kiss-ass trying to get on the school bully's good side.

Tablada's face was like stone when he said again, "What car?"

With lazy coolness, Rian turned her head to look at Harry. "His car."

Harry said, "The fuck you talking about?"

Tablada's eyes were fixed on Rian. "How much?"

"What?"

"What? What?" mimicking her. "You suddenly developed a stupidity problem? How. Much. Money."

"A lot."

Tablada pursed his lips and exhaled hard through his nose. "Simple questions, you know. Simple goddamn basic English. So lemme try again." He fixed her with a stare. "How much money did you leave in the car? And don't say a lot. How much?"

Rian came up with a number that seemed reasonable. "About a hundred thousand."

Tablada sniffed. "Hundred?" He nodded. "Okay, young lady." He took a cell phone from his shirt pocket and flipped it open.

"It's more than that they owe my pa," Harry said, his voice shrill, "but anyway, she's lying 'cause I'd know if money's in my ride. Where'd you hide it, huh? Where?"

Tablada had dialed and put the phone to his ear, looking down at Rian with a smug smile. "Don't you worry, all will be revealed in a minute."

"The truth shall make you free," Harry said to her.

Rian shook her head and said under her breath, "*Set* you free, asshole."

Harry said, "What?"

"Nothing. Talking to myself."

"Hello? Hello, Arthur?" Tablada pressed the phone against his ear. "Marlon here . . . Yeah, making progress. In fact that's why I'm calling you. I located her finally . . . a farm just outside Belmopan. . . . Yeah, she's right here, I'm looking at that cute little face right now, matter of fact. . . . Well, she's saying she left some of it in your son's car. . . . I know, but that's what she's saying." Tablada nodded. "Yes, I know, exactly why I'm calling you. . . . Yeah, he's right here. Hold on." Tablada turned to Harry. "Your father wants to know where's your car keys."

Harry frowned, stroking his goatee. "Um . . . let me think."

Beto said, "Remember you put them in your computer desk drawer?"

Harry looked at him. "No, man, that's . . . You sure?"

Beto shrugged. "I think so."

"But I never put the keys there."

"That's what I remember."

"I'm trying to think where else, 'cause–"

"Hey!" Tablada glared at them. "Goddamn, boy, your father's waiting."

"The computer desk drawer," Harry said, "tell him to check there."

Tablada did. He waited, grinning at Rian, the phone at his ear. "We'll see in a moment if you're telling the truth, cuteness."

The room was silent, everybody tense, Joel still staring at the floor, all downcast and beaten, still holding the wet towel.

Tablada said, "Yes, Arthur? Oh...okay." He drew the phone from his ear and looked at Harry. "The key isn't there. He wants to talk to you." He handed Harry the cell without looking at him.

"Dad?"

Everyone in the room could hear Arthur Rolle shouting on the other end. He went on and on. Harry lowered his head, slipped a hand in his pocket. "Dad, but...no, Dad...yes, I know, I know...I understand, man, but it's not mine..." Louder shouting. "All right, all right, yes...In my socks drawer, I think, no I'm sure that's where it is." Harry shifted from one foot to the next, glanced up sheepishly. His father continued to rant. "Yes, sir," Harry said and moved the phone from his lips. "Fuck." He swatted Beto on the shoulder. "You left the fucking bag a weed in the desk drawer, fool."

Beto pointed to his own chest. "Me? You the one had it last, remember?"

"Shit. Now he's talking trash how he'll kick my ass when we get back." Harry sucked his teeth, shaking his head.

Pathetic. That's what Rian thought looking at him, with his half-assed goatee and overlong baggy shorts and skinny legs. She looked at him and his long-haired lackey Beto and the evil, grinning Marlon Tablada and then at Joel, and she felt embarrassed for Joel and for herself. There they were talking yesterday morning about a new life together, the unspoken word *marriage* hovering above them like a dream, and look where they were now. Joel, the man she thought she loved, standing there humiliated into silence and she sitting as if in a principal's office waiting for the bomb to drop.

"Yeah, Dad, I'm right here. It's there?" Harry nodded at Tablada. "So ... how much money is ... You could tell me ... Okay then." Now it was Harry's turn to hand Tablada the phone without looking his way.

"Hello? Appears to be short, huh?" Tablada listened. "Good, I'll be right here." He slipped the phone in his pocket and smiled at Rian. "He found the cash under the front passenger seat. Says he'll count it out, call me back if it's short or not. Looks like it's short so far, he's saying. Believe in God?"

Rian blinked and didn't answer. Wanted to say, yeah, like in, god, this man is so tiresome.

"Better pray your lie comes true." He laughed, walked away, killing himself with his wit. He clapped Joel's shoulder, tittering as he went into the bathroom. "Got to take me a leak. You all don't go nowhere."

21.

THEY HAD BROUGHT the rain from the city with them. Miles leaned forward to peer through the downpour, the wipers beating back and forth.

"Right, take a right," Alicia said.

Miles turned down a narrow clay road that rose through a cluster of trees. The road broadened after a few hundred yards and the land on both sides cleared. Wire fences and posts marked the boundaries of farms. Then came a hill. Miles squinted into the rain. "Where the hell are we? I can't tell north from south, all these curves and turns and whatnot."

Alicia said, "I told you you wouldn't find this place without me. It's, like, really tucked away, probably why Rian and Joel wanted to go there." She touched Miles's arm and pointed. "There, down there, on the left. You'll see a gate."

The car felt like it was on ice, slipping down the hill. Miles tapped the brake as they rolled alongside the gate.

"It's open," Alicia said, and she didn't seem happy.

"Then cool, let's go in."

"I don't know. It's usually closed. Like usually you have to blow your horn for the watchman to come open it. Maybe we should blow anyway?"

Miles sat there, rain drumming the roof and beating a thought into his head. He didn't want to announce his arrival. If

Tablada and his crew were already there, he didn't want to give them the drop on him. Best try for the element of surprise, like they said in the movies. Yeah, well . . . He drove on in.

Alicia said, "You sure about this?"

"It's a gift. Let's take advantage of it."

"Maybe it bodes ill."

He looked at her, smirking. "You saying it's a portent of evil?"

"Yeah," she said, "like an augury."

"A what? Like an omen?"

"Aren't you scared? Because I am."

"I'm kind of shitting myself as we speak, actually."

They came around a curve in the two-track, and Miles said, "Jesus Christ," and mashed the brake.

An old man stood blocking their path, training a shotgun at the windshield. He was shouting something. Miles raised both hands as the man stepped unsteadily to the side, gun aimed at Miles's head. Miles said, "Who the hell is this, the watchman?"

The old man motioned for Miles to lower the window. Miles did, carefully. Rain poured in.

"What the hell you doing on private property?" the barrel wavering as the old man spoke.

Alicia leaned across Miles's lap, peered out the window. "John Paul? Remember me, John Paul?"

John Paul said to Miles, "Turn back and get off this farm." The gun moving, his gnarled finger trembling over the trigger, Miles thinking, Please put that thing down.

"John Paul," Alicia said, "I'm one of Laura's friends that used to come here to ride the horses. Don't you remember me?"

John Paul half-crouched for a better look at her. Recognition flickered across his face. He wiped rain off his face with one of his T-shirt sleeves, examined her again, Miles flinching whenever the gun moved. He felt Alicia's fingernails clawing into his thigh. The rain came down.

Then the old man broke into a three-toothed smile. "I remember your face, girl. What's your name?"

"Alicia. Alicia Gomez. I'm one of Laura's friends. I've been here before, I–" She put a hand to her chest. "Please, don't, that gun is making me nervous."

The old man looked at the thing in his hands. "Oh, Lawd, sorry, pet." He lowered it down by his leg. "Crazy day, I tell you. Crazy things going on here. What you doing up this way?"

Alicia took a second. "Looking for a friend. She said she was coming here. Rian Gilmore's her name. Is she here?"

"Yes, she's here." John Paul wiped rain out of his eyes. "Looks like she's in some trouble, though."

"Trouble? Like how?"

He looked off down the two-track. "Some men just now broke through the front gate. This girl's got some money belongs to them is what she tells me. Those men, they cut my padlock and drove right on in like nobody's business. The girl went to meet them at the cabin not fifteen minutes ago."

"Doesn't sound too good," Miles said. "How many men?"

"Don't know. They blew by here in a Land Rover so fast I couldn't see them right. About four?"

"A blue Land Rover?"

"That's correct."

Miles said to Alicia, "Tablada's here." He said to John Paul, "Think we can go to the cabin and pick Rian up? She's expecting us. And I know she'd rather have us for company than those guys."

The old man spat and stared at the ground. The rain kept coming down. He looked frail in his soaked clothes. "To tell you the truth, I don't like any of this one bit. I don't know if anybody's being square with me. You two included. But I tell you what. I'll give you twenty minutes to get her and those men and get off the property, take whatever business you all got off the farm. Or I call the police. The only reason I been hesitating is I don't want this getting back to Mr. Castillo, but believe me I don't care if I lose my job now, I just don't want any trouble, you understand?"

Miles kept eye contact with him and nodded, wanting to show respect by giving the old man his full attention, show he was being cooperative. He figured he'd need more time, but he told John Paul he understood perfectly. Alicia said they'd pop in, pop out, promise.

The old man nodded. "Go ahead," waving them through, "but make it quick."

They pulled up beside the Land Rover and stepped out into the rain, shoulders pulled high, heads tucked low. Soaking wet though they were, they didn't want to run, make themselves look like they weren't composed. When they reached the porch, Miles was shivering, but only partly from the rain. His mouth was dry from the Percocet but he was alert, his body thrumming. He had a hard bubble of tension in his chest. He said to Alicia, "Stand behind me." Then he knocked.

The door opened, and he recognized Rian Gilmore. She looked older than in the photograph; maybe it was the strain of the last few days.

From over his shoulder, Alicia said, "Hey, Rian."

Rian canted her head. "Alicia? Hey, girl," and she was about to step toward her friend when somebody behind her spoke. Rian opened the door wide and moved to the side.

Marlon Tablada was sitting on a stool in the center of the room, smiling. Two young men stood off to one side, and another young man, his face bruised and lumpy, sat on another stool by a kitchen counter. Miles hardly recognized Joel Tablada–looking as limp and dejected as the towel he was holding. Miles suspected it was his father who'd worked him over; no parent would allow anyone else to do that to his son.

"Well, well, if it ain't the pugilist," Tablada said, "coming all this way for no good reason I can see. What you doin' here, boy? Tell me you came for the fresh country air, for the scenery, 'cause I'm at a loss."

Miles stepped into the room, Alicia by his side. He gestured at Rian. "Came here to speak to this young lady. Question is, what're *you* doing here?"

Tablada laughed. "A boxer *and* a comedian."

"What's so funny?" Miles smiling.

Harry looked askance at Tablada. "Who dis?"

"This? This is a man that seems to have a problem doing like he's told. This is a man likes working for free." He watched Miles. "Didn't the lady relieve you of your duties? But you're committed, isn't that right. Committed to getting in my way. Listen, Mike Tyson. Turn around and go back where you came from, you and your girlfriend here. This ain't no place for you today."

Miles stared at him. Then he said, "The watchman by the front gate you broke open, he gave me twenty minutes to talk to Rian and for everybody to get off the farm, or he calls the police.

So I'm not leaving until me and Rian have a chat. In private. Then we all leave."

Rian said, "What the hell's going on here? Alicia?"

Miles lifted his bandaged hand. "See this? Half of my finger was sliced off this morning by a guy works for him," pointing at Tablada, "because I was hired to look for you."

"What?" Rian's eyebrows knotted.

The room was quiet. All eyes were on Miles.

"Your mother hired me to hunt for you after you took off with Joel. She said you stole money from her and she wanted it back and wanted you home. She gave me four days to find you before you turned eighteen and got married and left the country. Which is what she said you were planning."

Rian glanced at Alicia for help.

Alicia said, "It's true, Rian."

Miles continued, "Your mother hired me, but he," pointing at Tablada again, "he knew all the while where you and his son were, and I think your mother suspected that, too. Only problem was the price wasn't right for him."

Tablada stood up, glaring. "I think you've talked enough for now. It's time to shut the hell up and leave."

"Yeah," Harry Rolle said, grabbing at his crotch. He said to Beto, "This getting a little too complicated." He looked around at everyone in the room. "Don't know what the fuck this got to do with the price of milk in China."

Miles smiled at him. "I know who almost everybody else is here but I don't think I caught your name. You are . . . ?"

"Jesus Christ, Lord and Savior."

Beto chuckled.

Miles looked at Rian for the correct name. Not until Alicia turned to her did she catch the silent question.

"Harry. His name's Harry Rolle."

Miles took a second. The drug dealer's son. So the money . . . Oh yes, he was beginning to understand. Everything was about money here. He said, "Harry, my name's Miles Young. I think we're here for the same reason."

"Yeah? And what's that?"

"You want what's rightfully your dad's, I want what's rightfully mine."

Harry rolled his head lazily in Beto's direction. "Hail me when you solve that riddle." He folded his arms and studied Miles sullenly.

The gears in Miles's head were clicking, laying out a quick plan. If he could just follow through, his limbs all trembly with adrenaline. In a calm voice–to settle himself–he said, "Rian, can I speak to you outside a sec?"

"Nobody's speaking to anybody," Tablada said. "It's time to hit the fucking road. Say goodbye."

Rian scowled at him. "Who the hell are you to answer for me and tell him, me, or anyone who we can talk to? Sorry, but you're way outta line. You can't stop us from talking."

Harry moved toward her and lifted the front of his shirt, and they all saw the stainless steel pistol stuck in his waistband. "No, it's *you* who's outta line. *We* can stop you."

Miles heard a sharp intake of breath from Alicia. The gears clicked and turned again. His body was taut, breath flowing smoothly. He nodded, saying nothing. Forty-seven pro fights and seventeen years of training your mind to handle the stress of being under attack could lend you a calmness sometimes. In extreme situations when all you wanted to do was turn and run, you might find confidence. Under pressure some people froze; the only time that had happened to Miles, and only partially, was last Sunday in the ring, and he was embarrassed by that as much as he was frightened now. But he wasn't about to repeat it. He would not give this smirking son of a bitch with a gun for courage the pleasure of seeing his fear. He said, "You're here because you think Rian has your father's money, isn't that right?" Man, he hoped to hell he was right. When he saw something quiver behind Harry's eyes, Miles knew he was right.

He said, "Which is why I'm surprised you're not hearing what I've been saying, which makes me think you're not focusing on your father's welfare, with all due respect. Don't you see Tablada is playing your father like a fiddle? Didn't you hear me just tell Rian that he knew from day one where she and Joel and the money were?"

Tablada took one, two quick strides and clocked Miles in the jaw, Miles stumbling back. He caught his balance and squared his shoulders to deal with more if it came.

Tablada said, "That one is for business. The next will be personal."

Boxers say it's the punches you don't see that hurt you the most. Miles did not see the blow, but it did not hurt him. He gave Tablada a little smile. "Do that shit again, I'll answer you in kind and let's see if you're still standing after I'm finished. Harry here's gonna have to use that gun to get me off you, trust me." He said to Harry, "You heard what I've been saying? This guy could've helped your father days ago if he weren't looking to play Isabelle instead."

Miles heard something and saw Tablada's hand go up. Miles clenched his right hand and set his feet. Then he heard the cell phone chirping, Tablada reaching into a top pocket. He flipped open the cell. "Hello? Arthur? . . . Hello?" Walking to the other corner of the room. "Damn." He fiddled with the phone. It started chirping again. "Hey, Arthur . . . yeah, bad connection. So, how does it look?"

Tablada turned and gave them his back, listening, nodding.

Miles looked at Harry—he was slack-jawed, frowning, like a dull-witted boy trying to process two and two.

"I'm not lying to you, Harry," Miles said softly. "I can prove it." He had the perfect opportunity now. "Alicia, hand me your cell phone."

Harry's eyes moved from Miles to Tablada and back, like he was trying to figure out whom to believe.

Holding the cell phone, Miles asked Rian, "What's your home number?"

Harry said, "So you don't know it then?"

Miles liked that. Harry was paying attention. "Okay, let me think. Give me a second here." He was taking too long. "Give me a second. Okay, here we go, 3-3-1-8-8-6," tilting the phone so Harry could see him punching the digits.

"3-3-1-8-6-8," Rian said.

Miles pressed Clear and started over. "So I wasn't far off."

Three tones later, Isabelle Gilmore picked up. "Hello?"

"Hi, Isabelle. This is Miles Young."

Silence. Then, "Hello, Miles. How can I help you?"

"Well, that's an interesting question. Seems to me you weren't too concerned about helping me, considering what happened this morning."

Silence. Then, "I don't know what you're talking about."

"Please, let's cut the bullshit. Listen up, Isabelle. I'm here with your daughter, and Joel, and Marlon Tablada, the man you hired after you dismissed me. And Harry Rolle is here, too, that's Arthur Rolle's son. So you could talk truthfully about why you sent Stick to my house this morning or you could deal with Mr. Rolle yourself after whatever cover-up or game you and Tablada tried to pull."

Tablada turned around. He and Miles looked at each other across the room, the two of them holding cell phones at their ears. Tablada said, "What the fuck are you doing? No, no, not you Arthur, sorry . . . No, it's one of the boys here, no problem, everything's fine . . . I see . . ." Listening, he eyed Miles, then shot Harry a questioning glance.

Harry put up a hand to say he had things under control.

Tablada half-turned and continued talking to Arthur Rolle, but he looked worried and started to pace.

Miles said to Isabelle, "You listening to me?"

"I am. You're lying to me."

"Think so? Keep listening." He put his back to a wall so he could see the entire room. "I know now that you owe Arthur Rolle some money and wanted Tablada to find it but he wouldn't so you hired me to draw him out, then you dropped my ass cold. Then you sent that fool called Stick to make sure I stayed at home. Because you got worried when I told you I had a lead. Yeah, I know about Stick, and don't worry, I've dealt with him already. Keep listening, because this next part is important.

What I want, I want you to admit to me that you intended to hire Tablada all along because you knew that he knew where to find Rian."

Isabelle said nothing.

Harry stared at him.

Miles waited.

Tablada turned around to face them, with the phone at his ear. He glared at Miles before walking into the kitchen. "I didn't catch that, Arthur . . ."

"You're bluffing," Isabelle said. "You don't know anything."

Miles said, "Say hello to your daughter," and went to Rian, put the phone by her lips. Miles nodded to her.

"Hello, Mom. It's me."

Miles pulled back the phone. "That sound like a lie to you? I want you to say that Tablada knew. Tell me the truth."

"Put my daughter back on the phone. Put her back."

Miles said nothing. He watched Tablada stick a finger in his ear, fighting the bad reception.

Isabelle said, "Okay, Miles, if that's what you want to hear, yes, but I paid you well, don't you forget that."

Miles stepped toward Harry. "So you knew Tablada knew all along and you used me to lure him." Quickly he put the phone at Harry's ear, Harry's hand going up instinctively, then dropping slowly as he listened. Miles could hear her voice faintly. When he could no longer hear her speaking, he pulled the phone back and said, "Thank you. Hold on a second." He lowered the phone to his side and looked at Harry. "You understand where I'm coming from?"

* * *

Tablada was saying, "I got it...Not a problem, I'll see you soon." He flipped his cell phone shut and came toward them. "The fuck's going on here?"

Harry looked like a lost kid. He turned his head from Tablada to Miles and back, trying to decide what to believe.

Miles moved the phone to his lips. "Still there?"

Isabelle said, "Tell me what it is that you want."

"To be compensated for what happened to me. Thirty thousand. When I get back to the city, you and me, we'll talk."

Tablada said with a shark's grin, "Get off the phone."

Miles raised a finger to him, saying to Isabelle, "No, we'll talk later. I'll get back to you with time and place."

Tablada said, "Hang it up. I won't tell you again." He looked at Rian. "You didn't pray like I told you. Hundred thousand in the car, you said? Try forty. You're coming with us. Mr. Rolle wants to see you, says maybe he can impress upon you the urgency of this situation."

That snapped Harry out of his silence. "The money's not there?"

Tablada shot him a look of disdain. "I just said your father counted the money, didn't I? He's short several thousand." Then he looked at Miles, and this time he bellowed, "Get off the fucking phone!"

Something awoke in Harry. Suddenly the gun was in his hand and pointed at Miles's face. "Get off the phone, asshole."

Miles held his breath. Alica gasped, or maybe it was Rian. Miles lowered the phone.

Harry stepped forward and jabbed him in the jaw with the muzzle of the gun. It hurt, and Miles could smell the gun oil.

The reality of the danger hit him and his stomach churned. "Easy, easy," he said, raising his arms.

"I don't know what your game is but you better re*spect* me." Harry pushed the muzzle into Miles's neck. "And I guess me and you have to chat, Marlon."

No one spoke. No one moved.

Until Tabalda said, "You and I have nothing to chat about, Dirty Harry. We have business to conduct. We don't need this distraction. Now quit acting like a damn fool and put that thing away."

For a second, looking at Harry's face, Miles thought the boy was going to cry. His face went slack, his mouth opened, and he seemed to take on a slouch. Like some kid whose father had just shamed him in front of his friends. Then he stiffened, his nostrils flaring. He lowered the gun slowly and sneered at Tablada. "What did you say?"

Tablada shook his head and went, "Pffff," turning away, like he had no time to deal with this ass.

"What did you say to me?" Harry moved across the room and leveled the gun at Tablada. "You fucking dissing me?" He raised his voice, "After what I know about you now, you think you could *diss* me?" Walking forward red-faced, pointing the gun.

Tablada spun around to face him. "You outta your fucking mind, you little punk? I ought to slap–"

The gun exploded and Tablada dropped.

He lay on his side, blood spouting from a hole in his head, legs twitching.

Miles's ears were ringing; Alicia was screaming; Joel jumped off his stool and backed away, knocking the stool over, staring wide-eyed at his father; Harry stood over Tablada and squeezed off another shot, the floorboards splintering.

Then a sudden silence and gun smoke.

"Dad, Dad," Joel yelled and ran to his father. Harry stood holding the gun and watched Joel collapse over his father. "Daddy, Daddy." Joel pressed a hand over the wound in Tablada's head. Blood pumped through his fingers.

Harry spun around and shouted, "Fuck with me, go ahead somebody, fuck with me," spit flying, waving the gun wildly at everyone.

Miles stood still, muscles locked down. Alica was crying in her hands. Rian had found a corner to crouch in. Beto kept saying, "Oh God, oh fuck, oh God," while Harry raged on.

Tablada was dead. It was strange how Miles accepted it so calmly even though he'd never seen anyone shot before. Keeping arms raised, showing Harry the respect he didn't deserve, Miles knew this day would leave a permanent stain on him.

But to stand there like a statue while some young dimwit decided your fate? He just couldn't, so he resorted to a talking self-defense. "All right, brother, no one's gonna mess with you, tell us what you want us to do now."

Harry didn't seem to understand English anymore. His lips twisted and he said, "What? What?" and jerked the gun up at Miles.

Miles cringed, turning his head to the side. Softly, like he was talking to an attack dog, he said, "Harry. Harry, listen to me."

"No, you listen to *me*." But he had nothing to say, just stood there pointing the gun, breathing heavily.

"You get outta here now!" It was Alicia stalking forward, crying but angry.

Harry swung the gun on her. Alicia took a step closer, shouting. "Go ahead. How many people you gonna shoot today, huh?" and Miles put out a hand to stop her. "Alicia, please, Alicia."

Harry kept the gun on her. Alicia stared at him with her red eyes. "Is this the way your mother raised you, huh? Is it?"

Miles said, "The watchman, Harry. The watchman heard those shots. I swear, he told me I didn't get off the farm in twenty minutes, he'd call the police."

Harry aimed the gun at Miles now. His eyes glinted with tears as he searched Miles's face. His finger curled around the trigger.

Miles blinked, arms held high, and he saw little Lani's face clear and pretty and felt himself falling, falling . . .

"You're lying," Harry said, but his voice was high, shaky.

Miles said, "You could doubt me and take a chance. But why would you want to do that?"

Inch by inch, the gun came down and Harry watched Miles.

Beto said, "Hey, let's go, Harry."

Harry looked at Beto, then at the gun. "The watchman," he said, his voice dry and distant. "All right." He thumbed up the safety, fumbled around pushing the pistol in his waistband. Then he stood in a kind of trance while the room waited, and Joel knelt bawling over his father.

Harry walked over to Joel and looked as if he wanted to say something, but he only licked his lips, staring. He crouched beside Tablada and went through his pockets until he came away with a bunch of keys.

Beto opened the door and Harry followed him out, then in a careful show of manners, gently closed the door.

Through the window Miles watched them drive away in Tablada's Land Rover in the heavy, slanting rain.

Miles needed to think fast. How do you hide a murder? A body? Why would you want to? What would happen to them if they lied? And if you started a game of deception how do you get four people to handle ten thousand questions that would come flooding in without getting swept away by their own lies?

Rian had pried Joel off his father, and he knelt with his head in her lap as she sat on the sofa, blood all over their clothes. Miles brought a sheet from the bedroom and covered Tablada.

Alicia had thrown up in the bathroom and came out wiping her mouth with a towel, apologizing. She seemed stunned.

"It's all right," Miles said, "you don't need to apologize." He felt unreasonably calm, certain of himself. Because one thing was clear. He didn't have any sensible option but to tell the truth. And while the consequences of that might bring heat on him in the form of an investigation and maybe even payback from the Rolles—a real possibility—the alternative promised endless days of looking over your shoulder, sleepless nights worrying when the cops would come knocking at your door.

Miles felt tired, too. He wanted a peaceful future, for him and Lani.

He walked across the room for a closer look at the blood and the bullet casings, his shoes resounding hollow off the wooden floor. He turned and looked at Alicia awhile, the color creeping back into her face, and now he felt sorry he'd brought her here, complicated her life. "You okay?"

She nodded, wiping away the moisture under her eyes.

"We need to talk about what we're going to do," he said. "We don't have much time."

"Okay."

He said, "All right," and paused, bracing himself for everything that would follow, like a boxer before he rose off the stool for the final round.

Miles told her what they should do and she agreed. Rian and Joel sat there, holding each other. Miles sat beside them, told them his plan, which wasn't a plan at all, he said, but common sense. But Joel sat back on his haunches and said, No way, he wasn't leaving his father. Miles tried not to look at the bruises on his face and the broken nose his father had given him when he said that somebody would be there soon enough, his father wasn't going to be alone. Joel shook his head and said, "No way," so Miles turned his attention to Rian.

"I'm not going back home," she said, "so there. Go to the police if you want but I won't be there with you."

Miles nodded, looked away a second. "That's fine. You don't have to be there with me. But you and I have to talk. As it is, the watchman might've called the police already. So you want to leave here? I'm the only way out. You and I've got to have a quick talk first."

She gazed at him. "About what?"

"About this," Miles said, showing her his bandaged finger.

"You're saying that's what my mom caused?"

"You got it."

"What do I have to do with that?"

"Let's put it this way. Her money will be paying for it. And you have her money. Before you object, lemme just ask, where're you headed now? You say you're not going home."

She examined her fingernails, looked at him. "I don't know. Yet."

Miles sat forward, elbows on knees. "I was telling Alicia, I kind of understand what you're going through, you wanting to be with Joel, get away from your mother's control. My wife and I, before we got married, that's how it was with us. We eventually made the break. Left Miami, got away from her family. I guess what I'm saying, you can get away, too. But not in Belize. Here, your mother will always be close on your tail. I have a daughter myself and I can't say I'd condone her running away but, hey, every situation's different so I won't judge. But here's what I'm proposing. I'm offering, strictly business, a way that you get what you want, I get what I want." He paused, studying her.

"So what're you saying?"

"A house to stay. In Miami. You pay me rent, a one-time payment, it's yours to stay in for as long as you need."

Joel rose and went to sit on the floor, arms on knees, by his father's body.

Rian blinked, looked at Alicia. Alicia sat on the armrest and gave Rian's shoulder a squeeze. Rian stared at the floor. "How do you know it's my mother who's responsible? Know for sure?"

This wasn't the response Miles expected. He thought a second and said, "The dude that cut me told me it was your mother that paid him. Name's Stick. Joel knows who he is," glancing at Joel.

Rian lifted her chin. "Stick. He could be lying."

Miles leaned in. "You know your mother better than me. This sounds like something she would do?" He kept his eyes on her.

She had to look away. She exhaled, lowered her head, and covered her eyes with a hand. She stayed that way for a time. "You're probably right," she said quietly. When she raised her head, she said, "How much?"

Miles said, "Thirty thousand. Which is the exact amount I would've made for the fight, which your mother cost me."

Rian breathed in deeply. "Okay." She nodded. "Okay." She lifted her gaze. "Joel? Joel, did you hear?"

He sat staring at the floor. He said something. Then he straightened up and looked at her. "My father," he said. His eyes were glassy.

Rian waited. Then she rose and waited some more. Eventually, she turned to Miles and said, "Give me a minute to collect my things." And just like that, she and Joel were through.

Miles tried not to look at her face, not wanting to see her on the verge of tears. He and Alicia watched Rian bundle her clothes in a towel and tie it at the top. Joel kept his face down as she walked by.

Miles stood at the open door. "Got everything?"

"Except the money." She stopped and looked back.

Joel had put his forehead on his knees, and the moment of silence made him lift his head, a glazed expression on his face.

Rain blew in through the open door. Trees swished in the breeze.

"Bye, Joel," Rian said.

He swallowed. "Bye," he said.

Then they closed the door and left him there alone.

Miles pulled the bag of money from the well in the stinging rain. They drove off the farm and up the road back to Belmopan, the bag in Rian's lap, their clothes soaked. About a mile from Belmopan, Rian broke down and Alicia climbed into the back seat to console her. Rian sobbed for Joel, saying that she felt sorry for him and that she loved him so much. She cried and cried and all Alicia could do was hold her. And through her tears Rian said that because of her they'd killed that man, Escalante, because she'd stolen the money. Miles told her not to feel responsible for anyone like Raymond Escalante, it wasn't she who brought harm to him. People like this knew the consequences of the life they led, the pain they caused. He only half-believed that, of course. Because no one involved today was guiltless, not him or her or even Alicia; their actions today might have effects he couldn't foresee, he knew that. He intended to keep thirty grand of dirty money, and Alicia would keep her silence and they'd wish for the best.

Outside of Belmopan, he borrowed her cell phone and called emergency, said there was a man shot and killed on the Bamboo Bank Farm. He gave rough directions and hung up, stepped hard on the gas, and ignored his pounding heart.

His finger was starting to hurt again but he had no time for it. He hoped this would all be over soon, the longest week of his life.

22.

THREE DAYS LATER, on Saturday morning, he awoke to the sound of seagulls and the smell of fresh paint. Lani was asleep beside him, stuffed panda cradled to her chest. She'd crawled into his bed sometime in the night. He got up quietly, washed in the bathroom, and slipped into khaki shorts and a T-shirt. He had a meeting this morning and for the image he wanted to present, only casual attire would do.

He opened the curtains and gazed out at the harbor, sunlight glinting off the small waves. Seagulls hovered noisily over a distant barge. Next door, the neighbors' teenage son was painting their fence, his grandfather raking leaves under the almond tree. Another hot day.

Miles went downstairs to make coffee and was sipping a cup on the porch swing when the paper boy passed. Miles told him to hold on there, scooped change out of an ashtray on a side table and ran down to buy an *Amandala*.

A headline on the front page made him stop, sit on the stairs. *Police: Suspect in slaying of ex-inspector Tablada fled to U.S.* The story described how police went to the house of "prominent San Ignacio businessman and reputed drug trafficker Arthur Rolle to question his son in the shooting death Wednesday of Marlon Tablada." Harry wasn't there, the story said. He'd booked and his father claimed not to know where he was. "Police think Harry Rolle, 23, left for the United States on Thursday. Arthur Rolle is a U.S. citizen, originally from Evansville, Ind." The story continued on another page; Miles didn't. The less he thought about Harry and that day, the better he felt.

He and Lani ate French toast for breakfast, chatting about what they'd do today, where they'd go. The entire Saturday lay ahead of them like a promise. They'd spent the last two days on walks or playing in the yard. Lani loved strolling along the sea-wall, skipping ahead of him. He told her stones could skip, too, and tried teaching her how to skip them on the water. She preferred collecting them, oohing and ahhing over the shapes and colors. He was getting used to the city again, the narrow streets, too many cars, the bicycles weaving in and out of traffic, stray dogs, the heat.

"Want to go out this morning and get some ice cream?" he asked Lani.

She grinned. "Yeah, let's." She pointed to the last slice of French toast on the platter. "I want more piece of bread."

Content, he watched her eat. His daughter was healthy, he knew he'd always love her, and the world was close to wonderful.

The phone rang. He intended to ignore it. It kept ringing and ringing. He answered it in the hall.

"Miles, Manny Marchand here. How you doing?"

Miles exhaled, rubbing his eyes. "Manny, what's up?"

Manny said, "Well, truth be told, not a hell of a lot. I was thinking we could have lunch today. Considering we haven't yet sat down since this whole business with Rian blew over. What time should I pick you up?"

Miles slipped a hand in his pocket and leaned against the wall. "Don't waste your time. I'm not going anywhere."

There was a pause. Manny said, "I'm sorry about your injury, but you don't seem to understand. It's important that you and Isabelle clear the air."

"So why am I talking to you?"

"Miles, a lot has happened in the past week and some very important people are upset. For reasons of personal safety Isabelle has decided to make herself unavailable. Until affairs are ironed out, of course. This is why we need to talk."

"And what're you proposing to come talk to me about, the weather? Or maybe you plan to finally tell me the Miami fight was called off days ago."

"Miles–"

"Sammy called me yesterday, after Wahed's manager contacted him and wanted to apologize about Wahed failing the drug test. I wonder when you planned to share this with me. Maybe after I found the girl? Man, we've got nothing to talk about."

"We both know that's not true. A mother, Isabelle, is still grieving for a daughter she can only hope is still alive, and you're quite likely the last person to have seen her alive and–"

"Like I told you before, I don't know where Rian is."

"–not to mention the fact there are certain monetary considerations that have been left open-ended."

"I wish I could tell you where the money is."

Manny groaned. "Really, Miles, you read the papers this morning? Harry Rolle took off before they could arrest him. No Harry Rolle, no arrest, no one with information. Except you and Joel. But both of you are refusing to cooperate with me, answer some unanswered questions. As you know by now, a bulk of the money Rian took belongs to someone else, and, well, it may cause a heap of problems if this person–"

"Arthur Rolle."

"–yes, Arthur Rolle, if Arthur Rolle doesn't get his money returned to him on time."

"Heap of problems for who, Manny?"

Manny laughed dryly. "You need me to tell you that?"

"So here you are, coming to me requesting information, at the same time hanging a threat over my head."

"What I am giving you is a complete analysis of your position. You were entrusted with a particular responsibility that you were relieved of at a particular time, but what you did, you overstepped your boundaries in every which way. At this point, you're just a man who has rudely insinuated himself in a situation with business ramifications he does not comprehend. Four families have been affected by violence related to this matter, and you, a meddler, who's been left unscathed, you want us to believe you know nothing? You were on the scene when Tablada was killed, and Rian and the money disappeared, and you're saying you know nothing? Miles, Miles, Miles, we've known each other for a long time, so I'll be frank. You've put yourself in a dangerous position. You've got no idea, no *idea*, what kind of people you're fucking with."

Miles let the pressure build. He was cool because he held the high hand and this morning he'd lay it on the table. He said, "People like El Padron, that's who you mean?"

A long silence. "Yes. That's one, certainly. But you needn't go so far. Arthur Rolle himself is bad enough."

Miles said, "Don't worry about me. Tell Isabelle she ought to be concerned about herself. Anyway, Manny, it's a beautiful day and I'm about to head out, take a walk with my daughter and get some ice cream, and the less I have on my mind the better, you understand? You want to know where the girl is, who has the money, all that, fine. Give me, oh," looking at the clock in the hall, "till about three, we'll get this whole thing settled."

"I like the sound of that, Miles. Now we're getting somewhere."

"We'll meet someplace private we can talk. Your room at the Fort George is fine with me."

"Perfect."

"Give me your room number." Miles cradled the receiver on his shoulder and jotted down the number on a slip of paper. "All your questions will be answered soon."

"Great. That's all we want. Let's get this puppy wrapped up, spare everyone concerned any more grief."

Miles said goodbye and strolled into the kitchen to clear the table. He took his time washing the dishes. He helped Lani find her sandals, stood back when she insisted that she put them on herself, then he came in right before the tears to switch the sandals to the proper feet. "Wait here," he said, "be right back."

He went upstairs, opened his bedroom closet and lifted a heavy backpack from behind a shoe rack. He laid the backpack on the bed, zipped it open, and dropped the flap forward. He counted the stacks of bills, touching each as he went. Satisfied, he zipped the bag shut.

He trotted downstairs with the bag. Lani was by the door, eager for her ice cream mission. Miles had a thought: Was he doing the right thing here? A moment of doubt. He said, "You ready, baby?"

Lani nodded and opened the door. A gust of sea breeze greeted them as they stepped into the sunshine. He drove slowly down Foreshore with Lani buckled in the backseat and the backpack wedged under his. He decided, Yeah, I'm doing the right thing taking her with me; Arthur Rolle was a father, too. He'd understand that if Miles trusted him enough to bring Lani along, then he had no intention to play games. What father would put his little girl in danger?

Maybe the father who was trying to deceive, to create a wholesome impression by bringing his daughter along... Enough. Miles turned off the doubts; the game had to end sometime. He drove around to Regent Street and over the swing bridge and cruised past the post office. He parked two cars down from the Belize City Police Station gate.

He slung the backpack over a shoulder, and he and Lani crossed Queen Street traffic holding hands. At the corner of Queen and Hyde's Lane was Blue Bird's ice cream parlor with its huge plate-glass windows, and sitting at a table facing the station, as Miles had instructed, was a white-haired gentleman in dark glasses. The man was sipping a glass of water with a straw, meditatively, pretending he hadn't been watching them. Miles had seen him the moment he parked.

Arthur Rolle stood up when they approached the table. He smiled tight-lipped at Miles, and stooping a little, he said to Lani, "Hello there, what's your name?"

Lani drew closer, all shy, leaning against Miles's leg. She mumbled her name.

"That's a really pretty name." The old man looked up at Miles. "You have a good-looking little girl here, Mr. Young."

Miles said, "Thank you, Mr. Rolle."

Arthur Rolle stretched out a palm. "Step into my office, why don't you."

They waited until Lani had started on a small cup of

chocolate ice cream before they opened their conversation. Already Miles had made out the two shifty-eyed men sitting stiffly near each exit, full milkshakes in front of them. Rolle needed to train his people better.

"It's very decent of you to have contacted me," Arthur Rolle said. "Also very smart. My life's problems are of no concern to you, so I think it was wise you recognized that fact. I want to commend you." He smiled again, but who knows what his eyes were saying behind those shades.

Miles lifted the backpack and set it on the table. "Like I said when I called, I have nothing to hide. All I wanted was my money. I never meant to be in the middle of a squabble. Same time, though, I've got to take care of myself,"–a pause, a glance at Lani–"my little girl." He rested a hand on the backpack. "Two hundred fifty-two grand. Like I told you, I took my forty, the girl helped herself to some, spent some along the way. This is the balance. Plus what you found in the car."

Arthur Rolle sat back and laced his fingers on his stomach, gesturing with his chin at Miles's bandaged finger. "Been through a lot and you're handing it over to me just like that."

Miles nodded. "It's not mine, except for forty thousand. And I have that now."

Arthur Rolle lifted his drink, sipped from his straw. "My son, before he went on his trip, he told me you were talking thirty."

Miles shook his head, all confidence. "He must have heard wrong." Leaned back, folded his arms. "For the loss of a contracted bout. For the loss of a finger and medical expenses. For pain and suffering. Not a cent less. And I want Isabelle to know it."

Arthur Rolle squinted. He looked off to the side, cars passing by, people strolling the dusty sidewalk. He hadn't acknowledged the backpack yet. It was too soon for that. Measuring Miles, feeling him out, the way boxers do in the first round. Miles understood the game.

"Safety and security," the old man said, still peering outside. "Everybody wants to feel safe and secure." He turned to Miles. "That's a fundamental desire, no? A need, you could say. People don't function well, psychologically, if they live in constant fear. I don't blame you for coming forward. You want to live your life, not have all this," waving at the backpack, "baggage, carrying this baggage of problems with you. Peace of mind, right? What everybody wants, come clean, live life in the sunlight, free and clear. I mean, that's why we're here, sitting across from a police station, for safety, security. No, I don't blame you. See, the only problem I have is, what will a man do to maintain his security, and I'm talking about the deepest-down inner peace, too." Arthur Rolle slapped the table. "What will a man do? That's what I want to know."

Lani looked at her father with concern. Miles stared at Rolle, waiting, not wanting to speak unnecessarily. After a moment, Lani returned to her ice cream.

"Handing over this bag of problems is a smart decision. But talking to our friends across the street, giving details about an unfortunate incident that's no business of yours, you believe that's smart?"

Miles said, "More than one person saw this ... incident. More than one person was questioned. No one, including me, has anything to hide. From anyone. You said it just now, I want to live with peace of mind. That's the reason I'm here."

Arthur Rolle removed his shades with a show of deliberation and set them on the table. His eyes were a startling blue. He scratched his chin and smiled, but the smile didn't reach his eyes. With thumb and forefinger he tweaked the backpack zipper open. He peered in, zipped it up, and sat back.

"Looks like money," he said, eyes boring into Miles. "Smells like fear."

Miles handed Lani a napkin and used another to wipe the mess she'd made on the table. He balled it and set it aside and sat forward to consider the man.

"I came here dealing straight. When I called the other day, told you what I was holding, asked how much you had coming to you, you said two twenty, and I took that for the truth. Didn't have to. In fact, I didn't even have to come forward. But I'm here. Bringing you two fifty-two. I get my money, you get yours. We both win. You think it changes anything, you believing what my rationale is? Maybe, you consider your situation, you'll see Isabelle sitting in the palm of your hand. You'll notice you're not hearing El Padron's footsteps behind you, none of his people breathing hot and heavy down your neck. And why? Because I delivered. It could've been Rian Gilmore took the money and ran. Or, hey, nobody ever found it. Pick one. But I didn't go that route. No, sir, I came to you of my own accord, and this is because I will live my life with my daughter without any difficulties that don't pertain to me." Miles jerked a chin at the backpack. "Consider this a fee, or a gift, whatever. It matters to me not. The dollars don't change. You want it, it's there. You don't, it's still there. It's between you and Isabelle and El Padron, the way it was from the get-go. Only now, with Isabelle, you've got the upper hand." Miles looked at his watch, exhaled. "Anyway, I'm meeting a friend in ten minutes, so I better get going." He put a hand on Lani's shoulder. "Was that good?"

Lani nodded, smears of chocolate ice cream on her lips.

When Miles turned back to Arthur Rolle, the backpack was in his lap and his shades were on. He watched Miles stand up.

"It was a pleasure, Mr. Young."

Miles held Lani's hand. "In a way, it was for me, too." He removed a slip of paper from his pocket. "One of Isabelle's friends is expecting a visit from me about the money, this afternoon at the Fort George. Name is Manny Marchand. He helped plan the little game with Isabelle. This is his room number. I'd be honored if you were the one visited him instead."

Arthur Rolle nodded. "What a pleasant surprise. That's a meeting I'll most enjoy." He took the paper. "What a nice sunshiny day," he said, looking out the window. "Have a good life, Mr. Young."

Miles walked out of Blue Bird's holding Lani's hand. Waiting to cross the street, he glanced back. The two men were standing at Arthur Rolle's table. Miles watched Rolle rise, clutching the backpack to his chest. He made his way out, one man in front, the other at the rear.

Miles crossed the street and buckled Lani in.

"What are we going to do now, Dad?"

He smoothed back her hair, admiring her full lips, her pixie nose. "Be happy, my sweets. We're going to go home and be happy. But first we have one more stop to make."

At the gym, Sammy was reading the *Amandala,* feet up on his desk. In the ring behind him two frightened teenagers in headgear danced around, flinging punches at the air. A trainer standing by the ring apron barked up orders for them to ignore.

"Hey, hey," Sammy said, bringing his feet down, swiveling around in the chair. "How you doing, boy?" He came to Miles, took hold of his forearm and raised it so he could see the finger. "Damn shame," he said, shaking his head, "damn shame. When last you changed this dressing?"

"Going back to the hospital today, matter of fact."

"Taking your medication?"

"Twice a day."

"Been trying to get in touch with you for days after I heard what happened. Where you been? Now you call me outta the blue, tell me you want to see me this morning? What's going on, Miles? Everything okay?"

"Copacetic," Miles said. "Just needed some time to think, collect myself. I'm feeling good, Sammy. You shouldn't worry about me." He looked down at Lani, who was tugging at his pants. "What do you want, baby, I'm talking."

She pointed at a skipping rope on Sammy's desk.

"Go right ahead," Sammy said.

She ran and grabbed it, trotted over by the ring and wrapped the ends around her hands. Like Alicia taught her. She began skipping, grinning at her dad.

Sammy said, "And no more boxing?"

Miles shook his head. "No more boxing. That's okay, though. It was time for me to move on. But, listen, I have something for you is why I'm here." He drew a chunky white envelope from a front pocket of his shorts. He took Sammy's hand and pressed the envelope into his palm. "A little something for all we've been through, a small thank-you."

Sammy eyed him quizzically. He opened the envelope cautiously and peeked in. "Jesus Christ. This a lotta money here, Miles. What's going on here?"

"Justice," Miles said. "I know Manny owed you a pretty penny for that Frankie Cano fight. If you think that's too much in there, after your share, bless Toby if you want. After he sobers up, of course."

Mouth agape, Sammy ruffled the bills in the envelope. "And how much is this?"

"Not too much."

"Miles."

"Twelve thousand. All of it you deserve. The four for Cano, and your cut of what I would've pocketed if the Wahed fight went down."

Sammy kept shaking his head, looking at the envelope. "But that comes to only . . ."

"And a little extra."

Sammy studied the envelope. "Only because you are like a son to me I'd ask how you came into this windfall. But I won't ask."

Miles smiled. "Good. It's too long a story anyway."

"I'll take it if you tell me I shouldn't worry."

"Don't worry."

Sammy said, "I don't know . . . I appreciate this but this is a lotta cash."

"Take the money, Sammy."

After another moment of thought, Sammy said, "Thank you, Miles." He offered Miles his hand. Miles took it and pulled him into an embrace. After some backslapping, they withdrew awkwardly, self-consciously, batting each other's shoulders,

Miles mumbling, "Yeah, well, okay," Sammy saying, "Thanks, thanks."

Sammy walked them to the door when they left. He said goodbye to Lani, shook Miles's hand again. He said they'd see each other soon, but Miles knew better: This was a relationship that had served a particular purpose, and the time between their meetings would stretch farther and farther and the memories would fade, like the yellowing photos on the gym wall of boxers who had trained here, who had believed devoutly in championship dreams that never came to pass.

Alicia stood by the gate waiting when they pulled up. She was wearing a light blue sundress that fluttered in the breeze, looking prettier than sunshine. Miles rolled down the window. "Sorry I'm late. Been here long?"

"Not too. Still unloading my things." She motioned to the bucket and mop, the broom, gloves, and bottle of Mr. Clean by the fence. She said to Lani, "Hey, sweetie."

Miles said, "You didn't need to bring all that. I got that stuff."

"Makes cleaning faster," Alicia said, "plus your house is pretty big."

"I thought we'd, you know, clean together, take our time."

"We could do that, too." She smiled and they held each other's eyes. "I'd like it if we went slow, actually."

Miles nodded. "Really take our time, you're saying. I was thinking the same thing."

"Yeah, let's not rush it, Miles. Let's take our time."

He looked at her and was filled with a calm that had eluded him for weeks. He reached out the car window and she let him hold her hand.

They went upstairs together, and for a minute he was as self-conscious as a schoolboy. In the living room, before they began cleaning, she handed him a note. "An e-mail I got last night from Rian."

Rian wrote that she was writing this from a public library computer. She'd found Miles's house fine, no problem with the directions, but neighbors across the street, an old couple who were kinda nosy but nice, said that some kids had spray-painted graffiti on a back wall a few months back. Other than that, the house was fine, the trees in the backyard were loaded with mangoes. She wrote that she hadn't called her mother yet and didn't know when she would, she really didn't want to. She missed Joel, missed Belize, but for some reason it was her dad she missed most of all. Like she knew she wouldn't see him again, and it made her guilty she hadn't said a proper farewell. She spent a lotta time at the mall, caught the bus there. Didn't have much else to do. She was planning on getting a car, but then maybe not, she needed to stop spending. She needed to get a job soon. Her first ever! That was making her nervous. She was planning on going back to school, too. Get her diploma. Or maybe not, just get a GED. She'd have to look into that. She thought Miami was okay, just as hot as Belize if not for the fact everywhere was air conditioned. She had to go now, she'd write again soon, or maybe call once she got the phone hooked up. Sometimes, she said, it gets lonely.

They cleaned the living room, the hall, then the kitchen— dusted, swept, mopped, vacuumed. Lani helped by putting her toys away and rearranging the knickknacks Alicia had just carefully arranged. Miles took down his bedroom curtains, dusted the louvers thoroughly, threw open the windows. Light flooded in, a breeze that felt like rain. Over the bed was a huge photo of Miles and Abigail sitting in a swing. He couldn't recall where it was taken or when; he'd stopped seeing it months ago. On his night table, next to the clock, was a small photo of Abigail Lani had put there a couple weeks after her mother left. On the dresser, more photos of Abigail.

Miles removed the photos from the frames, putting them face down in an empty cardboard box. He took down the one from the wall. He started dusting, trying hard to act like all this shedding of his past was just another task.

When Alica tapped Miles on his shoulder, he was on his knees, staring at a photo in his hand. "Hey," she whispered. "Want to take a break?"

He must have been there a long time. "Yeah," he said. "Sounds good."

They sat on the verandah swing, rocking gently, staring at the sea. Rain clouds had darkened the sky, they could see the streaking showers on the horizon, a blue-black shadow. The breeze gusted cool on their skin.

"I know you probably heard stories," Miles said. "About me and Abigail. I just want to say thanks for giving me space. Respecting my privacy."

She said, "Okay."

She didn't deny her knowledge. That would have been disastrous to the moment. This moment that he wanted to share his history, let her through another door of his life. He said, "The second I met Abigail, I liked her. She wasn't like the other patients on the floor. She was pretty normal. Except for the fact she seemed a little sad sometimes, you wouldn't think there was anything the matter with her, you know? We really hit it off. We were always talking. Religion, society, politics, the little I knew. I'd never had that inclination before, to really sit down, get to know another person like this. She was intelligent, and pretty, I thought she was pretty."

"She was. Is." Alicia canted her head at the photo that was still in his hand.

"Yeah. I was attracted to her. And I knew she liked me. After two weeks, one night I went to her room, to give her an extra blanket. They always kept the floor freezing, man. So I went there on the women's side of the ward, should have had a female nurse with me before I entered but . . . you know how that goes. Rules were broken all the time. So I went into her room, and we started talking. It was about three or four o'clock in the morning maybe, and we just talked, sitting really close to each other on her bed. And like I knew what I was doing was questionable, but it never occurred to me that it was . . . that it was *wrong.* I respected her too much." Miles breathed in the air that smelled like rain, watching the shower advance over the tossing waves, breathing in the memory of his wife, breathing it out.

Softly, Alicia said, "So what happened?"

"They found us asleep a couple hours later in her bed. We'd kissed, talked, nothing else. Our clothes were on." Light rain began pelting the roof. Miles stared at the lighthouse across the harbor sheathed in rain. "When the hospital suspended me, it didn't matter. When Abigail's father pressed the issue and they fired me, it didn't matter. Being with Abigail, getting to know her better, that was the only thing that mattered to me then." Miles looked at the photo one last time, then placed it between them on the swing. "We wanted a family. So we got married and started one. And now she's not here anymore."

The rain moved fast across the seawall and was over the lawn and the house, and they sat there half-sheltered, letting the cold drops hit their legs, their arms. "You still have Lani," Alicia said.

Miles looked at her. "I do," he said. "And now you."

Turning to him, Alicia said nothing. She wiped the rain from his bicep and traced the veins in his forearm with a fingertip. She clasped his hand. "Let's go inside," she said. "Lani must be hungry."

He nodded. "Yeah." But he didn't move right away. Then he got up, holding her hand, and she led him into the house, and they closed the door, as the wind picked up and the rain fell harder, washing across the railing, the swing, the photo that had fallen to the floor, the rain drumming the tin roofs of the neighborhood, bringing relief from the wicked heat that had plagued the city that long week.